CH00952050

Kiwis Sinners and Saints

Tall tales under canvas

Robert C W Pyper

Copyright © 2014 Robert Pyper

ISBN-10: 1500767352
ISBN-13: 97800767358

Dedication

To all those field geologists who have struggled mightily to find a great prospect worthy of developing into a mine.

Author's Note:

Like all fiction—despite author protestations, the characters in this book are based on real people, however I have had to make them a little less uncouth to avoid offending the reader. As a result they have become unrecognisable to all except perhaps their mothers, who no doubt were blind to their many faults and always saw them as they are pictured here.

Inquiries should be made to:

Robert Pyper

283 Huntingdale Street

Pullenvale, Queensland, 4069

Telephone 617 33742443; Mobile 04 19661342

E-Mail: robert.pyper@bigpond.com

Website: www.robertpyper.com.au

Contents

Acknowledgement

Cover Design by Tanya Kryger

My sisters, Alison and Joanna for comments

Jim, Art and Chas for the inspiration

Robert C W Pyper

Chapter 1 The Kiwi

I had no sooner stepped inside the squash centre than my daughter, Wendy, confronted me, a challenging grin on her face. "Hi," she said. "We were beginning to think you had chickened out."

There comes a time in the perception of teenage children when dads are no longer Gods, to be respected, worshipped and emulated, but rather to be shown up as quaint relics with a use by date that has just been exceeded. This was to be my fate today on the squash court, where in gratitude for my patience in instructing them over the years and demonstrating my superiority in all things, especially squash, my two teenage children intended revenge.

"Ian's already on court having a lesson from Jim someone," she said as I joined her upstairs. "He's seems pretty good."

"You should get one too; give yourself a chance," I said, looking down on the court. I noticed with rising hope that Ian had turned pink and was about done in. I would challenge him the moment they finished.

They noticed me and stopped playing. "Hi," Ian said, between gasps. "Dad, do you know Jim?"

Little did I guess as I waved casually that he was to play a major part in my life for the next 18 months. He was about thirty, well built, with a permanent reddish-gold stubble and thinning blonde hair and he had barely raised a sweat. We had not met but he had turned up at the courts recently doing maintenance, mainly painting and repairing damaged walls. The courts currently looked as if they had developed Chicken Pox as he had yet to paint over the repairs.

"Hi," he said. "Just giving Ian a few pointers. We'll finish this game off, then it's your turn, Wendy. I hope you're a bit fitter than your brother." He turned as he spoke and served a rocket before Ian realised the game had re-started.

"Hey!" Ian protested.

"Seven love," Jim said. "Stay alert. Move around and boast them off the side wall like I showed you."

By the time Jim had finished with the two of them, neither had the energy to play me. With my God-like status still intact I shook Jim's hand in gratitude and was about to leave when he said. "Your turn."

"Yes, give him a game dad," Wendy said. "See if you can win a point."

Jim was one of those extrovert characters who acted with strangers as if they were old mates. "Tell you what," he said, before I had time to start on the reasons why I couldn't play. "I'll give you seven points start and ten to one odds. How much can you afford to lose?

I normally only bet on near certain winners but to refuse would be to lose face. "Fifty cents?"

"Done."

"I could be playing A grade," I said. "What makes you so confident?"

He chuckled. "I saw you play in the fixtures last week."

Jim gave me the first serve, which, in my nervous state, came off the racquet frame but just managed to reach the corner where it flopped down tiredly, almost unplayable. Although he somehow got to it, his return hit the tin below the red line. I had only one point to make to win the game. I served again, a lightning-like drive that he lined up with utter contempt and smacked into the wall so hard it impacted like a rifle shot, loosening a chunk of plaster from one of his recent repairs and upsetting the trajectory. It rose up and landed in the gallery.

"Game over," I said as my kids looked down in disbelief. "Let me buy you a cold drink with your five dollars."

I didn't realise it at the time but Jim's loose bets were going to net me quite a bit of cash over the coming months. Jim turned out to be a friendly character. He was from New Zealand, an unemployed Kiwi butcher who had come to Brisbane a month ago looking for work and had been doing the repairs in return for free games. His coaching lessons were free also.

"What do you do, Bob? He asked, after we had talked for a while. "With your luck at squash you probably don't need to work."

"Now that I've discovered you I'll probably retire," I said. "Up to now I've been a freelance geologist."

He looked puzzled. "Doing what?"

"Working in the bush looking at rocks and finding gold."

His eyes lit up. "Any chance of a job?"

It so happened that I had just taken an 18-month contract with a mining company, Hunter International, looking for gold in North Queensland. I had Chas, my trusty field assistant, already lined up in Charters Towers but I needed another field hand, and Jim had already impressed me with his enthusiasm and energy.

"Could be," I said.

"I'm your man then. What do I have to do?"

"Take samples, plot up results, do a bit of cooking, set up campsites, keep track of supplies, maintain vehicles, look after the geo, things like that. It will be four to five weeks work northwest of Charters Towers, in northern Queensland, then a bit of time off before heading out again for another month or so."

"Piece of cake then," he said exuding confidence; then he frowned. "Except maybe for looking after the geo?"

"That's more important than the rest put together. Ever camped in the bush before?"

He scratched his chin for a moment. "What's the bush? I've visited a few parks in New Zealand and I camped with the scouts as a kid."

"You sound over qualified but I could make an exception."

"What's the pay?"

I mentioned a figure, then said. "All expenses are paid too."

He looked incredulous. "You mean free tucker?"

"All free."

He leapt to his feet and shook my hand in a crushing grip. "Let's go."

* * *

Jim hung onto the door as we bounced through a water-filled mud hole, swerved round a clump of eucalyptus suckers and sideswiped a white ant's nest. "We're lost, aren't we?" he said. "The great Australian geologist has got us lost."

It was a week later and we were heading to the campsite. I could hear the unease in his voice; he was in an alien environment, for he had never lived outside a city before, and we were certainly not on the tourist route—possibly not on any route. We probably were lost but I was not about to admit it.

"There's something you should know," I said, as I peered into the rain-swept darkness—the mud covered headlights barely illuminating the overhanging branches let alone the supposed track. "Geologists are never wrong. Keep that in mind at all times, and why would you think we're lost? Just because we're off the map and the track's a bit hard to see."

"Hard to see?" He pushed his new bush hat to the back of his head. "There's no track and there hasn't been since we turned off the Towers road miles back."

It was 1986, before mobile phones and GPS systems and we were in the middle of thick scrub, north of Charters Towers and miles from anywhere, on a track that was mostly in my imagination—a strung out series of less overgrown patches—but which I hoped would lead us to the exploration campsite. I had driven to the area the previous year doing some reconnaissance work, but a lot of vegetation had sprung up since then and spending an uncomfortable night in the cab waiting for daylight—for I doubted we could ever find our way back in the dark—was looking more and more likely.

"The campsite's probably round the next bend," I said, twisting the steering wheel to the left, then to the right, as I negotiated a fallen tree.

"Another bend?" He leant out the window, yelling into the darkness and waving his hat. "Another bend? My God! I can't believe it. There's another bend!" His exuberance was cut short as the scrub on either side closed around us. He pulled his head in, looking sheepish. "Back up. I've lost me hat."

Jim and I had flown up to Townsville that morning, then driven to Charters Towers to meet Chas, who rented out the camping gear we needed and who would be bringing Art out the next day with more gear. However, on our arrival, Kerry, Chas' wife, had no idea where he was. Rather than wait for him to turn up—which, knowing Chas, might never happen—we used the time to pick up the food we needed.

As we walked down the aisles of the supermarket, I produced two typed sheets and gave one to Jim. "That list is for the essentials—matches, rope, mantles for the gas light, fuel for the generator, salt, pepper, fly spray—Can you be trusted with our survival for four weeks?"

"What's the other list?"

"Food and a few luxuries."

His eyes lit up. "Like what luxuries?"

"Chocolate, tins of cream, soft drinks, biscuits, fruit cake, juices, the usual thing to make life pleasant after a day's work."

"You mean we can eat what we like?"

"Within reason."

"Who defines reason?"

"I do."

"Great," he grabbed the second list. "Caviar, oysters, chocolates, malted milk, nuts, dried fruit. Let me at them."

"Just remember we won't have a fridge until Chas brings one out tomorrow."

He grinned. "It'll be all gone by then. Chas can bring out some more."

After our purchases we sat in a coffee shop. Jim had already slipped into his role of field assistant. He wore a pair of old boots, tattered blue jeans, a Canadian lumberjack shirt and a wide-brimmed hat. His unshaven face sprouted a reddish-brown bristle, transforming it into something that would have looked good on a wanted poster.

"What a life," he said, sucking on a strawberry milkshake. "Thank you, Hunter."

"If their accountant finds the receipt for your extravagance in the pile I send in he may write you a querying letter."

He stifled a burp into a long, punctuated growl and bit into a chocolate bar. "I can't work if I'm gnawed at by hunger pains."

There was actually no chance of the food bill being queried, for just as it is well documented that a large supply of beer is critical to the morale of troops in wartime, so is the quality and quantity of the food in an exploration camp critical to its running.

We eventually located Chas but by the time we had his equipment loaded it was getting dark, which is why we were driving late into the night to our rendezvous with paradise, camped by the Star River.

Sometime later, and with great relief, I recognised the site I was looking for and slowed, then turned off into a cleared area and stopped. The lights lit up a depressing scene of straggly scrub, dripping gums and white ant nests. After a short silence Jim spoke.

"Why have we stopped?"

"This is it."

"Is what?"

"Our destination."

"We're going to spend a month here?"

"Camping spots don't come any better. Were you expecting a

power point and hot shower?"

"I want out." He bumped his head against the dash a few times in mock disgust.

Although it was only late March and quite warm, the sodden and gloomy surroundings possessed a certain ability to chill the mind if not the body. Luckily the rain had eased to a fine drizzle.

"You could have picked a place with fewer rocks." Jim said. "What funny shapes."

He was referring to a few cone-shaped, smooth brown objects, some reaching knee height. I stifled a groan of incredulity and the thought that my new fieldy might turn out to be quite useless crossed my mind. "They're termite mounds, Jim—white ant nests. Are you saying you've never seen one before?"

"Never." He got out and undid the sides of the Landcruiser tray, his shock already forgotten in the excitement of this new and strange environment. "Okay, what now?"

"We'll unload the gear, clear the funny rocks, and erect the tent."

"No worries! Take a break while I fix everything."

"You're going to set up on your own?"

He gave one of his wide grins. "Can't be too hard, surely, and I've got to look after the geo. Isn't that what field assistants do?"

I could not believe my luck at finding this gem. No field assistant in my experience had ever expressed such a desirable sentiment, but wisely I declined Jim's offer. Setting up our big tent was no job for one man.

An hour later, we had most of the gear stored out of the rain and the tent erected. The tent was a square design with a centre pole, corner poles, and double canvas and fly screen walls that could be rolled up or let down.

"For an ex-butcher you didn't take long to learn how to set up a camp," I said, eying the muddy footprints all over the inside walls.

"That's really good," Jim said, testing one of the camp stretchers. "Rain was nice too; don't need a shower now." His stomach growled. "What are we going to eat? I'm famished."

"Ever cooked before?"

"The odd barbecue. Don't mind learning, though. An old geo like you must have picked up a few clues."

"I was a natural," I said. "Find me a tin of baked beans and some eggs and I'll demonstrate 30 years of practical bush knowledge on the gas stove."

Jim disappeared outside and I could hear him grumbling in the rain until there was a crash of tins and cutlery. "Thank you, Bob!" he called loudly. "Thank you for the wonderful job, the wonderful weather, and for inviting me to spend a month in this wonderful arsehole of a place."

He came back with beans, eggs, a tin of fruit, some pressurised cream and a sodden cardboard box that had once been full of assorted packets of biscuits, nuts, dried fruit and other delicacies until the bottom fell out.

He munched on a biscuit, then opened a packet of mixed nuts and poured them down his throat. "Everything's lying in the rain but we don't have a tarp so stuff it. When do you expect Chas to turn up?"

I tipped the beans into the frypan "Early tomorrow."

"That's really good." He found a bar of chocolate and began to demolish it. "It's good that the company pays for the tucker. Do you eat like this every time you go bush?"

I cracked the eggs onto the steaming beans as he searched through the carton for more food. "Never. Until I saw you I thought it was impossible."

He looked into the frypan. "Only four eggs? Aren't you having any?"

* * *

The next morning we woke to find the wet bush glittering in the sunshine and the Star River gurgling in the background. After putting the finishing touches to the campsite we scouted the few tracks in the area while waiting for Chas and Art, who finally turned up late in the afternoon.

"Got a bit delayed," Chas said.

Chas, who was about Jim's age, was solidly built and dressed as always in newly washed blue dungarees covered with fresh grease and oil stains. He was a phlegmatic character who never let life's turbulence and setbacks upset his composure. I expected him to be a stabilising influence in the camp, for where Jim saw every change and obstacle as an exciting challenge to be probed, queried, confronted and conquered, Chas merely moved on like a deep ocean roller.

As Chas was employed on another contract, he had brought out Art Fenman, his cousin, to take his place. If I had known anything about Art he would never have been given the work, but by the time I realised just how useless he was he had become a sort of black sheep of the family, not wanted but hard to get rid of.

"Where's the caravan you were going to bring?" I asked.

Chas gave a sheepish grin. "About 20 km back in a creek. The tow bar broke. I can get it welded at the station and bring it out tomorrow before I head back."

The old Landcruiser tray top he drove had a well used look with scratches and dents and bits of the bush hanging off every projection. In a wildlife park it would have made a brilliant hide. Jim was already circling it, checking out the equipment. It was so down at the back from the weight of gear it carried that it looked almost sporty with its headlights pointed to the treetops. "Is this all your stuff, Chas?" Jim asked.

"Yep."

Jim took in the deep freeze, generator, fridge, power cords, hand winch, roo jack, and numerous boxes of food with an admiring and calculating eye. "You could have put a bit more on. The springs aren't flat yet."

"The rest's in the van."

"So you do a bit of contracting then?" Jim asked, keen to get the inside running on making money in exploration, although with Chas, getting any sort of information required skills beyond the reach of most.

Chas lay on the ground and wormed his way under the Toyota with a spanner. "Yep."

Jim squatted down. "Get much contract work?"

"Some."

"What sort do you do?"

"Bit of everything."

"We're hiring your gear, eh?"

"Yep."

"So how much can you make by hiring it out?"

"A bit."

"What else do you do?"

"Whatever's going."

Jim might have tapped this fount of information all afternoon but I began to unload the gear and he got up to help. He grabbed the generator and turned to Art who was sitting on a box drinking a coke. "Give us a hand here, Art."

Art was about twenty, grossly overweight, with tight curly black hair, thick lips, deep-set eyes, triple chins and puffy cheeks. It was a face that looked as if it had already plumbed the depths of corruption and enjoyed the experience enough to want to sample more.

"Sorry, mate" he said, squinting up at Jim. "Me back's a bit crook; I might manage some of the lighter stuff. The springs in the bloody Tojo are shot. I need to rest up a bit."

Later that night, when Chas had driven off, Art carried his bedroll into the tent and surveyed the space between the two camp stretchers. "Why didn't you guys clear a flat spot?" He turned to Jim. "What about loaning me your mattress? You've got a stretcher."

"Get real," Jim said. "Anyway, you'll be out like a light after doing all that heavy lifting."

I took pity on Art and lent him mine. We turned in about eleven but Art had a snore that needed so much pressure to wind its way through the adenoids, pharynx, larynx and other obstacles that it vibrated the ground as well as the eardrums. We didn't get much sleep.

"Anyone ever tell you, you snored?" Jim asked the next morning.

"I only snore if I'm uncomfortable. If you'd of loaned me your foam I'd have slept like a baby."

"I'm talking about snoring, not sleeping. Why didn't you go back with Chas and sleep in the caravan?"

Art gave a snort. "You reckon I snore. You should hear him. Things fall out the bloody cupboards when he gets going."

Jim turned to me, munching on a wedge of toast dripping with butter and strawberry jam. "What's on today?"

"Sampling the drainages for gold."

"That's really good. I'll make the lunches. What does everyone like?"

"A couple'a hot pies, fries and tomato sauce, washed down with a few beers is all I need," Art said.

"Dream on," Jim said. "And we don't have any beer."

"I've got eight cartons in the van."

I looked at Art in amazement. "Chas is teetotal," I said. "How come he lets you load his van with beer?"

"I didn't tell him."

Jim chuckled. "Probably why the tow bar broke."

Chas turned up later with the caravan. "I fixed the tow bar," he said. "Bert reckons the property is overrun with feral pigs."

"Who's Bert?" Jim asked.

"The cow cocky."

"Cow cocky?" Jim mulled over the terminology. "You mean he's the owner of this farm we're on and runs cows?"

"What planet are you from," Art said, derisively. "It's a station not a farm. You must be a Kiwi. You talk like one of those refugees."

"And proud of it," Jim said.

"Poor bastard," Art snorted. "Did you hear about the Kiwi who was pulled over by the traffic cops. 'Sorry officer', he said. 'I'm not much good at making a U turn but I can sure make its eyes bulge'."

"That's enough, Art," I said, concerned for the smooth running of the camp. New Zealand, our closest neighbor, was reputed to have more sheep than women, which was a great stimulus for generating crude jokes, and because our unemployment benefits were so generous, Kiwis—named after their famous New Zealand flightless bird—arrived here in droves.

"Bert has the lease on a few thousand acres," Chas said, getting back in his Toyota to leave. "They're known as cow cockies as they mostly run cattle. He said he'd call by later." He waved goodbye.

* * *

Bert turned up in his Landcruiser the next evening with three pig dogs. "I'm going to cull a few pigs, they're ruining the land," he said after yarning for a while. "Want to come along?"

Jim was in the back of his Toyota in a flash, joining the excited dogs. "Reckon we could catch a baby one?" he asked. "Wouldn't mind keeping one as a pet."

"Stone the bloody crows, are you ridgi-didge?" Bert said, scratching his head "Should be a few little 'uns about, for sure."

It didn't take us long to find some pigs. The dogs were excited but not nearly as much as Jim, who jumped out with them, waving his hat and yelling.

The dogs circled, rounding up half a dozen that came tearing past the Toyota, Jim in close pursuit. A half-grown black boar with small curved tusks, collided with a dog and Jim launched himself forward and caught it by the back legs.

"Mad bastard", Bert said. "He must be a quid short in the bank; it'll have him for breakfast if he lets go."

It looked as if Bert was going to be right for Jim not only had the pig to contend with but one of the dogs, that thought this squealing and shouting combination was a new type of animal to be attacked.

"I've got it," Jim gasped, as it jerked him along the ground. "He's mine."

"More like he's got you, mate" Bert said, as we ran over. He threw a sack over the pig and knelt on it, fighting off the dog. "It's as mad as a cut snake. Bring some rope, Art."

"Oink, oink," Art replied between laughs. "Oink, oink."

"These bloody things are dangerous," Bert said, after he'd trussed up the pig. "He could have ripped your guts out."

Jim brushed himself down and patted the pig. "Never saw black ones before."

"What are you planning to do with it?" Bert asked.

Jim looked at it dubiously. "It's probably a bit big to tame. Maybe I'll fatten it up for eating."

Bert tried not to laugh. "You can't tame these, they're naturally wild, but there's a pen you could keep it in if you want."

We took the pig back to the homestead and Jim fixed it up with straw and water as if he were putting a baby to bed.

"Jim's missing the four legged woollies," Art said. "He'll be in there with it soon. Oink, oink."

* * *

A couple of weeks later we accompanied Jim on his evening trip with the camp scraps, to feed the pig.

"It's getting tamer," Jim said, as we leaned over the sty. "Used to squeal and carry on, now it just watches."

"Sounds like you've fallen in love with it," Art said.

"It likes its new name." Jim clicked his fingers. "Here Artie, come to Jimmy." The pig didn't move. "It's getting fatter, too. Its barrel shape and the way it eats the leftovers gave me the idea for the name."

"You're probably scared of it, that's why you named it after me," Art scoffed.

"Who'd be scared of a tub of lard?"

"Okay. Bet you're not game to climb in there."

"You reckon?" Jim took a piece of sweet corn and straddled the railing as the pig glowered at him from the far corner.

"Ever see the film Razorback?" Art said. "Pigs love human flesh. I know of a bloke broke his leg and was stranded in the bush overnight. The pigs found him. All they left was the skull."

Jim edged over the railing and crouched down inside, then held out the corn. "Here Artie. Come to Jimmy."

The pig, after considering its options for a moment, took him at his word and charged. Jim leapt the rail with a yell.

Art doubled up laughing. "Oink, oink," he honked. "Oink, oink. Bloody Kiwis."

Jim took a ragged breath. "Another week and he's mince meat."

"I thought you wanted to tame it?" I said.

Jim shook his head. "Bert reckons they can't be tamed. Think I'll kill it next Sunday. Bert's got an old bath we can use and the nights are pretty chilly. It'll be just right for setting the meat."

* * *

Bert supplied a tractor, a.22 rifle, an old bath and a couple of forty-four gallon drums of water the following Sunday, and we had the water heating in the late afternoon as the evening chill set in.

"We need to scrape off the hair before we can cut up the meat," Jim explained. "There's a critical temperature for the water. Too hot and you spoil the meat; too cold and you can't get the hair off."

When the water in the bath was close to boiling Jim picked up the rifle. "I suppose you're a crack shot?" he said to Art.

"Once cleaned out a guy in sideshow alley with a point 22," Art said. "Took the rifle off me after I'd won most of the prizes."

Jim dropped the pig cleanly with a single shot, then using a tripod mounted on the tractor, he hauled it up and dunked it in the hot water. After that, Jim and I began scraping the skin down over the bath while Art made useful and enlightening commentary as he warmed his backside by the fire.

"That water looks like one of your soups, Jim," he said, coming over to inspect our progress and staring in distaste at the murky and evil looking black brew in the bath, now full of mud, rotting food scraps, hair and blood. "Probably taste a bit better though."

He poured himself a cup of tea from the billy on the fire and stood close to the warmth, for it was a clear starry night and getting quite cold. "Should've had the water hotter though, mate. The hair isn't coming off as readily as yours has been falling out."

Art was right about the skin. The evening chill and the size of the pig had cooled the water too rapidly and we now had to work hard to clean the hair off but Jim was so preoccupied that he seemed not to hear Art, so Art had another dig.

"They reckon young bald Kiwis never get the women and they become homosexual as a result. I hear they kick the homos out of New Zealand and they come over here in droves."

This sally too, went unanswered.

"Used to work in an abattoir once," Art said. "Butchering is a mug's game if you ask me. No wonder you quit and came over here."

After we had scraped the pig down, we used the tractor to move it off the bath and I watched as Jim, now back in his trade, started to gut it expertly, using the set of butcher's knives he always carried with him.

"Don't know how you could kill something you were in love with," Art said, throwing some wood on the fire, which blazed up. 'You should stick to sheep like a normal Kiwi. Never known a Kiwi to take a shine to a razorback before but I guess it takes all types."

It was this sally that finally seemed to get through to Jim. He stopped cutting and looked down at the carving knife he was holding. It glinted in the firelight as he twisted it about, testing the blade with his thumb. The knife was a long carbon steel number with a slight curve that put me in mind of a sultan's scimitar. He turned towards Art, who, from the grin on his face and the wobble of his double chins, was clearly pleased with the effect of this final barb that demonstrated yet again that he was a man of clever wit.

Jim seemed to make up his mind. Giving the pig a push that set it swinging on its tripod, he changed his grip on the knife from one of cutting to one of stabbing, fixed Art with a particularly malevolent stare and headed towards him.

My God! I thought, Art has pushed him too far. It had happened before in exploration camps. The heat, flies, camp food and primitive living conditions can send a man 'troppo' and now Art's crude humour had pushed Jim to breaking point.

Art obviously thought so too. His mouth opened, his eyes widened, and with each measured step Jim took towards him, everything opened wider. A dark stain appeared down Art's right trouser leg.

I took a step towards them but the swinging pig would have moved faster. I was caught in a moment of paralysis just as Art obviously was. As time seemed to slow in anticipation of death, Jim stopped in front of Art, then bent down and picked up his sharpening stone. He chuckled as he began to hone the blade.

"Had you going then, didn't I? Thought you was going to faint."

"Faint." The squeak in Art's voice diminished his bravado somewhat. "I was just about to give you the chop. Lucky you stopped in time."

He glanced at a dark stain on Art's trouser leg. "I think you wet yourself."

"Spilt me tea, that's all."

I breathed a sigh of relief but as the contract still had another 17 months to run I was not certain they would both survive. Jim went back to work until the pig was cleaned to his satisfaction before he packed his knives away.

"It's a well known fact that feral pigs are full of worms," Art said, having recovered from his near death experience and enjoying the warmth of the blazing fire on his back. He was clearly keen to get in a few more sallies and make up for the ultimate embarrassment of wetting himself, especially now he knew Jim was harmless.

"That's why you'll never find the locals eating them," he continued. "I guess a Kiwi would find that the best part though. Oink—oiiiow." The grunt of derision suddenly turned into one of pain. "Shit!—I'm on fire!—God!—Help!" He began to jump about in panic before rushing over to the bath. He flopped in on his back, immersing himself in the muck with a hiss of steam as his burning boot sizzled.

I could see Jim's mouth working as Art hauled himself out of the glutinous brew and squelched over to the Toyota. It was a golden opportunity for a smart comment but Jim couldn't get going at first, all he could muster was a faint, "Catch that porker, Bob—Don't … Don't let it get away, oink, oink."

Chapter 2 The Savoury Omelette

The pig was nicely chilled the next morning. Jim cut it up, giving half of it to Bert, and taking the rest back to the camp.

"Where are you going to put that?" Art said.

"In the fridge."

"There's no room."

Jim opened the fridge door and surveyed the interior. It was showing signs of neglect. There were half-empty tins starting to rust through the zinc plating and past meal remnants, originally wrapped in Alfoil, now loose and working their way down through the shelving like a series of coarse sieves with the smallest items congealing on the bottom. Some baked beans on a plate had formed a solid greenish crust. A lump of cheese had cracked and dried out to a hard yellow rind. Two tubs of margarine minus tops, with added jam and vegemite smears, jostled with assorted fruit drinks minus labels and bleached remnants of unwrapped chocolate. The steak thawing for the evening meal was already bleeding over the few remaining slices of stale bread.

Jim chewed his lip for a moment. "You're right, it's chock a block."

"Told ya," Art said. "Anyway, that pig is so full of worms there'll only be bones left by tomorrow. If you put it in the fridge they'll probably eat everything else in there too."

Jim's frown of concentration lightened as he searched the interior further. "No worries," he said; "we'll get rid of these." He heaved out Art's carton of beer. "Plenty of room now."

Art looked shocked. "You can't do that, my beer will get warm."

"Yeah, but it won't go off like pork will."

"You can't drink warm beer you cretin, it's undrinkable."

"So learn to rough it like Bob and I do."

Art's chins sagged and his mouth gaped. "Rough it? So what are you giving up? What about taking out all those bottles of water?"

"I can't work without cold water. It's natural anyway, not like beer."

"What's wrong with warm water?"

"We'll vote on it," Jim said. "Bob, you're in favour, right? So it's two to one. Democracy in action."

"I might have to drink it all now, before it warms," Art said.

"We'll clear a space in the chest freezer each evening," I said. "Enough to fit a couple of cans in; they'll be cold in twenty minutes."

Jim turned to me. "And while he's drinking those he can have two more cooling. It'll do him good to drink at half his normal speed."

* * *

We had got to the stage in our exploration where we were now working a fair way from the camp and I planned to sample the creeks for gold using the air photos as a guide. I gave Jim the compass before we set off.

"What does it do?" he asked, fiddling with it.

"Gives you a direction."

"How?"

I was amazed at his ignorance. "North and south. North's this way." I pointed. "It's magnetic. Didn't you do geography at school?"

Jim shook his head as he looked through the compass sights. "So where's south then?"

Art groaned. "Ignorant Kiwi wouldn't find a whore in a floss house. How'd you get this job, Jim?"

"He got it by being a top squash player and coach," I said.

Art grunted derisively. "So you're a brown nose, Jim. Been nice to the boss and got yourself a job. You'd never find me brown noseing. If you can't get a job on your own merit then you don't deserve to get it."

"Cut the crap, Art and let me concentrate, Jim said, fiddling with the compass.

"I suppose you let Bob win a few games of squash too?"

"I only ever played Jim once and beat him nine love," I said. "But he gave me a generous handicap."

"I'll have to give youse a game sometime, Jim. I play A grade in the Towers."

"My God!" Jim said. "With that physique I should've guessed. Is there anything you can't do?"

Art shook his head. "Dunno; haven't been around long enough to

16

find out."

The country we headed into was typical of sub-tropical coastal Queensland. The rainfall was high enough for substantial trees to grow, mostly iron barks, grey box and wattles, but the undergrowth was easy to push through, except along the creeks. I drove as close as I could to the nearest creek that drained into the Star River and drew up under a tree.

"We'll need the crowbar, shovel, sieve and sample bags."

Art demonstrated his bush experience by grabbing the bags and sieve, leaving the iron-ware.

We had to push through a lot of dense bush and when we finally got to the creek, somewhat hotter and well scratched, Art dropped the gear on the rocks with a groan. "What a bastard," he said. "I hope we don't have to climb any higher."

"Sorry," I said. "There are two more sample sights further up." I turned to Jim. "This is a good trap. Lever out a few of the loose rocks. We'll clean it out to bedrock and bag up the gravel to pan off later."

Jim attacked the rocks with the crowbar. "It jars the hand a bit," he said, as sparks flew.

"There's a technique in using a bar," Art volunteered, from where he sat in the shade of a scrub wattle.

Jim pushed his hat back and leant on the crowbar. "What a load of crap."

"Fact."

"Show me then?" Jim held out the bar.

"You're the one needing the practice. You don't need a demo from me, you need work experience."

It hadn't taken me long to form an assessment of my two workers. Jim exuded a raw energy and exuberance for living and learning. It radiated from him in the form of energetic movements, wide smiles, loud laughs, bursts of song and excitable conversation that never let up. Art was the antithesis of this. The two of them put me in mind of a sun circling a black hole in the galaxy with Jim the sun and Art the black hole. Art sucked energy out of the environment just by his presence.

After Jim got down near the bedrock I gave Art the job of shovelling the gravel into a plastic bag. I produced a small whisk when he'd finished. "The best chance for finding gold will be right on the bottom so sweeping up the fines is critical for a good sample." I showed them what I wanted then passed the brush to Art.

Art got down on his knees with a grunt and began sweeping.

"Don't strain yourself," Jim said.

"No chance if I follow your example."

"Done much field work, Art?" I asked.

"Been all over," he said, giving the impression the question was impertinent.

"Like where?" Jim asked.

"Mostly gold mines. Drill supervisor Mt Leyshon. Leading hand at Pajingo."

"You'll be a useful man to have around, then."

"Reckon."

"Done any of this trap sampling before?" Jim asked.

"Plenty."

"Could've fooled me."

"Reckon anyone could."

Jim squatted down. "What do you do when you're not chief sampler and leading hand, apart from bludging that is?"

"I'm into a few business ventures." Art dropped the brush and eased himself onto a boulder. "That should do it." He lit a cigarette.

Jim picked up the brush and began to go over what Art had done. "You left most of it behind. No point in half doing a job."

"No point in being a bloody old woman either. You could be here all day cleaning one rock."

"Jim's right," I said. "There are no short cuts. Gold gravitates to the bottom. What you've left could be where it's concentrated."

"So what sort of things are you into then?" Jim asked.

"Bit of everything."

"Like what?"

"Prospecting, mining, drilling."

"A Jack of all trades?"

Art nodded.

"And master of none."

"I know a lot about plenty."

"Sounds like it. You married?"

Art laughed. "Think I'm stupid?"

When we had finished, Art scrambled to his feet and grabbed the crowbar and shovel, leaving the large bag of gravel for Jim. I was about to make a comment but Jim forestalled me. "Let him go," he said. "I can handle Art, besides, with food like Hunter puts on I need the exercise."

I did not doubt that Jim could handle Art. Jim had a sarcastic wit that more than matched Arts and it tended to make you laugh rather than take offence, which was just as well, for he loved to exercise it.

When we had gathered enough samples we returned to the campsite where Art raided the fridge and Jim and I headed to the river to pan them off and check for gold. The Star was smoothly flowing and darkly clear, and the late afternoon sun on the clouds was reflected in the water with an almost gold colour. I took it as a good omen.

"This company, Hunter, that we're working for," Jim said. "Are they just looking for gold?"

"Gold is their main interest, but there's also a lead anomaly here that they want to investigate."

"What's an anomaly?"

"Anything that gives an unusually high assay. In this case they took samples of stream sediment which came back with lead values that were higher than they were expecting."

I had given Jim a panning off dish, and after watching me he began to pan a sample too with infinite care, being careful to tip the rejects into another dish. "What happens if you find a large nugget?" he asked.

"What do you reckon?" I said.

"Into the pocket and back up the creek for some more. Goodbye Hunter, hello Jim." He chuckled. "So why are we getting samples assayed back in Charters Towers when we can find the gold right here in the dish?"

"Just a precaution in case we miss some gold."

"Hey! Wash out your mouth. You've got the world's number one panner here now." His face suddenly lit up with delight. "Gold!" He pointed to a yellow speck. "How do I get it out?"

I took the dish and removed the heavy ironstone it was sitting in, then counted three medium colours."

Jim threw his hat in the air with a yell. "I can pan gold. Is he any good or is he any good?"

I picked up the dish he'd just panned his sample into. "Let's see what you washed out."

"Why, don't you trust me?"

I concentrated the sample down again and passed the pan to him. "Two pieces of lead shot—that'll be the cause of the lead anomaly probably—one flat coarse colour, two medium colours and some fines."

"Oh my God!" he groaned. "Let me try again."

On returning to the camp, Jim picked up the camp oven, a heavy cast iron cooking pot with a flat lid. "I'll cook the evening meal. How do I use this thing?"

Art ripped the tab off a can of beer. "We're going to be poisoned for sure. Never known a Kiwi yet who could cook."

"It's not a problem," Jim said. "I'll just cook for Bob and me."

Art screwed up his eyes in sudden thought. "Just joking; want a beer Jim?"

"No. I need to concentrate." Jim hovered about the fire like a caveman afraid it might go out and let in the wild animals. It was so big and hot that it nearly burnt through a guy rope on the annex. Jim's quick application of Art's half finished can of beer cured the problem but started another round of sarcastic comments from Art.

We tried out Jim's concoction later. It was actually much later as we couldn't get near the coals for a long time to put anything on them. There were potatoes, carrots, beans, cabbage and meat all together

"It's delicious," I said, helping myself to seconds, and removing a parchment-like cabbage leaf. "Pity you took the lid off to look at it though. Charcoal is great for cleaning teeth but does nothing for the texture."

"Can this man cook?" Jim said proudly.

"Any tit wit can cook with a camp oven," Art scoffed.

"I didn't see you volunteering," Jim said. " Besides, you'd be too drunk. How many cartons have you sunk while Bob and I've been working?"

"It would take mor'n a carton or two to put me under," Art said with spirit. "I was near born in a pub."

Jim gave a snort. "Yeah, and with a crowbar in your hand. Listen to yourself; you're already incoherent."

"Incoherent? Your problem is you don't speak English."

As we sat round the caravan's rickety table, Jim looked around. "This van's a heap of junk," he said, eying the torn screens, chipped cupboard doors and other broken fittings.

Art grunted assent. "I told Chas that already. This is my last job for him unless he gives me a better deal."

"I'd put up with a lot for a job like this," Jim said. He turned to me. "You must save a fortune with the company paying all expenses."

I nodded. "There are other tax advantages too."

His eyes lit up. "How do I get on to them?"

"Get to know a geologist."

"I do. So what's next?"

"Make yourself indispensable to him."

Art looked up from his Playboy magazine "From what I've seen, you'd be a natural at brown nosing, Jim."

"So what else?" Jim said, ignoring Art.

"I could do with a cup of tea?"

"My God! It's started already." Undeterred, Jim hopped up and put the kettle on.

"I'll have another beer while you're at it," Art said.

"I'm only working for info, Art. What are you offering apart from the usual drivel?"

"I know a few tax rorts."

Jim shook his head. "I should have known." He got out the milk and sugar and later passed me a steaming mug.

"Thanks, that's really good." I said, mimicking his clipped New Zealand accent and favourite expression.

He sat down again. "So what else do I do?"

"You form a company. It would need a catchy name."

"I could call myself Shafer something— Jim Shafer's ...?" He paused in thought. "What goes with S?"

"Shonky, slack, sick, suspect, stupid," Art interjected.

"Settle down!" Jim thought a moment. "Shafer Superior Services?"

"That's not bad," I said. "But what are you offering?"

"Any suggestions?"

"What about a biscuit to go with this tea?"

He pushed over a packet of ginger nuts."

"I'd prefer the Chocolate Montes you stashed away earlier on."

He got up and extracted them from the cab of the Landcruiser and, handed one to me.

"So what am I offering?" he said.

"Not too bloody much, from what I've seen so far," Art said.

"What do you want to do?" I asked

"Contract myself out at say one-forty a day."

Art let out a belly laugh.

"That's twice what you're getting now," I said.

"It's probably what you're charging Hunter for me; anyway I'd be worth it."

"You'd need to be very experienced to charge that."

"I will be. I could buy a four-wheel-drive to hire out too." He found a pencil and did some figuring on a biscuit wrapper before glancing up. "This is really good. I could hire out all the camp equipment, too."

"Chas already beat you to it."

"Stuff Chas. I'm your friend."

"You mean mate?"

He groaned. "I hate that word. Everybody's a mate over here. Mate this, mate that. Ow're yer goin', mate. See ya, mate. So long, mate. Good on yer, mate." He munched through another chocolate biscuit, then said. "I could also hire field assistants to you?"

"They'd want to be pretty good for me to use them."

Art chimed in. "My oath they would. I'm on sixty-five a day but I'm giving Chas a special mates deal. Normally I'd be on twice that."

It was Jim's turn to laugh. "If Art is the standard then I could pick up any no-hoper sleeping in the park. Say I charged them out at seventy a day and paid them forty, which would be twice what Art's worth. That adds another thirty a day to my income."

"In your dreams, mate." Art said. "No one will work for a Kiwi over here, anyway. Not even for a two hundred a day."

Jim got up and rifled the deep freeze and refrigerator and piled his plate with tinned fruit, ice-cream, glace cherries and a topping of raspberry sauce and pressurised cream before returning with his overloaded plate and a block of chocolate.

Art, who was drinking another beer, lit a cigarette. "How can you eat like that? It's disgusting."

"You mean you don't have any vices?"

"None that are worth mentioning."

"What about the beer?"

"A few tinnies after a hard day's work isn't a vice is it Bob?" He turned to me for backup.

"A few?" Jim said. "A man doesn't get a beer gut like a bloated whale with BO from just a few. More like a few dozen and what about the smokes? You've been puffing all day. You're a chain smoker."

"Bull."

"Thirty a day. That's your second pack."

"Who's counting?"

"What about all the women you were boasting about? That's a vice."

"That's natural. Sex with women is only strange for Kiwis. I suppose you reckon you don't have any vices."

"Vices are for slobs who can't get motivated."

I stood up. "If you two are going to argue all night I'm leaving."

Jim, who'd managed to argue and eat at the same time, pushed his plate aside and produced a pack of cards. "What about a game of poker?"

"That's another vice," Art said. "But if you want your money ripped off, I'm ready."

"I don't want anyone losing a month's pay cheque," I said as we sat around the table. "Twenty cents will be the maximum raise and we'll stop after an hour."

"We'll play Manila," Jim said, dealing the cards. "I used to play this all night back home. There'd be 500 dollars on the table sometimes and the only way to survive was to go for it."

"Bloody peanuts," Art said, staring at Jim through a haze of cigarette smoke. "I've been in games that went all week. You had to have 500 just to open. Good way to make a buck though."

"So you're a gambler too," Jim said. "You forgot to mention it before. Were you born holding a pack of cards?"

"I been gambling since I could count." Art threw twenty cents into the pot with a flourish reminiscent no doubt of the way he'd disposed of hundred dollar bills. "Probably forgotten more about gambling than you ever knew, mate."

"I'm not your bloody mate," Jim said, irritated by the term and by Art's indifference to the truth. "Stupid Aussie slang."

Art cracked opened another beer. "Sorry mate."

Cards have a fascination that is unknown to the generations brought up on TV and computer games. Playing cards for money lends an added edge and time slipped away effortlessly. It was only when the generator ran out of fuel around midnight, that play ended.

"I'm four dollars fifty ahead," Jim said, as we packed up in torchlight. "What about you, Bob?"

"Just over three dollars up," I said.

Art totted up his stake. "I've won five or six bucks."

"Amazing," Jim said. "Everybody won, can you believe it?"

Art nodded. "I believe it, mate. What do you believe?"

Jim's eyes narrowed. "You're full of bull. Someone puts shit on me then I do it to him. Be warned."

"You should'a stayed in Kiwi land, matey," Art said. "That's where it all piles up." He yawned. "Talking of which I gotta have one." He grabbed a toilet roll and went out into the night.

I turned in and had nearly dozed off when there was a brilliant flash, but instead of a following thunderclap there was a burst of distant swearing from Art. Moments later, Jim tore into the tent with his Polaroid camera and threw himself on his stretcher, laughing so much he could barely talk. "I caught him in the act," he said between heaving gasps. "He might cut down on talking so much crap when he sees how much he produces."

Jim displayed the photo the next morning. The dunny we had set up was a bit on the nose and Art was draped over a log instead. The well-located white ant's nest that happened to be in the picture as well, with its pointed top, looked like the proverbial pile, hot and steaming. "I knew it," Jim smirked. "You're full of it, Art. This is the proof."

Art made a grab for it but Jim was too quick.

* * *

"When are we getting out of this dump?" Art asked at the end of our fourth week. "I'm down to me last carton."

"We should be finished in about three days."

"Art's face brightened. "Beaudy; I can drink nearly eight cans a night then. It'll be bloody good to get back to the Towers and off this rationing."

My estimate was optimistic, however, and we were still working on the fourth day, with a lot to finish if we were to leave the following morning. The cold water was gone by mid afternoon and Jim was drinking warm water with no apparent ill effects, but by the time we were back at camp anything cool was welcome. As Jim and I drank iced water from the freezer, Art, having finished his beer ration, searched throughout the camp in case he had mislaid a tin. Finally, he located a half-full can of coke from the back of the fridge, placed there in the distant past, and guzzled thirstily.

"Your hand's shaking," Jim said. "You've got the DTs."

"Bloody have not," Art said.

"Look at your hand. How are you going to get through the night?"

"You're talking bull!"

"Hold out your hand then."

Art held it out. It did have a slight tremor. "That's from carrying all the sampling gear back."

Jim gave a cynical laugh. "A couple of empty bags and a sieve"

"Show us yours then."

"I don't drink so what's the point?"

"Worms have the same effect as DTs. They get into the brain, although being a Kiwi you might be safe from that problem. Wormy

24

meat can eat your guts out too."

"That reminds me," I said. "We'd better roast that leg of pork. There's nothing else to eat and it'll go off soon."

"Off?" Art said. "It's never been on. You guys are mad."

"What are you going to eat then?" I asked.

"It won't be pig, that's for sure. You can smell it every time you open the fridge, it's bloody disgusting."

"That's not pig," Jim said. "It's the stew you poisoned us with last week that no one could eat."

I got the fire going and when the coals were ready, I put the pork in the cast iron pot, along with a few other ingredients. It was a two-and-a-half-hour wait and as the pork cooked a delicious smell wafted through the camp.

"Can you imagine this meal," Jim said as we sat there getting hungrier and hungrier. "A bottle of red, thick gravy, crackling." He smacked his lips. "What are you going to have, Art? I think I saw a packet of salt biscuits in one of the boxes. They could be nice."

"The bottle of red sounds all right," Art said. "Almost as good as a beer, 'cept we don't have any, but a man would have to be near death from starvation to eat wormy pork."

"You might have to live off that larder you've got round your waist. I reckon it's cost the company a few hundred dollars to put it there."

Art heaved himself up. "I've lost weight on this job. It comes from doing the work of two men." He began to hunt through the fridge. "Ah!" He pulled out a crushed egg carton. "I'll have some of these—beaudy. One cheese, tomato and onion omelette coming up."

"It's amazing what you find when the fridge gets empty," I said. "I thought we had more eggs somewhere but I couldn't find them."

"They were squashed behind Art's carton of beer," Jim said.

The egg carton had become glued shut. Art sawed it open to reveal only two whole eggs, the rest had been crushed to a putrefying slime.

Jim laughed. "That explains the smell."

"What a waste." Art stared at the mess sorrowfully. "I could still be tempted. I reckon an omelette made from this mess would still be better than what you're having."

"You've still got two whole eggs," I said. "If you add the tomato and onion you're in business. There's nothing else left except tinned two-fruits."

"Yeah," Art said, looking at the carton with renewed interest as hunger pains gnawed. He gingerly dug the two eggs out of the pungent mess with a spoon. After washing the eggs, he fried the onion over the gas stove and salvaged the last of the tomato and cheese by pruning off the bad bits and cutting them into small slices.

"Talking of amazing things," Jim said. "It's amazing what hunger can do to a man. Art's been here four weeks and the only thing he's cooked is his backside. Now we find he's a cordon bleu chef."

"Eat your heart out, boys," Art said, scraping the golden brown onion to one side. He grabbed an egg and cracked it on the side of the frypan.

From past experience I can confirm that there is nothing more putrid than a rotten egg. While the crushed eggs in the carton had ponged at a high level, their rating on the Richter earthquake scale had been somewhat reduced by gradual leakage into the fridge. The un-cracked egg, however, had retained its full 100 per cent potency. There was a sort of popping noise, reminiscent of a tired birthday balloon going off a few days after the happy event, quickly followed by a strangled gasp from Art, who staggered back a few paces as the contents exploded. An indescribably disgusting smell then pervaded the cool night air. For a moment, Art stood there transfixed as if the yellowish gloop, now covering both him and the stove, had the powers of paralysis. It might have stopped Art in his tracks but not us. Jim and I vacated at speed.

Although Art was in temporary shock, it did not stop his tongue from working. The string of oaths that enlivened the night, however, was drowned out by our laughter. Jim's face was the colour of the nearby coals, his body contorted in the ecstasy of the moment.

By the time Art had showered and consigned his clothes to a sack tethered in the river there were three plates of roast pork on the table with all the trimmings. Jim and I were already making inroads into our share.

"Pull up a seat, Art," Jim said. He sniffed. "On second thoughts, take the plate and sit somewhere else. You've always been a bit on the nose but there are limits to the pain I can put up with. Why didn't you have a shower?"

"I had a bloody shower."

Jim sniffed again. "It must be the usual BO then. I thought I was used to it."

"Very funny." Art sat down and dissected his pork carefully with a knife, before he took a tentative bite, but his hunger was too great; soon he was eating it with gusto. "What a bastard," he said. "I'm reduced to the level of a Kiwi. Who'd have thought an egg could do that. How old do you reckon they were, Bob?"

"Chas mentioned something about them being free range."

Jim chuckled. "They had a bloody good range all right. I reckon you'd smell them a mile upwind. Not even Art has that range." He began to laugh again. "I thought that was how you liked your eggs Art; that you were angry because it missed the pan and landed on you."

Art leant over and carved another large slice of pork. "Now I know why they send the Kiwis over here in droves; it's to get rid of them and their stupid humour."

"Tomorrow, we'll get an early start," I said, as we cleaned up after the meal. "We should be packed and ready to go by seven. You reckon you can get out of bed by five-thirty, Art?"

"Course I can. The pork will probably give me nightmares. I may not even get any sleep."

"Join the club," Jim said. "I've only managed two hours a night because of your snoring." He patted his stomach and burped contentedly. "But after that superb meal I reckon I'll be dead to the world before I hit the pillow."

Art gave an assenting grunt. "We'll all be dead after eating that pig."

Later in the evening Jim lay on his stomach on his camp stretcher, his favourite position. "Think I'll write a letter to my girl," he said as I wrote up the day's results at the portable card table.

"Didn't know you had one," I said. "A Kiwi?"

"Wish it was. Australian girls are the pits; too immature."

"How come you're writing to one then?"

"She's one of the better ones. Trouble is she has two kids; little terrors." He pulled a photo from his wallet and passed it to me. "Katy."

"Not bad. She looks about forty though. A virile specimen like you should be able to find a young chick with the looks of a film star."

"Think I have. I put my name down with a dating agency before I came up here and met a real stunner." He passed another photo over. "Kirsty, she's into squash, wind surfing, cycling. We got on well on the first date. Early thirties, long dark hair and a nice smile.

"Kirsty could be the one then. A future Mrs Shafer?"

"No way, she's not a Kiwi."

"You'll only marry a Kiwi?"

"Kiwi girls are different. I was married to one for a while, just after I left school, but we were kids looking for continuous sex and fell out."

"You mean wore out."

He chuckled. "I like a woman who's mature."

"Has Kirsty got kids too?"

He groaned. "Three. Think I'll write to her too." He started writing and I was soon asleep, only to be woken later as Jim shone his torch in my eyes.

"Bob. You awake? Listen to that."

"What?" I muttered in sleep-drugged annoyance.

"Art, snoring in the van. Every time he eats too much the volume goes up. I've been tuned in for about an hour. I can't sleep with that racket going on."

The van acted as a sound shell and Art's efforts were particularly good this night. "So what did you wake me for; to share in the enjoyment? It's after midnight for God's sake."

"I just had a brilliant thought. I reckon I've got a cure."

Jim disappeared outside and after some surreptitious rustling I heard a dull pop. He reappeared soon after, barely able to contain his laughter and bringing with him an unmistakable odor.

"You broke that other egg?" I said.

"Right under the van. It'll either wake him up or take him out." Sure enough, Art's snoring began to falter, then stop. There was the sound of the van rocking as he turned over in bed followed by a few muffled groans, then the snoring started again.

"Un-be-lievable," Jim said in utter disgust. "Can you imagine sleeping through that pong?"

"No I can't," I said. "Did you check the breeze before you broke it? I think we're down wind."

"Oh my God," he groaned. "You're right."

The smell of rotten egg and Art's racket was a combination that had amazing sleep-depriving power. We were up soon after four. It was the earliest I had ever struck camp and Art was like a zombie, virtually useless, as he needed a good eight hours rest to function at all. "That bloody egg," he mumbled as we loaded up in the darkness. "Couldn't you guys smell it? The pong kept me awake all night."

Chapter 3 The Saint

Jim spent the ten days break in Townsville and on my return from Brisbane he picked me up at the airport in a Toyota tray-top rental.

"How was your holiday?" I asked. "Did you see all the sights?"

"It was the best," he said. "The hostel was full of female Swedish backpackers. I never left it. Man, it was great. I need a few weeks in the bush to recover. Where are we going this time?"

"Back to the Star River, but to a new site. There are a few things to do in Townsville first though. We won't make camp until after dark."

He groaned. "Not again. Why do we always set up in the dark?"

"It's ok. I sent Chas a map and arranged for him to flag a route in, set up the tent and buy a heap of supplies. He and Art should be heading there right now. All we'll have to do is turn up, eat the meal they've prepared and go to sleep."

A wide grin split his face, well covered with reddish stubble. "That's really good. The Shafer-Woodhouse team swings into action again. You can't have the company's two top explorers wasting time getting lost and then having to set up camp in the dark as we did the last trip. "So we're working in a different area?"

"Yes, the Little Star, higher up in the ranges. It should be a real tourist Mecca. The road in isn't much good though. There are a lot of creeks. I asked Chas to fix the worst sections on the way in."

At around ten o'clock that evening I had reason to reflect on my earlier confidence, as with Jim driving, we ground slowly through innumerable washed out creek crossings in low range, low gear. As we clambered out of each creek the roo-bar caught on the jump-ups and the tow bar left a great furrow behind. We were making slow progress trying to follow Chas' faint tracks, alternately losing and finding them through the partly bulldozed scrub and waist high spear grass interspersed with hidden anthills and fallen logs.

"Chas has done a great job fixing up the rough bits," Jim said as the sump hung up on a rock and he was forced to back off and find an alternative route. "He hasn't shifted one single rock or touched one bank with a shovel. I can't believe that guy can drive where he does."

"He's good value when we don't have a track to follow. You'd be surprised at the size of a tree he can push over."

"See any flagging?" He was referring to pieces of yellow flagging that Chas had used to mark the route. "You'd think the track those two dimwits made would be a bit clearer if they only came in this morning."

"It does look a bit old. Maybe it's not their track."

"What if it isn't?"

"We'd have to go back to the road and look for another lot of flagging."

"You're joking! We could be looking all night. We've got no food either."

"A night without food is nothing to a geo," I said.

"You could have fooled me. Every time I put something in the fridge to finish off later you do the job for me."

"Yes, but hunger doesn't scare me like it does you. Talking of which, I remember the time when I was a student in the fifties, working summer vacations for the Tasmanian Mines Department. They put me to work in southwest Tasmania."

"I've never been to Tassie."

"Well this place here is like the manicured lawn of a prize Toowoomba garden in spring compared with the southwest. Even in summer, storms blow in two days out of three; the wind knocks you off your feet if you stand upright and there are no tracks to follow because the place is or was an unexplored wilderness. Near the coast the scrub is so thick and stunted you have to hack your way with a machete, and inland, the hills are so craggy you need a rock climber's experience to go in."

"Sounds like New Zealand, but not as rough. What's this got to do with food?"

"They flew me in by helicopter with Steve and Pete, a Polish geologist and Polish prospector. We had to map the country on foot using air photos and carry all our gear with us. As we moved camp nearly every day, Steve had the clever idea of the helicopter making three food drops at carefully selected points. That way we'd have only a week's food to cart about."

"A week's tucker? I'd be carting 200 kilos."

"It was great until the start of the third week when we couldn't find the drop zone."

"So you radioed for new supplies."

"No radio."

"You flagged a car down on the road."

"No road."

"What if you fell ill then?"

"You died."

"So what did you do?"

"We searched until hunger pains got the better of us. Then we walked to the fourth drop and lived on half rations for two weeks."

"That would be okay by me," Jim said. "There's no will power needed as there's no temptation. What a great way to diet."

"You'd have eaten your share in one week and then starved." A piece of fluttering yellow caught my eye, tied to a wattle branch and not much bigger than a butterfly. I pointed. "There, flagging."

"He doesn't believe in using much, does he? Maybe he thinks we might see it."

"He's of a conservative nature."

"Well I hope he spends a bit more on the tucker than he does on flagging."

"I sent him our usual list of supplies."

"That's really good. The only thing going for this job is the food and the fact that you can't spend money on anything."

"You certainly made the most of the food. Playing squash must be quite a hassle now with that stomach you've developed."

He grimaced. "I've got to cut down this trip."

"Or work harder, or do both."

"Settle down." Reaching into the glove box he pulled out a sesame seed bar, ripped the cellophane wrapping off and began to chew. "It's after ten and I'm starving. I wonder what Chas cooked for us?"

"Maybe a roast."

His eyes lit up. "Yeah, roast chicken with crispy chips—maybe green peas, gravy, followed by ice-cream and chocolate topping."

"With everything set up for us we'll be ready to spring into action first thing tomorrow."

Jim fingered the Jade Tiki that hung around his neck. "First thing? I might have known there was a catch. Every job I do for you is the same. It takes a sixteen hour day and I'm working for peanuts."

"Suxteen hours?" I said, taking off his New Zealand accent. "You were an out of work Kiwi butcher on the dole and I've turned you into a top geological assistant and camp cook."

"You had it easy though; you were working with genius. Show me once and I had it figured." He paused to engage low gear as the tracks dipped steeply into yet another creek. He eased into it, then scrabbled up a near vertical jump up on the other side, the wheels spinning and the Toyota crabbing sideways. "How much further to go do you reckon?" he said.

"We must be close. The Star River should be just ahead. I asked Chas to set up near it. We should see a light any moment."

"I think I can smell that roast."

As branches whipping across the windscreen I glimpsed something. "Stop. Reverse back."

He reversed, then swung the wheel so that the headlights floodlit the scrub just off the track. The tent and numerous cartons of unpacked gear were stacked in an untidy heap beneath an ironbark. A small piece of flagging dangled above them.

Jim broke the silence first. "My God!" he said, his voice rising. "Sucked in again. I never learn."

We got out and looked around in dismay. A note was on one of the food cartons, held down by a rock. Jim read it to me in the glare of the headlights "Got a late start and have to return to lop trees for the Greenvale Shire this week, back with Art, Tuesday 9am."

Jim scrunched the note up. "It's good that he marked the site so well. No chance of missing all this flagging in the dark. Nice of him to supply a written apology too."

"Very polite."

Thoughtful of him to stack all the gear right here; we only have to cart it fifty metres to a flat spot.

"Very thoughtful."

He walked over to the tent, lying in an untidy roll and kicked it. "And good that he's reliable."

"My word."

"And that he lets you know exactly what's going on."

"Right."

He surveyed the now collapsed pile of split cartons that had clearly been there for some time and had been well soaked by a passing storm, possibly a cyclone, judging by the look of them.

"And that he's stacked the cartons so the rain and ants can't get them."

"Yes."

"You'd think he could at least have put them under the tent."

"Or even in the tent," I said.

"Give the man a break. He would have had to put it up." Jim shook his head. "The man's a dickhead." A thought struck him. "Hope he can play cards; he's not much good for anything else."

"I don't think he plays cards."

Jim looked aghast. "So what did you hire him for then?"

"He's a good worker."

"Yeah? Maybe for the Greenvale Shire."

"We've had a slight setback," I said, "but the Woodhouse-Shafer team is not defeated."

"The Shafer-Woodhouse team is bloody disgusted though."

"We'd better put the tent up. It looks like rain."

"Stuff the tent," Jim said, still full of aggression. "An army marches on its stomach. Give me food." Moments later he was scrimmaging among the cartons.

After some searching he found a carton of orange cordial, a carton of canned two-fruits and a carton of cornflakes, but not much else in the way of food.

"It's not a problem," Jim said later, sitting on his camp stretcher in the tent and spooning cornflakes and two-fruits into his mouth. "We've got a deep freeze, a barbecue plate, cutlery, 3KV generator, an electric toaster, a griller, table and chairs—who needs food?"

"Why the sarcasm? I asked. "Your compensation is high pay and a month in a place tourists would kill to get to."

He nodded. "You're right about killing. Death is very close. Chas will be the first."

The following morning, after a late start getting the camp set up, and with no sign of Chas and Art, we began to sample the streams. After about an hour, Jim leant on the crowbar and fanned the flies away with his hat

"So this Chas," he said, opening a topic that was clearly preying on his mind. "Is he another Art?"

"He's nothing like Art."

"Could have fooled me. It'll be nice if he turns up. Good that he's reliable isn't it. He said nine and it's only eleven-thirty. That's what I call reliable."

"He might be at the camp. Maybe we didn't hear the Toyota?"

"Okay." Jim said. "Put your money where your mouth is. I'll bet five dollars he's not there."

I shook my head. I'd known Chas for some time and knew this was a very risky bet.

"Five dollars he's not there by twelve, then," he persisted.

"No way."

"Okay, we'll name three times, the nearest one gets the bet."

This was more to my liking. We wrote the times down separately and then compared notes. "I've got one o'clock, five, and 1 am tomorrow morning," I said. "What about you?"

A look of shock passed fleetingly over his face. "What's with this tomorrow? I thought you trusted this guy?"

"I trust him to make me a lot of money. What have you got?"

He scowled. "I should have remembered that bet you won at squash. Brains and skill can't beat luck. I've been sucked in again. Twelve, two, and four this afternoon."

Jim parted with five dollars as we sampled more two-fruits and cornflakes that evening. "Easy money," I said. "Do you want double or nothing?"

"No. I need to study the odds for a few days. Chas is worse than betting on the dogs but I'll forgive him if he turns up right now with some decent tucker. What do you reckon? Thick juicy steaks, mashed potatoes, ice-cream, nuts, chocolate. If he brings a dog it could be joining the steaks in the camp oven the way I feel. What idiot said cornflakes was a meal?"

"Why don't you try fishing? The river is big enough to have a few crocs. I've got some fish hooks."

He leapt up. "Why didn't you say so before? Let me at them."

I found the fishing tackle and for some time after that I could hear Jim down by the river swearing. He came back later empty handed.

"There's fish there," he said, "but the turtles beat them to the bait every time."

"So we'll have turtle soup."

"No way; they're too cute to kill."

Chas and caravan turned up about an hour later, just as Jim was snacking on a few more cornflakes. "Running a bit late," he said. "The van got stuck in a creek or two."

"Or five or six," Jim said, examining it critically. "If it had been me, I'd have abandoned it and claimed the insurance. It's an even bigger heap of junk than it was last time."

I shook my head in disbelief. "How did you get it across all those creeks, and why in the name of God did you bring it anyway? We've nearly finished the program waiting for you. What's wrong with a tent."

"Why bring a tent when you can rent Hunter a caravan," Jim said, admiration and envy in his voice. "Don't forget this is our mobile casino. It's great Hunter sends it out each field trip.

Chas gave one of his shy grins that sat incongruously on someone six feet tall and nearly as wide. "Thought it might be useful. Won't charge much for using it."

"So what are you charging for it?" Jim asked.

"'Bout a hundred a week."

Jim looked astounded. "A hundred! What a rip-off. You could get a lot you more if you made it half decent. Some glass and fly screens would help, that'd be worth another twenty. Fix up the hole in the wall and the leak in the roof, another twenty; give us a table that doesn't have to be supported on beer cartons, a half decent stove and a fridge that actually cools things down—say another sixty; proper bunk beds and sound proofing for Art; that's over two-fifty a week, Chas."

Chas gave an indifferent shrug. "Yep."

"Where's Art?"

"He's been delayed."

"That's the best news I've heard yet." Jim began searching the back of Chas' Toyota, which normally looked like a metal recycling bin but today was almost obscured with vegetation that had come adrift from scrub bashing and which had ended up in the tray. Twigs, leaves, bark and broken tree limbs, some of considerable size, now filled it. Numerous species of ant ranged aggressively over the lot, dragging morsels of squashed insect and other windfall delicacies in a vain search for home.

"Food Chas. Where is it? Don't tell me you forgot it."

"It's in the van. Couldn't bring the tucker when I left the gear here last week. Not enough room. I had to buy it this morning."

"No need to apologise," Jim said. "I don't mind eating cornflakes and bloody two-fruits three times a day and setting up camp in the dark. I don't mind having to cook the meal you were supposed to cook and doing all the work you were supposed to do and finding all the cartons out in the rain, not to mention setting up the tent and getting no sleep after an 18 hour day. Just show me some real food and I'll forgive everything."

We waited patiently as Chas cut the wire holding the caravan door to the frame. "The door fell off," he said, by way of explanation.

Jim pointed to the dangling remains of a fly screen and a snapped copper pipe. "Window fell off too, and the gas bottle."

"Bottle's in the Toyota. It came loose at that last creek crossing."

Chas propped the door against the wall, pulled out the step and Jim fell inside as the step collapsed under his weight.

"Oh my God!" Jim said, his voice rising as Chas and I crowded in behind. The fridge had toppled over but not before it had emptied its contents. The oven was upside down, but still attached to its gas pipe. Spread over the floor was a jumble of broken cartons heaped into a loose pyramid that floated in and was held together by a greenish ooze of detergent, cordial, flour, milk, biscuits, potatoes, broken eggs and red dust. Surrounding the pyramid and well coated with the products of disintegration were scores of tins and bottles, mostly without labels.

Jim lifted a cardboard carton off the top of the pile that was oozing a dark fluid. The words 'Ice cream cake' could just be discerned.

"Good choice Chas. One of my favourites." He pulled back the flap and let the liquid pour into his mouth.

"Are you going to bog in now?" I said.

He looked at the oozing pile, showing remarkable restraint, given his hunger. "I'm tempted but I think I'll settle for cornflakes and two-fruits."

Chas shrugged. "Track was a bit rough."

This bare acknowledgment of the culinary supply crisis facing the camp awoke Jim from his mood of resignation. "Rough?" he said with gathering spirit. "You were supposed to fix it. Did you have to drive like a maniac over it though?"

"I needed a bit of speed for some of the creeks."

I had seen something of Chas' driving and I suspected that the caravan had probably spent more time in the air than on the ground.

Jim pulled a mattress off the food pile. It had acted like blotting paper and soaked up a goodly amount of liquid. A thought seemed to strike him. "Where are you going to sleep, Chas?"

"I'll bunk in with you until I clean this up."

"If Bob cooks the meal I'll give you a hand to do it now."

Chas looked impressed. "Thanks," he said.

Fortunately the core supplies like meat and vegetables were fairly intact and Jim burped in contentment when the meal was over.

"What's for dessert, Chas?" He asked.

Chas selected a label-less tin and began to lever the top off with a can opener. "Soft ice-cream and something," he said, peering into the tin. "What about soft ice-cream and beetroot?"

"Pass."

He reached for another label-less tin and went to work. "Soft ice-cream and—baked beans?"

"Pass."

He tried again. "Soft ice-cream and—three bean mix?"

Jim got up in disgust. "Can't you tell the difference between fruit and vegetables?"

"The meek shall eat and be satisfied, Jim."

"Bloody right, but first I need to eat, then I'll be satisfied. Give me a go."

He selected a tin and shook it violently. "Right," he said, attacking it with the can opener. "We'll have melted ice-cream and—yes, jackpot, fruit!" He peeled the top back and then recoiled. "Bloody two-fruits!"

Afterwards, as we got ready to turn in I thanked Jim for helping Chas clean up the van.

He chuckled. "Did you notice that I also moved the caravan from where he parked it?"

"You mean you had an ulterior motive?"

"My oath. If Art can't sleep for Chas snoring can you imagine having him in here with us?"

* * *

After Jim's breakfast of porridge followed by bacon, eggs and eggshell, we discussed the program. "There's a fair bit to do in the next four weeks," I said, "and this place has its own weather system, which is mostly wet. One decent thunderstorm could see us bottled up until the creeks go down next year. If we want to be out on time we'll need to split up as much as possible to speed up the work."

Chas, who was listening with half an ear while tinkering underneath his Toyota, crawled out looking a bit dubious. "Might be best to stick together for now, my fuel pump's playing up and could leave me stranded. I can pick up a replacement when I get the next supplies."

Jim kicked one of the tyres on the vehicle. "Only the fuel pump? You'd be flat out getting a wrecker to salvage this for spares."

"It'll run better than yours," Chas said, adding water to his leaky radiator.

"How do you work that out?"

"You've got a flat."

After a late start we began sampling a tributary of the Star. "Tell us about Art, Ba-er-Chas" Jim said. He sometimes became confused with names when his mind was preoccupied and he started to say Bob before he realised his mistake and corrected it in mid stream. "What was that about him being delayed?

"He was caught growing marijuana."

Jim burst out laughing. "What happened?"

"He was given a warning and is doing community service."

"You mean he has to work?"

"Yep. *A prudent man sees the evil but the simple are punished.*"

"That could kill him. I hope he's supervised. It would be a full time job for three people, keeping Art working. So what does he have to do?"

"Paint our church."

"Yours? How come?"

"He's a member."

Jim's mouth opened in shock. "Art's in a church? You have to be kidding me? You mean he actually turns up, each Sunday?"

"I wouldn't say each Sunday."

"So what would you say?"

"He turns up occasionally, but I'm working on it."

"You must be working bloody hard. I reckon the only way you'd get Art into a church is in a coffin for the final service."

"Probably."

"Why would anyone want to go to church anyway?"

"*The Lord giveth wisdom: out of his mouth comes knowledge and understanding.*"

"Sure, but you must have some hold on him?"

"He's a relation."

"My God, I'd keep that quiet. So you're trying to convert Art?"

"Just showing him a better way."

"You got that part right; anyway would be better than the way he's going now. Has it had any effect?"

"It's a bit early to tell"

"So how long have you been trying?"

"About ten years."

Jim chuckled. "Only ten years? I see what you mean. That's not very long. I think it'll need about fifty at the very minimum. So what do you try and teach him?"

"What Christ said. *I am the way, the truth and the light.*"

"I reckon that religions are just a rip-off. In return for this spiritual feel good they want to take everything you've got."

"Giving is voluntary."

"So what do you give?"

"A tenth."

Jim, who had started to heave out a rock that Chas had loosened, stopped in amazement. "What! A tenth?" Jim was clearly troubled by the enormity of this information. "So if you've been clearing say 20,000 for ten years, you've given the church 20,000."

"Well done Jim," I said. "If you can apply such power of concentrating on the work here we'll be finished in a few days."

Jim was not to be distracted by sarcasm. "Twenty thousand, Chas?"

"Yep."

"That's a new Toyota."

"It would pay for the shed I'm building."

"What shed?"

"A light industrial project I'm setting up. Should be able to rent it for about 3000 a year."

"You would have to be a dickhead, Chas. You could be earning another 5000 a year if the shed was built and you weren't giving away your savings."

"Yep."

"So what else do you do when you're not ripping off Hunter, going to church, building sheds and giving away your money?"

Chas leant on the crowbar for a moment, considering. "Bit of everything."

"Married?"

"Yep."

"Any kids?"

"Yep."

"How many?"

"Four."

"Four! So what are you, Catholic?"

"Nup."

"What then?"

"Mormon."

"Mormon! That's one of those weird religions isn't it? Six wives; no sex outside marriage, no grog, no gambling, that sort of stuff?"

Chas gave a shy grin. "The six wives are out. It's just living as we're taught in the Bible."

Jim pushed his bush hat back and looked at Chas aggressively, hand on hip. "That's crap. Nobody can live like that. So you're perfect, eh?"

"I try to be."

"You're not tempted?"

"*They that wait upon the Lord shall renew their strength,* Jim"

"You don't drink?"

Chas shook his head. "No drugs, alcohol, tea or coffee."

"Does that make you a Christian?"

"Helps."

"Do you smoke?"

"Nup."

"You've never smoked?"

"I used to, and a few other things."

"Like what?"

"Smoke, drink, gamble, but that was before I was a Mormon."

"So you've sinned?"

"Yep."

"What about working on a Sunday?" Jim said, levering the rock out. "You drove out here with some gear."

Chas nodded. "Sometimes you have to."

"Sounds like a double standard to me."

A faint frown creased Chas' brow. "Possibly. It depends."

"Yeah, it depends on how much money you can make."

"No, it depends on who you inconvenience by not working."

The two of them toiled in silence for a while—Chas secure in his beliefs, which had the certainty of the sun rising and setting—Jim wrestling with his disbeliefs, which were outraged at this phlegmatic simplicity. "This Art," he said finally. "How can he be in the church when he's into every sin in the book? He bludges, swears, tells lies, takes drugs, cheats at cards, fornicates. You name it, he does it."

"We're all sinners. The church isn't for saints."

This revelation had Jim stopping again, "But you're close to being perfect, by the sound of it."

"Hope so."

"So what sin have you committed today?"

Chas thought for a moment. "Probably had a few bad thoughts."

"Bad thoughts!—that's disgusting Bo... er... Chas. What do you think about that, Bob?"

"I think we should finish here and move on."

Jim turned to Chas. "What sort of thoughts?"

Chas shrugged.

"They're private," I said. "Chas doesn't want to corrupt you."

Work resumed for a short period until Chas opened the next round. "So what about you, Jim? What do you believe in?"

Jim, who now had the crowbar, struck sparks off a rock as he stabbed down. "Do unto others. Just as it's written in the Bible. Someone gives me a hard time then I return the compliment. An eye for an eye."

"That's a bit twisted and out of date," I said.

Jim grinned. "Suits me okay though."

"Married?" Chas asked.

"Was once."

"You actually found a woman who would live with you?" I asked.

"Hey! Settle down. What is this, get stuck into Jim week?"

"Month," Chas said.

Later, as the billy boiled for lunch, we listened to the stock exchange report on Jim's portable.

"Hunter's gone up to 47 cents," Jim said. "Soon as I get some cash together I'm going to buy some shares. There has to be a better way to make money than this sampling work."

"Have you ever invested in the stock market?" I asked.

He chuckled. "No, but I read something about it recently. It said a lot of money had been made by investors with gold shares."

"The market's starting to heat up," I agreed. "Penny stocks are rising."

"So how do I make money?"

"Do you mean quickly or securely."

"Quickly, of course."

"You pick a penny stock that's going to double in price."

"How do you know which ones? You'd need to be a geologist?"

I shook my head. "No way. Geologists know that only about one in 300 companies gets to find anything of real value so they miss out on all the dubious companies that have nothing but whose shares increase spectacularly."

"So how do I find one of them?"

"Find one with a board that will promote itself."

"How?"

"By watching their share price. It tends to fluctuate greatly over time but nothing is actually discovered."

"What about Hunter?"

"They've got some good projects and good management."

"So if I buy a thousand dollars worth of Hunter they could double or triple in six months?"

"Or they could be worth nothing."

"Settle down. Hunter won't drop. Not with the Shafer-Woodhouse team in action."

"What about Chas and Art though," I said. "They work for Hunter too?"

He was silent for a moment, then chuckled. "You're right. I might have to re-think. The shares would be valueless if it depended on those two dickheads. Have you bought any Hunter shares?"

"A few."

"What did you buy them for?"

"Twenty-eight cents."

"And they're forty-seven now." He groaned with frustration. "So if they go to a dollar you can retire."

"I think I'd need more than 10,000 dollars in my retirement fund."

"I've got to get some. How do I go about it?"

"You need to ring a broker. I'd keep well clear of mining stocks unless you have surplus funds you can afford to lose. Stock markets that get overheated, always crash, and not many investors get out in time. You'll be the same as all the rest, sitting on paper profits of thousands but ending up losing the lot."

"What about you. Are you going to take your own advice and sell now?"

"No. I'm going to hold on to them and lose the lot."

"Not you. You'll make a fortune. You're going to be my financial guru."

"For a share of the profits I'll advise anyone."

Jim turned to Chas. "What do you reckon Chas? Is it a good way to make money?"

"*Incline thine ear unto wisdom, Jim, and apply thine heart to understanding.*"

"Yeah, so what do you reckon?"

"You'll go bust."

"Thanks for the vote of confidence." He dropped the crowbar and pulled over the esky, our battered plastic cool box. "Lunch time," he said, rummaging around in it for food. "What is this?" he held up a tin of camp pie, a tin of two-fruits and two tins of sardines that had been cushioned from the knocks and dents of the morning's journey by a packet of now pulverised dry biscuits. "Who packed this crap?"

"I did," Chas said.

Jim poured out a handful of powdered biscuit. "How're we supposed to eat this?"

"With difficulty?" I volunteered.

"What about a little imagination, Chas. What about a little variety?"

"There's two types of sardines and if you don't like fish there's camp pie," Chas said.

Jim sighed. "I mean: we've got lettuce, ham, dried fruit, nuts, cheese, chocolate and all sorts of fruit drinks—and they're still back at the camp."

Chas nodded placidly. "You can have them tonight."

"I'll make the lunches in future," Jim said. "If no one's responsible we'll get nothing."

I squeezed some condensed milk into my tea. "A cup of tea is all I need on a hot day. I notice you're not a tea or coffee drinker either, Jim. You sure you're not religious?"

He snorted. "No. I never touch the stuff but I'm just exerting free will, not mindless religious black magic."

"*As a man thinketh, in his heart so he is,*" Chas said.

"So what's that supposed to mean?"

"It means that the power of the Lord is working in you."

"Chas is right," I said. "You could be on the road to salvation. Your willpower over these insidious drugs indicates major character reformation is possible."

"Food and greed go hand in hand, Jim, and gluttony is a sin," Chas said, becoming quite eloquent. "You've made a start but you need to go further."

Jim gave another snort. "I'm starting to feel reformation working, but it's not voluntary, it's due to your inability to pack a decent lunch. No one could suffer the sin of gluttony with you in charge of the tucker." His eyes lit up suddenly and he grabbed the tube of condensed milk I'd been using, rolled on his back and squeezed the tube into his mouth, a look of bliss on his face.

"Hey!" I said. "That's for my tea."

"You should learn to share," he said. "Besides, tea's a drug. Take more notice of Chas, give it up and become a Christian."

Jim's religious forays continued throughout the afternoon but no matter how canny his arguments, how aggressive or how scathing, Chas sailed serenely through them, confident in his beliefs.

Back at the camp that evening Chas did the cooking and as night descended we ate barbecued steak to the erratic throb of Chas' generator, which made the lights flicker like candles in the wind. Afterwards Jim belched.

"Good cooking, Chas." he said, his voice mellowed by repletion. "What's for pud?"

"Tinned fruit," Chas said.

"Tinned two-fruits, you mean," Jim said, remembering a sore point. "That's the last time you do the shopping. How can a man have so little imagination that when he's got the whole store to shop in, all he buys is two-fruits, cornflakes, sardines, orange cordial and dry biscuits."

Chas gave one of his shy grins. "Didn't want to spend too much of the company's money."

Jim put his hands on his hips and tilted his head back. "But what about ripping the company off for a caravan we don't want, a generator that's clapped out, a freezer that melts ice-cream and a vehicle we can't use. That's all right is it?"

"You use the caravan every night for gambling."

"Yeah, well... maybe it has some use but the rest is clapped out junk."

"It's still working." Chas collected the salvaged ice-cream from the freezer and spooned some over his two-fruits, then said. "Think I fixed the fuel pump. We should have two vehicles tomorrow."

I picked up the can of pressurised cream and passed it across to Jim. "Goes well with two-fruits."

Jim's eyes lit up. "Stick the two-fruits. If I ever see another can I'll puke." He shook the cream vigorously, opened his mouth and pressed the valve.

"*The drunkard and the glutton shall come to poverty,*" Chas said, helping himself to Jim's portion of two-fruits.

"Oh my fod!" Jim said, foaming at the mouth.

With the dishes washed Jim turned to me. "The casino's set up, what about poker?"

"Suits me."

He turned to Chas. "You right for a game?"

Chas shook his head. "Don't gamble."

"Don't gamble?" Jim looked as if Chas had uttered a profanity. "What if I give you half of everything I win?"

"Nup."

"You could give it to the church."

"They already get ten per cent."

"So give them some more."

"Nup."

Jim rolled his eyes. "My god! What is this man? How are we going to survive four weeks in the bush without playing cards?"

"I could loan you my Book of Mormon."

* * *

It took Jim a few days to come to terms with Chas and his ways and he had to spend his evenings lying on his stomach on his camp stretcher writing letters to his girlfriends. Just as the camp was beginning to work smoothly the generator packed up.

"I can't work without cold water to drink," Jim said, giving the impression a major disaster was shaping up. All our tucker's going rotten too, if you can call the rubbish Chas brought out last trip, food."

"I'll head into the Towers now, if you want," Chas offered. "I could get the generator fixed and pick up some supplies and be back tomorrow night."

I handed him a list of things we needed but Jim grabbed it. "Let me check this for essentials first," he said, whipping out a biro. He scanned down the list. "Make that ten pressurised creams and ten tubes of condensed milk for starters, and no two-fruits, Chas. Get raspberries, blackberries, cherries—I mean use your imagination. Bring back a proper generator too, not some heap of junk you can rent out at rip-off rates same as everything else you've hired."

"Yep."

Jim turned to me as Chas drove out of the camp later. "Okay, five dollars on when he gets back. Give me some times."

* * *

"It's a four hour trip to the Towers," Jim said the following evening after the meal. He was lying on his stomach on his camp stretcher again; a position he found helped him the most in his contemplation of life.

"Four hours to shop, an hour to kiss his wife goodbye—better make that two—that gets him here at seven o'clock, which is my first guess. I'm looking good, right?"

I laughed. "No way. Add in a problem with fixing the generator, a delay delivering the samples, a couple of punctures, a flat battery, boiling radiator, blocked fuel line, crook fuel pump …"

Jim smacked his head and groaned. "If he costs me another five dollars I'll kill him."

Late in the night the headlights of Chas' Toyota woke us. Jim switched on the torch and checked his times. "Just got five dollars back," he chuckled. "Thank - you - Chas."

"What've you got," I said sleepily.

"Twelve-thirty, and it's ten past. What about you?"

"I had midnight. I win by five minutes." There was a short silence. "Chas!" Jim yelled.

A moment later Chas poked his head in the tent. "Yup?"

"Why the hurry to get back?"

"I had a few problems. Broke a spring."

"Is that all?"

"I thought you might be waiting for the food too."

"I was, but I fainted from hunger three hours ago and Bob revived me with some cornflakes and two-fruits. I just wanted to tell you," his voice rose a little, "that you've just cost me another bet. You are - a - dick - head."

"Yup."

"Is that all you can say?"

"I brought Art back with me too."

There was a momentary shocked silence. "Correction," Jim said. "You're not a dickhead you're a bloody idiot."

"Yup."

We had just got back to sleep when the quiet of the night was shattered by the generator; all the lights came on.

Chapter 4 Caravan for Hire

The Star River area has its own weather, which bears little resemblance to anything predicted by the weather bureau. Although it was late May, the so-called dry season, it had been getting wetter and wetter. On the last day of our program, the rain came down in earnest.

"I think I'd better get the van out before the creeks come up too much," Chas said, holding a raincoat over his head from which water cascaded.

"I hope you don't intend to charge the company for the week it'll take to tow it out," Jim said.

"Only take a day to shift."

We had Chas loaded up by mid morning with his freezer and generator and most of the samples, as well as the trusty van hooked on behind. As he began to drive out I stopped him and pointed to the rear wheel where two of the six studs attaching it to the back axle were missing and the rest were loose. You'll never make it out."

Chas got out and tightened them. "That might do it. I'll still have front wheel drive."

"You're forgetting about Art." Jim said. "That's a lot of dead weight to be carrying."

Art stuck up a finger. "Break a leg."

Jim turned to me as they drove off into the grey mist of rain. "Okay. Five guesses for how far he gets. Ten dollars gets me my money back."

Two hours later we had the rest of the camp gear stowed on the Toyota and we set off after Chas. The rain had intensified and was now sheeting down relentlessly. We stopped at the first creek crossing and got out.

"What do you think," Jim said, as we stood hunched under

raincoats looking at the swirling water, which was about knee deep. The creek had steep banks, making access difficult.

"There's no sign of Chas' tracks," I said. "He must have found another crossing. I had him stuck at this creek as my first guess."

"Good work Chas me old mate," Jim yelled, in no particular direction. "Don't let me down."

"What's this 'old mate' business?"

He shrugged. "It's a good Aussie term for dickheads."

"The banks are a bit crumbly," I said. "What about wading across to check for washouts. I'll drive behind you."

"What about you wading across?"

"You're wetter."

"You're taller."

"This needs superior driving skills," I said. "I know I've given you a good grounding in bush survival but maybe not enough for this sort of driving."

"Try me."

"What about your philosophy of doing everything for the geo?"

"That was when I was a field assistant."

"What are you now then?"

"Assistant geo, two IC."

This standoff was ended by a shout and Chas loomed out of the rain-drenched landscape. "I'm stuck at the crossing up stream," he said. "Only got front wheel drive."

"I don't believe this guy," Jim said as we detoured with Chas riding in the back. "Another minute and we'd have been on our way and he'd have been left behind. Nothing worries him."

"I'm more bothered than he is," I said.

"What about?

"Your ability to pay. That'll be ten dollars, thanks. That makes twenty all up. Armaguard Security will have to follow us around the way you're losing bets."

Chas had his Toyota half way up the far bank, blocking the track, with the caravan nicely positioned in the middle of the creek.

After driving across to the other side we stopped about twenty metres past Chas' vehicle. As is to be expected under Murphy's Law there were no trees of any size to attach a winch rope to and we were on a steep slope. After chocking the Toyota wheels with rocks, we attached Chas' winch cable. The wire rope had been well misused in the past with kinks, frays and strands hanging off it and we all stood well clear as Chas started up. The winch was motor driven and after some revving it was clear that nothing was going to happen.

"The winch pin has sheared," Chas said. "I'll put in a temporary one."

"Everything on the vehicle is temporary," Jim said, blowing water off his dripping nose. This will be a temporary, temporary pin."

Half an hour later Chas started up again. The pin held, the rope tensioned, things that were about to happen finally did. The rope parted with barely a twang.

"I could put a knot in it," Chas said.

"This is a pretty dismal performance," I said. "If you tie a knot it won't go round the drum. But tie a knot anyway and we'll try to tow it out with both vehicles." By now we were so soaked that we'd abandoned the raincoats. Even keeping our footing on the muddy slope was difficult. Sometime later we were ready again.

"Let her rip," I said, giving a hand signal. Jim spun his wheels and Chas engaged his front drive and both Toyotas settled a little deeper into the mud.

"That's really good Ar-chas," Jim yelled. Anything else we can do before we head for the Towers without you?"

Chas gave an apologetic grin. "We could try the Tirfer hand winch? It's in the back."

The Tirfer is a portable winch of French design, which comes with a 20 metre coil of steel rope and can exert a pull of over two tonnes. Chas had to unload everything in the back of the Toyota to find it and soon most of the campsite was sitting beside the creek.

"Good planning, Chas," Jim said from the relative dryness of our vehicle where he'd stationed himself. "If you get a puncture I suppose you always unload everything to get the tool kit out?"

"What a bloody wasted day," Art said. "All we've done is move the camp one kilometre in the rain."

"What's this 'we've' business," Jim said. "All you've done is sit in the cab."

With the Tirfer attached to a small tree we were set once more however there was still a problem. The Tirfer needed a lever, a metre length of pipe, to work the mechanism. There was no sign of it.

"Can't find it," Chas said, after a fruitless search.

Jim left the shelter of the Hilux with some reluctance and joined us in the downpour. "You're going well, Chas," he said. "What about pulling a pipe off the roo bar. It might do the job?"

This was a good bit of lateral thinking. Jim grabbed a shifter and began to dismantle the bar, which was held together by rusty bolts and fractured welds. After turning the hexagonal nuts into circular washers without getting a single one off, he lost patience and attacked the top pipe with a sledge hammer, breaking one end so that he could lever it off. There was a cheer from Art as he handed it to me although Chas wasn't too impressed. It turned out to be too small to fit over the winch lever and Jim smacked his forehead in disgust. "That's it then, the caravan stays in the creek."

A clever thought struck me. "The jockey wheel for the van. That should be big enough."

Chas waded into the creek, now over half a metre deep and rising steadily, and unwired the caravan door to get inside. The rain was still pelting down, backed by a cold wind, but above the noise was something else, a distant but growing roar. Moments later a bore, a metre high wall of water, sticks, logs and other dead vegetation, swept round the bend in the creek. Chas grabbed the jockey wheel and splashed back up the bank just as it engulfed the caravan.

The van rocked as water poured in through the open door and it then began to jiggle downstream, while the tree to which the winch rope and everything else was ultimately connected to began to pull out by the roots.

"Get me an axe," Jim said, madness in his eye as he looked around for something with which to sever the tow rope, but by the time he was armed the bore had swept past and the danger was over.

The steel tube on the jockey wheel was a bit short for good leverage but it fitted the Tirfer and after the creek had dropped back sufficiently for the van to drain, we got to work. I levered the winch while both vehicles ground away in low gear. Slowly we moved clear of the water.

"*The Lord on high is mightier than the noise of many waters,*" Chas said as we surveyed the van's interior, now full of mud and sticks.

Jim chuckled. "Washing the van's carpet has probably killed all the fish from here to the Pacific." He turned to me. "But where did that wall of water come from?"

It gets dammed up behind an obstruction that suddenly lets go. We were lucky it wasn't bigger.

Jim and I did a quick reconnaissance of the track. The next impassable creek was only another kilometre away.

"We're marooned," Jim said on our return. "Good one Chas."

It was still raining hard as we set the tent up on the highest ground and it was then that I made an ominous discovery. Sticks and grass were caught up in the trees above our heads. I pointed it out to Jim. "That's from the last wet."

Jim looked shocked. "What if it keeps raining?"

"We'd have to lash a heap of trees together and raft out."

"My God! I thought Art was bad but Chas is a disaster.

"A top worker though. In a couple of days, if it stops raining, we'll be out of here and on the plane to Brisbane."

"A couple of days? Okay, five guesses for a ten dollar pot for the closest time we get airborne."

Jim cooked a huge meal on the gas stove and afterwards we sat in the caravan dodging dripping water from the leaky roof.

"What do you reckon, Chas?" Jim said, looking around the sodden interior "This rain could be a blessing. It might get you to fix things up."

"Blessed are the frugal, Jim, for they shall inherit the Earth."

"I suppose that means that all you'll do is hose it out you cheapskate. What about a bit of new carpet? That would only cost fifty bucks. Claim it on insurance."

Chas turned to me. "Maybe I'm covered for insurance through Hunter?"

I shook my head. "No chance. You're a contractor. You take out your own insurance."

"That's it, Chas," Jim said, getting quite excited. "Insure the van for a couple of thousand, then after the next trip you can make a claim. The assessor would only need to get within a hundred metres of it to write it off."

"But what shall it profit a man if he should gain the whole world and lose his own soul?"

"You could sell it to me," Art said. "I'd put in the claim and we could split the take."

"Nup," Chas said, closing the financial speculation.

"The table's still okay though," Jim said. "That's the most important part. Who's for poker?"

Jim, Art and I played poker for a few hours in wet clothes, listening to the rain and the steady plink of water dripping into containers.

"Good thing Chas is with us," Jim said after a particularly heavy downpour. "Only God can help us if this keeps up."

Chas looked up from his Toyota manual and pointed down.

"That's where you should look for help, Jim."

"I've got no worries; lady luck is looking after me," Jim said, chuckling as he pulled in his winnings from another pot. "I know she's around because I'm still ripping the guts out of Art."

Art sucked on his lower lip for a moment. "Gotta be that," he said sourly. "You can't fight blind bleeding luck. Normally you wouldn't have the skill to win against a bunch of bare-arsed blind bawling babies with the DTs."

"Another game then, Art? It's early."

"No way. I'm not fighting a lucky streak like that."

Jim stretched and yawned. "Think I'll write a letter to my girl then."

Art grunted. "To some dumb Kiwi chick?"

"Jim likes the married ones," I said. "He found one on a blind date."

"Jim's blind dates are for real," Art said. "The Aussie girls are either blind or blind drunk or both. I've heard that if they're blind and on a pension they sometimes fall for Kiwis, as long as they think they have plenty of money."

* * *

The rain cleared overnight and the creeks began to subside quickly. Jim and I drove over to the station homestead and borrowed their tractor to get Chas' van out onto the main track. It took us most of the day. We left Chas and Art heading for the Towers while Jim and I returned the tractor and slept over at the homestead.

"I'll bet he doesn't make it to the Towers without breaking down again," Jim said, eyeing me hopefully. "Want a bet?" I just laughed.

We caught up with Chas and Art the next morning, still on the gravel track and about ten kilometres from where we'd left them the night before. "G'day Chas," Jim said as Chas stuck his head out from under the vehicle, a shifter in his hand. "Now I know why you tow the van everywhere. You need the accommodation."

"Yep," Chas said. "I stopped to clean out a fuel line. Couldn't get started after that. Battery's flat."

"What amazing bad luck," Jim said. "Couldn't happen to a more deserving guy." He turned to Art. "You're looking a bit peaky."

"So would you be if you'd been sitting beside the road for a day and a night, feeding the fucking mossies."

"We had a lousy camp too, didn't we, Bob?" Jim said with a chuckle. "We were at the homestead. A roast dinner last night, soft beds, bacon and eggs for breakfast, a cut lunch for the road."

Art brightened. "What about a bit of that cut lunch?"

"I ate it."

"It's only bloody ten o'clock."

"When you're working you get hungry."

Art turned to me. "What about you, Bob?"

I shook my head. "Jim ate mine too."

After we started Chas with the jumper leads, I told him to go first. "We'll follow," I said.

"And pick up anything that falls off." Jim added.

The trip over the rest of the gravel track was slow but uneventful and on the highway we were able to bowl along at eighty. We were only a half hour drive from Charters Towers when a wheel parted company from the caravan and went flying down the road past Chas. He must have been watching some nearby kangaroos for he didn't appear to notice.

"I don't believe this guy," Jim said, honking the horn as the van's brake drum cut a neat white groove in the blacktop, creating a shower of sparks and the caravan began to zig-zag and sway. "He won't hear you. His muffler's half off. He's probably deaf by now."

"Surely he'll feel something."

"Not with all that weight aboard."

"He'll see it then."

"He's got no rear vision mirror."

"I can't pass him. What'll we do?"

There was no need to respond to this query because at that moment the other wheel came off and even Chas felt the jerk as the van, with tow-bar still attached but not to the Toyota, planed down the road in a shower of sparks. It came to rest on the verge as if it had been parked.

"You should have left the jockey wheel on," Jim said as we surveyed the damage. "Might have made it to the Towers on its own then."

Chas gave a sickly grin. "Guess I'll have to pick it up later."

"Darn right," Jim said. "The company has a few thousand invested in it already. At least no one's going to steal it and there's nothing worth salvaging inside it."

We made it to the Towers by late evening and unpacked the gear the next morning. Chas wanted to talk to a contractor in Townsville about the long-term rental for the shed he was building and offered to drive us to the airport. I rang the airline to find the flight times and make a booking for our flight to Brisbane.

"It's a strange thing," I said to Jim as I dialed. "The only flight that will be available will be the one that goes out at six pm."

"How come?"

"Because that's the one that wins the bet for me."

"Hey! Every man has his price but I thought yours would be a bit higher than ten dollars."

"It's not the money; it's the nature of the bet. I couldn't bear to lose to someone with so little betting skill."

Unfortunately for me we were able to get on the mid-afternoon flight and Jim made a great show of getting his ten dollars, the first time he had won a bet. "Lady luck," he said, kissing the note. "She loves me still."

We made good time down the range with Chas but twenty minutes out of Townsville the motor began to cough.

"I'm a bit low on fuel," Chas said.

"You're showing empty," I said, noticing the gauge for the first time.

"I'll switch over."

"But the reserve's on empty too."

We began to leapfrog down the road in short bursts as the motor began to miss. "You realise the plane leaves in sixty minutes?"

"Sure," he said, with no trace of emotion.

"There's a jerry in the back," Jim said.

Chas nodded. "It's empty."

Jim rolled his eyes. "I don't believe this."

"Pull in here," I said as we came to a complex of buildings beside the road. It was a government research station. "Maybe they'll sell us some fuel." We turned into a broad driveway as the motor died.

The first building Jim and I rushed into was a laboratory. It reminded me of the Marie Celeste. The lights were on, music was playing, but every office was empty. We hurried through three buildings before we found someone. Getting petrol though, turned out to be almost impossible as the key to the bowser was with the person in charge who was in Townsville. After half an hour of waiting the key was produced and we staggered back to the Toyota with a full jerry to find Chas winding up a siphon hose.

"Won't need that," he said. "The reserve tank was still quarter full."

He must have seen something in our expression because he actually offered an explanation.

"Reserve doesn't pump out when it gets low. I just siphoned it out and put it in the main tank."

We missed our plane and after waiting only as long as it took us to book the evening flight, Chas gave us a cheerful wave and headed out to the car park. "See you fellows next trip."

"No need to apologise, Chas," Jim said. "It could have happened with any dickhead, not just you."

"I'm not complaining," I said. "Now about that ten dollars."

Jim scowled. "I'd have won if he hadn't pulled that last stunt with that clapped out heap of junk; and you're not getting the money until we take off. My last bet comes good at 6 tomorrow morning."

Three hours later, as we took off, he handed over the money and stared morosely out the window. Suddenly he laughed and pointed. Below us was the car park and a battered Toyota. We knew it was Chas' because there was someone working underneath it wearing blue overalls.

Chapter 5 The Entrepreneur

It is great to be home after weeks in the bush. I lived on a few acres of land and one morning, as my wife, Judy and I were working in the garden, we heard what sounded like distant gunfire. It quickly became a rattle mixed with intermittent backfires and moments later a battered Toyota Hilux came up our gravelled driveway, trailing a cloud of dust and blue exhaust fumes. As it pulled to a stop, a grinning face poked out the driver's side window. "G'day mate," a voice called.

It was Jim, although barely recognisable without the ferocious reddish-gold stubble and the battered felt hat.

"What do you think?" he said, as we came over.

I put my hand to my ear. "What?" The noise of the rattling metal sides of the tray made it hard to hear.

He switched off. "What do you reckon about this? I bought it second-hand."

"Second-hand?" I took in the cracked windscreen, warped step, missing rear vision mirror and the buckled and dented sides. "It looks almost new."

He beamed. "Yes. I got it for a bargain price too, but it needs a bit of work."

"Like a new body and motor?"

"Settle down. I'm getting a roo-bar fitted, new rings for the motor, off-road tyres, long range fuel and water tank, a tool box to hold our equipment, an electric winch, a tow bar, maybe even a two-way radio. By the time I've splashed a bit of paint on it I can charge it out to Hunter as a nearly new vehicle."

"Do you think it'll have the power to haul all that extra weight around?" We'll be in some rugged country next trip."

"This baby will go anywhere." He started up and gunned the motor. "Listen to that raw power."

As a fog of blue exhaust blasted out we stepped back. "Not bad for one active cylinder," I agreed.

"This is Judy," I said. "She's heard a lot about you."

"Come in for a cup of tea?" she said, shaking his hand.

The racket died again as he switched off. "A glass of water will do, thanks."

We went into the kitchen and Jim opened the refrigerator door. "On second thoughts," he said, "make that a glass of milk." He found a glass and filled it.

"Hunter agreed to hire your vehicle then?" I asked.

He nodded. "Shafer Enterprises is in business. That baby will bring me in another twenty-five dollars a day profit."

He extracted a block of chocolate from the fridge, broke off a large piece and handed the rest to me. "Want some?"

"No thanks. So you reckon you can make money then?"

"Mine won't cost as much to run as Chas'."

Abandoning the fridge he moved to a jar of macadamia nuts on the kitchen bench and munched on a handful.

"It'll take you three years of work to pay for all the extras," I said. He grinned. "No way."

"We start in two weeks. You haven't much time."

"Not a problem. Are Chas and Art coming?"

"Yes."

Jim's eyes narrowed thoughtfully as they did whenever his thoughts turned to business and the making of money. "So this Chas," he said. "Do we need him?"

"Yes, he's a good worker. He's also a useful contact. I hire men and equipment from him."

"Used to hire," Jim corrected. "Shafer Enterprises has just muscled in and is about to take over."

"You'd have to undercut his prices to interest Hunter."

"I reckon I could match his prices—and Hunter would be getting top gear, not the heap of junk Chas hires out."

"And you'd also have to be as reliable."

He burst into sarcastic laughter. "Reliable? Shafer Enterprises is worth another fifty a day already. Keep talking."

"He does have trouble getting to the job on time," I conceded, "but once on site he's great."

"Yeah, he's great when he turns up about four weeks after the job's started. He'd be an expert at taking down campsites. I bet he's never set one up though."

"And Hunter would have to get to know you better," I continued doggedly, against these telling arguments. "At the moment the only information they have about you are astronomical food bills for ice-cream, chocolate, dried fruits and nuts."

"Not a problem. Their top geo is going to tell them what a great bloke I am."

"I'd like to help but I'm not that good at lying."

He chuckled. "There has to be a better way to make money than doing field work. I found an accountant who got me a shelf company.. What I need to do now is to have Shafer Enterprises hire out a heap of gear to Hunter and charge them for my labour. I'll be able to claim a swag of tax deductions."

"There's no chance of hiring out your labour."

"Why not?"

"Because I'm charging you out. I'm not letting you go."

"That has to be a rip-off. How much are you making on me?"

"No more than is fair and reasonable for a man of your calibre."

He thought for a moment. "I'm worth at least a hundred a day but I'm only getting seventy. You must be getting about thirty bucks a day for me?"

"I'd like to tell you but I can't."

"Why not?"

"Well—supposing I was making seventy a day out of you."

His mouth opened in shock. "Seventy?"

"See, that's why I can't tell you. If I told you I was making seventy a day, you'd get a swelled head. But if, on the other hand I said I was only making five, you'd be insulted, so I can't tell you."

"Try me, I can take it."

"Look at it this way," I said. "Without me there's no Shafer Enterprises; there's just the dole. Which reminds me, I also want a percentage of the rate you're charging on the Hilux?"

"*Wash out your mouth.*"

The conversation proceeded along similar lines for some time during which Jim discovered and ate the remaining half of a chocolate cake baked the day before but unfortunately left in a tin near the nuts. After this we returned to his Hilux.

"Listen to this radio and tape deck I've had installed," he said. "It'll blow you out of the water."

Although we were well away from the nearest neighbour I could foresee problems if the racket continued. Using sign language I got him to turn the volume down. He pulled out the ashtray, which was full of green powder.

"Take a whiff. It's pine scent. I can smell the bush even when driving in the city."

I wrinkled my nose in distaste at the overpowering artificial smell. "The bush is full of gum trees, not pines."

"A tree's a tree. Who cares what sort."

"You're going to drive this all the way to Townsville and pick me up on Monday week then?"

"Yep."

"You'd better allow three or four days to get there. It's 1200 kilometres."

"Settle down. I'll leave early the day before."

* * *

Despite my concerns, Jim was waiting for me at the airport on my arrival.

"It went like a dream," he said, before I could ask. "Hunter International is getting a bargain. They get the four-wheel drive and me for less than the plane fare nearly. Do you reckon they'd refund a speeding ticket?"

"I could ask for you. You realise they sacked their last speedster?"

"Don't bother then. I'll charge it to fuel."

I raised an eyebrow. "Thanks for letting me know. I'll keep a lookout when I get your expenses."

"You'll never find it," he countered.

Out in the car park a transformed Hilux stood waiting for me. "Like it?" he asked.

"How do I get into it?" It had so much protective pipe work on the outside that it looked like a jungle gym. The motor sounded quieter when he started up and the exhaust was relatively clear.

"Goes like a rocket," he said, as we headed towards the city. "Bit of a shimmy at one hundred but it dies at one-twenty. I think I'll raise the hire fee because of all the extras I've put on, like an electric winch and tow bar. Do you reckon Hunter would come at that?"

"Depends on how useful the extras are to the project." I switched on the air-conditioning knob but nothing happened. "What's with the air-conditioning?"

"It blew up."

"What?" I was appalled. "Turn round and take me back to the

airport. I'll hire another Toyota. One that is fully functional."

"Settle down." He pulled out the ashtray and the odour of artificial pine filled the cabin. "Take a whiff. That's better than any air-conditioner."

I closed the ashtray and hung my head out the window for a breath of Townsville elixir. "I'm putting in a complaint to Hunter. Geos can't work in summer without air-conditioned Toyotas."

"Chas hasn't got one either."

"I don't ride with Chas."

"I'm renting this to make money not to mollycoddle the geo."

"What happened to your philosophy that the geo was to be looked after?"

"It's secondary to making money." He turned onto the highway. "So what do we do now? I'm loaded with fuel and water. Shafer Enterprises is ready for action."

We're heading to the Sellheim River. We'll pick up a bit of gear, collect Chas and Art at Charters Towers and overnight there, then head out with him next day and call in on a few of the locals where we'll be working."

"I'm thinking of buying a generator," he said. "That clapped out thing of Chas' reached its use by date in 1950. At twenty-two dollars per day rental it would pay for itself after a month, Hunter would save a few bucks and we wouldn't keep losing our frozen food."

"Go for it."

"Thanks. What else can I rent out?"

"A gas cylinder and light."

"Beauty. Reckon you could loan me a hundred?"

* * *

It took another day to get the rest of the supplies, collect Chas and Art, and then call into the homesteads at Pyramid and Ukalunda, with a side visit to the Sunbeam alluvial gold mine. We reached our camping site in the evening and slept under the stars, ready to set up camp the next morning.

"A top spot," Jim said during an early breakfast. We were on sandy ground among shady gums and black wattles and looked down at the broad sweep of the river some twenty metres below, which flowed just enough to keep the sandy pools full of clean water.

"No chance of a flash flood getting us," I said, "and there's plenty of shade. We can cart drinking water up to the camp and wash our samples at the river."

"We need a water pump," Jim said. "I should have bought one in the Towers to rent out."

"I brought a pump," Chas said.

Jim looked heavenward for a moment. "That'll be another company rip-off."

"Hunter can use it for free, it doesn't owe me anything."

Jim gave a groan. "That's all I need to hear. It'll take a day to start if it goes at all."

"It's in good nick."

"Yeah like your caravan." Jim's eyes moved to the van then widened in mock surprise. "What have you done to it?"

Chas looked pleased. "Gave it a coat of paint, changed the carpet, fixed the door, put on new screens, fixed the cupboard hinges. Foot pump for the sink works, lights work, gas stove works."

Jim and I went over to the van to have a look. "Not bad for a mobile casino," Jim said. "You could have put in a bit of sound proofing though; I'll still be able to hear the midnight orchestra tuning up and you could have put in a new carpet instead of more rat eaten underfelt. I suppose you've upped the rent?"

"Another twenty a week."

"Twenty! I thought you followed Christian principals?"

"Try to."

"So if you touch up all the rust spots on the deep freeze it means you'll charge the company more for that too?"

"Probably."

"And a new spark plug in that clapped out generator? What's that worth—ten bucks?"

"Yep."

Jim turned to me. "So how do I get on the gravy train?"

"You're already on it," Art said. "Wish I could get paid to do nothing."

"Chas deals direct with Hunter," I said. "He's an independent contractor, same as me."

"Well if he can rip them off so can I."

"Bob tells me you've already started by hiring your own vehicle," Chas said.

Art gave a derisory laugh. "That wrecker's reject? Is that yours, Jim?"

Jim turned to him. *"Wash out your mouth.* It's a top machine and it's got the lot—roo bar, tow bar, winch, spare fuel and water tanks, roll bar, spare tyres, protective bars ..."

Art broke in. "You'd need all those the way you drive, and it blows so much smoke the cow cockie will think there's a bushfire every time you start up."

"Settle down."

"At least when Jim's lost in the bush we'll be able to find him," Chas said

"Yeah," Art countered. "Just as long as the motor's running, which is probably a big ask considering it sounds as if it's about to cark.

This was the truth; it had developed a few unusual noises since its shake-up on the track in.

"It needs a new muffler and an air-conditioner if the geo is to travel in it," I said.

Jim put his hands on his hips. "For what Hunter is paying me for it I'm tempted to pull all the extras off. They can have the motor and chassis, which is about all the hire covers."

"That's all they'll end up getting anyway if it was you did the work on it," Art said, showing what turned out to be remarkable prescience. "If you want extra money you have to give value."

This comment seemed to irritate Jim. "My God!" he said. "Coming from you—a man who reckons getting the dole is hard work—that's a bit rich. And that reminds me." He turned to me. "I reckon I'm due another ten a day as camp cook."

"Ten a day for poisoning us?" Art chortled. "They should pay us for letting you experiment."

"Ten or I quit as camp cook and Art can do a bit."

"I think I could arrange that for you," I said. "It's blackmail to threaten us with Art's cooking though."

"Great." He did some quick mental calculation. That puts me on eighty a day. Another sixty for the Hilux, twenty-two for the generator and I've started my share portfolio with a few Hunter shares, which are already up ten cents. I'm rich and getting richer."

Art turned to Chas. "If he can get a raise I want one too."

"Nup," Chas said, as Jim doubled up laughing.

"Why not? Jim already gets ten a day more than me and he's next to useless."

"When you start to show some responsibility I'll pay more."

"Like what bloody responsibility?"

"Work a bit harder. Cut down on the beer, the smoking, the gambling, the swearing. Everything we've talked about."

"My God," Jim said. "Art would need a complete change of personality."

Chas nodded. *"Go to the ant. Consider its ways and be wise."*

"Never mind the bloody ants. "I'll quit the church if I don't get a raise."

Jim chuckled. "How come they haven't kicked you out already?"

"Quit and I won't employ you at all," Chas said.

"Don't care whether you do or not. I'll go back on the dole."

"How's that going to support a life of debauchery?" Jim asked.

"If you want more money," I said, "there are two choices: a life of crime, or work a bit harder and start impressing the people who employ you."

"Looks like a life of crime coming up or a life in gaol, more likely," Jim said.

Art snorted. "Could make a living gambling if I wanted."

Jim let out a raucous laugh. "Better not play Manila then; you've lost every time we've played. You sure you don't mean pimping?"

"I already make a quid out of that."

"Listen up," I said. "Craig, the exploration manager, will be here tomorrow, all the way from Perth. Today is a reconnaissance day to assess problems such as access to creeks, state of tracks, any fences in the way, things like that. There are a couple of target areas to locate so we can take Craig directly there with minimum hassles."

The terrain in which we were working was more difficult than at Star River. There were patches of lancewood, which were nearly impenetrable and the sure death of tyres, for the timber splintered into razor-like shards. There were a lot of small woody shrubs too, called shitwood by the locals, that you could run over a hundred times and they would spring back up unmarked. If you were scrub bashing and wanted to follow your track back they were bad news. There were also half hidden stony outcrops that could damage a sump and there were numerous steep hills and gullies.

The next morning I gave Chas a set of air photos with places to check out and stream sample positions marked. After he'd left with Art, Jim and I set out for a different area.

"This will test the Hilux," I said. "You sure you don't want me to drive? You're turning down thirty years of finely honed driving skills."

"This baby understands me," he said, hugging the steering wheel like a lover as we bounced over the ground. "Funny thing though. It wants to steer to the right."

"You've probably got a flat."

"What, already?" He stopped and leant out the window. "Bloody hell. That tyre cost me eighty bucks. It better not be ruined."

"That's one of the joys of contracting."

We replaced the tyre and set off again. "A flat in the first few minutes is not a good sign," I said. "We could end the day running on the rims. Do you have a repair kit?"

"Does the sun shine? Does grass grow? Does..."

"Okay. I get the message. Ever used one?"

"Er—no."

There was no sign of Chas and Art when we arrived back at the campsite at around four. Craig had arrived and along with the latest laboratory assays for last month's work, had brought with him a carton of beer, two bottles of Hunter Valley red, and a gold jig to take the labour out of panning down large samples.

"Five guesses as to when Chas turns up," Jim said, after the introductions. "You in Craig? Cost you five dollars."

Craig raised an eyebrow as he passed us a beer. "Aren't we paying you enough, Jim?"

"Jim has requested a raise," I said, "as he does the evening cooking for the camp on top of other duties. I've agreed to ten dollars."

"With four in the camp plus visitors." Craig mused. "I could even go to fifteen. I'll let you know after I test the quality of the chef."

"How does roast chicken sound?" Jim said. "With roast potatoes, carrots, parsnip and peas?"

Craig shook his head. "I have two bottles of red to drink. Chicken doesn't appeal too much."

"Well what about a mixed grill with chops, bacon, eggs, tomato and steak, followed by chocolate ice-cream, glace cherries, whipped cream and raspberry syrup?"

Craig raised his beer in salute. "The first part sounds perfect."

Jim was getting smarter with his bets on Chas. His latest time was midnight but I had Chas down for ten the next morning and he didn't turn up in the night.

After breakfast, and after I'd collected another five dollars from Jim, I went off to see if the local station owner had a plane. It turned out that there was a mustering plane available and I was soon airborne in a single engine Piper. It took us half an hour of searching before a flash from the ground alerted us and we zeroed in on Chas, standing out from the brown vegetation in his light blue overalls. He waved casually as we flew over, looking for all the world like a tourist on a day trip.

"He's in the middle of a dry rocky creek about an hour's drive from here," I said later, when we I got back to the camp. "Best way to get to him is via Conway. He had a crowbar in his hand. It could be that he's hung up on a rock."

"Know where I'd like to hang him," Jim said. "He's cost me another five dollars."

Jim and I set out in the Hilux and it soon became painfully clear that it was going to take more than an hour to get to the site. Jim paused at the top of a washed out gully and stared at the tracks Chas had left behind with his mouth open. "You can only die once," he said putting the Hilux in low range, low gear."

"Do you mind if I get out?" I asked.

"Yes. The Shafer-Woodhouse team stays together."

Jim nosed the Hilux down the bank until the roo bar snagged on the rocky bottom. "Bloody roo bar," he muttered. "It's either the roo bar or the sump or the tow bar gets stuck."

"Or all three at once."

"Yeah—Chas is bloody mad." With a roar, he forced the Hilux forward and we stalled between the boulders on the creek bed.

"I think the spotter plane will be up searching for us next," I said.

Jim inched forward again, but as we climbed the jump-up on the other side the tow bar caught in the rocks and we shuddered to a stop, the wheels spinning. He backed off and tried again with even less success. "Bloody tow bar," he muttered again.

We got out and inspected the problem. Although the rocks were big, they were in loose sandy material. "Not a problem for Shafer Enterprises," Jim said. "I'll dig out a better slope. We'll be out in a flash."

"Hunter should be paying top dollar for all the gear you've got," I said, impressed.

"Make sure they get the message then." He began to search through the glove box.

"What are we waiting for?"

"I can't find the key to the tool box." He gave up searching, jumped up on the tray, and rattled the lock, which would have done justice to a bank safe. "Stuff it. Give me your hammer."

I passed my geology pick over. "This action you plan is going to reduce value, Jim. The rental will have to drop."

He bashed the lock off, flung open the lid and grabbed a short handled shovel. Five minutes later, we were on our way again with the roo bar leaning a little to one side as a result of its collision with too many rocks.

A few creeks later we stalled in deep sand in the middle of Chas' tracks. "He has more power than the Hilux," I said.

"I've got the technology though." Leaping out, Jim unwound the wire rope from the electric winch and wrapped it around a tree. "This'll do the trick." He set the winch into motion. As the Hilux began to plough slowly through the loose sand, he sniffed. "What's burning?"

"There's smoke coming from the winch." At that moment the roo bar rode up on a boulder and the front bumper, roo bar and winch tore off the chassis with a groan of stressed bolts."

He switched off and rubbed his thinning hair. "Bloody hell! What now?"

"We'll put this lot in the back, let the tyres right down and try again."

When we finally made it up the other bank we stopped to re-inflate the tyres. "Where's your Menzel pump?" I asked.

"What's that?"

"It screws into the spark plug. The compression pumps up the tyre."

"Now you tell me. All I've got is a hand pump."

I sighed. "A hand pump is perfect as long as you're not the one pumping. I suggest 50 pumps in each tyre until we're out of these sand traps. As a concession to your ignorance I'm prepared to help this time."

We followed Chas' tracks into a patch of spear grass and a moment later the Hilux jarred against a hidden stump and stalled, spinning the steering wheel and throwing us forward.

Jim sucked his thumb that had been bruised. "I should have bought a bulldozer not a Toyota. Bloody Chas! He could have found a better way in." In a sudden burst of frustration he revved the motor up and backed off, crunching the back bumper against a wattle.

"I think we're on his wheel marks," he said, thrusting the Hilux aggressively back into the waving spear grass. "I've bent the steering arm too, I think; it's not as free." There was a screech of rending metal and he stopped again and poked his head out the window. "Now it's a bloody log." He backed, got out, and yanked something off the Hilux and threw it in the back. "Those aluminium steps are a heap of junk," he said, getting back in. "They're as thin as alfoil."

"You're running out of room in the back. If anything else falls off we're going to have to leave it."

He scowled. "I'm going to hit Hunter with a repair bill. This is ridiculous."

From the spear grass, we progressed through some thick bush, which put Jim's protective jungle gym of piping to good use until an overhanging tree branch applied too much pressure, breaking the weld and peeling one of the bars back.

"Stop," I said. "You're clearing a new track on my side with this piece of metal."

We pulled the pipe off and it too joined the ironware in the back. Jim surveyed his jungle gym gloomily. "It's become a bit rickety without the roo bar and that strut for support," he said, "but it's still better than nothing."

We made good time crossing some relatively flat and scrub-less ground until a pothole jolted the Hilux. There was a bang and a series of radial fractures starred across the windscreen as the rest of the protective pipe-work broke loose and collapsed against it. Jim got rid of a lot of frustration ripping it all apart and it joined the hardware in the back. He took a long cold drink from the water bottle when he'd finished. "Surely that has to be it?" He said.

"I hear something," I said. "If it's not a snake hissing then you're getting another flat."

The secret of changing tyres was to get at them quickly before they became so flat that the jack would not fit under the chassis. If that happened a hole would have to be dug, and in hard, stony ground it meant using a shovel and crowbar.

"That's the last spare," I said. "It's the repair kit the next time."

"No worries. Chas should have a few spares; we're nearly to the spot where you saw him."

I thought I had Chas' position accurately plotted on the photo but there was no sign of him when we arrived at the site. Diligent searching located faint tracks and the usual trail of oil.

I looked at the tracks in some dismay. "He's taking a shortcut over the range."

Jim put the Hilux in low range. "If he can, I can. Besides we need his supply of tyres."

We climbed steadily, with the trees thinning out as the rocky outcrops grew larger. Eventually we came to a narrow, steeply sloping ridge of scree, with a rock wall on the left and a near vertical drop-off on the right. The tracks continued up.

As we got out to evaluate our position, Jim groaned. "This guy's a maniac."

"How's your insurance cover?"

He climbed back in, a determined look on his face. "Let's go."

I kicked the back tyre. "You're getting another flat."

A long time later, now much hotter and less well tempered, we lurched and slithered sideways up the slope, the left front wheel nudging the outcrops loose, the sump pulverising them and the back wheel sending them spinning into the canyon. We stopped at the top and sat for a moment thankful to be alive.

"Listen," Jim said. He leant out the window, then began to mutter and bang his head on the dash. "Thank you Chas."

"What now?"

"We're getting another flat."

Chas was at the camp eating a can of two-fruits when we returned, and Art was drinking beer with Craig. It was not a sight to overflow the heart with joy and goodwill.

"Hope you had a peaceful night, Chas," Jim said, as we pulled up. "We've only wasted the morning following your tracks."

"I got hung up on a rock," Chas said. "Ran out of water too. We had to walk seven K to a tank last night."

Jim began to search the fridge for a cold drink and a snack. "Glad to hear that you suffered a bit. Good that you took that easy short cut out too; instead of going back the way you went in and meeting us. Didn't you think we'd come looking for you? I needed your spare tyres too."

Chas gave a shy grin. "I had to finish off the sampling in the hills. Managed to get it all done. I used the two spares getting back."

"That's good. We're only a few days behind now because of you. Hunter is only out of pocket a few thousand dollars and I'm only out five bucks, three tyres, a windscreen, a winch and a front bumper. What do you have to say to that?"

"This is the day that the Lord hath made. Rejoice and be glad."

"You look a bit weary," Craig said, as Jim cast around in his brain for something to top Chas' comment.

"If you ever try to follow Chas," Jim said, getting himself under control. "Don't do it in your own vehicle."

As Art walked around the Hilux he began to shake with mirth. "I see you decided to do what you threatened, Jim." He said.

"What was that?"

"To rent Hunter the chassis and motor only."

Chapter 6 The Sinner

A spell of wet weather a few days after Craig left turned the country a bit greener and Art became quite excited when he found a crop of mushrooms. He brought some in as Jim cooked the evening meal.

"Look at these beauties," he said, revealing his hoard. "They're hallucinogenic."

Jim wrinkled his nose. "They look poisonous."

"These are safe. I've had 'em before. Add salt and pepper, bit of lemon, drop of milk and flour—beautiful. They make you feel as if you've got religion."

"How would you know, you've never had it?"

"Bull. I do unto others and all that crap."

"You're mad. You've abused your body for so long it'll take anything."

"These are harmless. The natives use them to get into the Dreamtime." Once Art had fried them to a brown mess he tipped them onto a slice of toast and ate them with much smacking of lips.

After the meal, Jim pushed the dirty plates towards him. "It's your turn to wash up. Make it quick because I want to rip a few more dollars off you and Bob."

Art was still washing up half an hour later and Jim went over to see what was taking so long.

"What are you doing?" he asked.

"Washing up."

"You've only done one plate."

"I've washed a pile."

"The same one ten times. The water's stone cold."

Art reached for his beer. "Water was near boiling."

Jim added some more hot water from the kettle, then put his mouth next to Art's ear. "Wash up!" He stood there then, handing plates to Art who ran the dish mop over them like a paintbrush.

"What's the trouble?" I asked becoming tired of shuffling cards.

"Art's in dream land." Jim handed a plate back for a second run in with the dish mop.

"Nothing wrong with me," Art said.

"You're spaced out further than Pluto. You've poisoned your brain."

"I'm as sane as the next man." Art took another mouthful of beer. "Might have had too many tinnies, but."

The poker session got going finally but it quickly faltered as Art became fascinated by the design on the back of his cards.

"We may as well give it away," I said.

"I'll play for Art," Jim said. "I can see everything he's holding anyway." He took three cards from Art and dealt him three more. "What's your bet?"

"Fifty."

Jim found a pencil and paper. "Okay, fifty bucks." He made a note. "I'll see your fifty and raise another fifty."

Chas looked up in alarm from his bunk. "What are you doing?"

"I'm teaching Art a lesson."

"What's wrong with him?"

"He's got religion, just as you wanted, Chas. He's spaced out on mushrooms. It might do him good if he thinks it's cost him a month's wages."

A short while later Art owed Jim 700 dollars and me nearly 350.

"That ought to do it," Jim said. "I want you to sign this IOU, Chas."

Chas nodded. "Sure."

Jim waved the paper in front of Art. "You owe us a thousand dollars."

Art looked as if he was sobering rapidly at this damming evidence of his stupidity for as his dilated pupils came into focus he turned pale and perspiration bespangled his brow, but his malaise went much deeper than this. With a sudden groan he clutched his stomach, rose to his feet and sprayed us with partially digested mushrooms. They were tinged an interesting blue, although we barely noticed it at the time.

After we'd had our second shower that night, Jim rewrote the IOU on a clean sheet of paper, raising the ante to 1500 dollars. "That'll cover our dry cleaning costs," he said as he had Chas sign it once more. "Where is the fat sod?"

"He headed for the bush with a toilet roll."

A pale and sickly Art appeared at breakfast the following morning and sat down with his head in his hands. Jim got up and banged a few pots about. "Bacon and eggs, Art?"

Art turned to me. "Think I might have to go back to bed. Me guts are crook. Be all right if I take a day off?"

"No way will you get a day off for self inflicted damage."

Jim sat down and admired a length of fried bacon dangling from his fork. "See any angels?" He asked.

Art shook his head. "No way was I in heaven. You were there in my dreams so I couldn't have been."

"You put on a good show at cards last night."

Art got up to make himself more coffee. "Don't remember much about it."

Jim effected amazement. "What do you mean you don't remember? You went wild. At one stage I had to get an IOU from Bob for 400 dollars to cover myself."

Art paused in the difficult act of stirring his coffee; such was the tremor of his hand. "Four hundred? Bull; there's a twenty cent limit."

"Not last night there wasn't. Don't tell me you've forgotten?"

"Forgotten what?"

"You were on about those five hundred dollar games you play in the Towers so we upped the ante. Pity you lost."

"Pull the other one."

"You owe Bob three hundred and me twelve hundred."

"Bull."

"Chas has the IOU. Show him Chas."

"Jim's right." Chas said, digging the note out of his blue overalls. He passed it across. "Fifteen hundred dollars. I told you gambling was a sin."

Art lit a cigarette. "I'm not paying nothing. Youse guys are bloody crooks."

"No need for you to pay," Jim said. "Chas will pay us out of your wages. At a seventy a day you'll have it paid off in twenty days. No, sorry. I forgot the tax. Thirty days."

"Yup," Chas said.

Art looked even sicker if this were possible.

"There could be a let out," I said. "You claim to be a man of great willpower. Give up the cigarettes, limit yourself to one can of beer a day and co-operate better around the camp and I'm prepared to forgo my share. What about you Jim?"

"Settle down," Jim said. "Don't make it too easy. What about cutting down on the food too?"

"No way," Art said. "I'll go back to the Towers if I have to do that."

"How are you going to get back, walk?"

"I want some work out of him," I said. "Beer and cigarettes is enough."

Jim nodded reluctantly. "Okay, but you're making it too easy."

Art sensed he'd been had but was too ill to argue. After a day spent collecting samples in the hot sun, most of the poison sweated out of him and he returned to the camp dying for a beer and a cigarette. Jim commandeered them first however and handed over one can.

"I'm numbering every cigarette packet and can. If you're ever in camp by yourself, I'll know if you've touched any. One puff and its fifteen hundred bucks."

"I'll smoke cow dung. That's not a cigarette."

Jim shrugged. "Fine, sleep in the stuff too."

Art settled into his new lifestyle with remarkably poor grace and a growing bad temper, but he did manage to work a bit harder and I commended him after a few days.

"It proves you were wrong about gambling, Chas," I said. "Art's benefiting from its effects."

Chas didn't look too impressed. "It's a short term effect. The sin isn't regretted. Without repentance he can't reform."

Jim chuckled. "It's the cow dung he's smoking. It clears his brain."

"Take no notice of them, Art," I said. "In a couple more weeks you'll be down to a hundred kilos. You'll be slimmer than Jim. He won't be laughing then."

Chas had left three large bagged samples behind in a creek system that he'd spent nearly an hour to reach by foot, as it was too rough and thickly overgrown to drive. He'd marked their position on the photo, and Jim, Art and I drove out to collect them the next day. It was an area of dense scrub and steep gullies and we had to park the Hilux about a kilometre from where they were.

"How are we going to find the Hilux again?" Art said, as we prepared to walk in. "You can't use a compass or flagging here, the bush is too thick."

"You're an experienced field hand. How would you do it?" I asked.

"Take three more samples from right here and pretend they're from the creek?"

"What about you, Jim?"

"I'd send Chas back to collect them?"

"What a pathetic lot of no hopers. Call yourselves prospectors? It's a sunny day, so we'll take a few compass bearings and use the sun angle and tree shadows as a guide. And we'll also turn Jim's radio on full bore which will give us a bullseye of about 200 metres radius to return to."

We located the creek and after much searching eventually found all three samples. Despite each of us having to lug a heavy bag back up the hills to the Hilux, Jim and Art still had enough breath to get into an argument. They were going full bore, paying no attention to where they were heading, when I stopped them.

"Where are you guys going?"

"Dunno; we're just following you," Art said.

"But I'm walking behind you."

"Well you're still with us, so it must be all right," Jim said.

"Can you hear the radio?"

They listened. "No"

"Do you know why?"

"Because we're lost?"

"Because we've gone past it and are now out of earshot. I was just testing you. You guys would have been hopelessly lost without the geo, wouldn't you?"

"Settle down," Jim said. "I deserve half the credit for providing the radio."

We spent a few more days in the hills getting samples. It required a lot of walking in the rising humidity, but we managed to build up a small pile and had them down by the river ready for jigging the next day and that night we turned in early. In the middle of the night Jim woke me.

"Bob, you awake?"

"No."

"I've been lying here listening to that wind getting louder—hear it?"

I listened. "That rushing noise?"

"Yes. It's not moving the tent. Why's that?"

I leapt out of bed. "You nong. That's not wind; that's water. There's been a storm in the hills: the river's in flood!"

I grabbed the torch and we went outside. Below us faintly visible in the starlight was a rushing blackness tinged with flecks of white foam.

Jim groaned. "There goes three days sampling."

"There goes our water pump."

"There go our panning off dishes."

"There goes the polypipe and jerry can."

In the light of day we surveyed the damage. The pump had been high enough up the bank to survive but most of the samples were gone.

A few days later, we had the samples collected again and it was time to try out the gold jig Craig had brought.

"Why send us a jig when the Shafer-Woodhouse team's on the job?" Jim said as we tried to figure out how it worked. "Hunter has the two best gold panners in the state."

"The jig doesn't replace us," I said. "It concentrates the sample down from about twenty kilos to a few hundred grams for panning off. It'll save time and effort."

We discovered that setting the jig up wasn't a simple procedure, especially getting the water pressure right and it took a lot of trial and error to get it to run properly. The sample had to be fed in slowly and the pump pressure was absolutely critical to get a good jigging action.

"Do you reckon you could take charge of jigging these samples?" I asked Art, once we had it working.

"No worries. I like this technical stuff."

"Since when has bludging been technical?" Jim asked. He turned to Chas . "I hope you guarantee the quality of the field hands you supply. We don't want to have to collect these samples again."

"Yep."

"Art's up to something," Jim confided to me as we left. "You see the way he heads out every evening with the toilet roll? Nobody's that regular. He's got a cache of beer or a carton of cigarettes hidden somewhere. One of these nights I'm going to spring him."

A few days later, about mid afternoon, we noticed a column of smoke appear in the direction of the camp and it grew bigger and blacker very quickly. We roared back to find the bush alight, the caravan blackened but intact and the tent in a collapsed heap looking rather charred. Art was beating at some burning grass with one of Jim's shirts he'd grabbed off the line. Chas made for the water pump while Jim and I beat out the flames around the tent. By the time the pump was going the fire had died from a lack of new things to burn.

I looked inside the caravan, which was a little sooty.

"Okay, Art" I said. "How did you stuff up this time? This better be good."

Art wiped an arm over his blackened face; he looked a bit groggy. "I was just cooking some sausages on the gas stove. The fat caught alight and I threw it outside."

"And burnt the place down."

"I thought it was better than burning the van."

Jim scowled. "You burnt it anyway you dickhead, as well as burning the tent and our things. That's going to cost you. A thousand bucks should about cover it."

"No worries," Art said.

"No worries? Have you been eating mushrooms again?"

"No way."

Jim grabbed him by the shoulders. "You're still off your brain, I can tell by your eyes."

"I'm as sane as you."

A check of the camp showed that things weren't as bad as they looked. The tent had only collapsed because the ropes on one corner had burnt through but our gear was intact.

While the others cleaned up the camp, I went down to the jig and panned off the concentrates Art had prepared. They were just sand with no trace of any heavy minerals. I marched back with the evidence and confronted Art in the caravan.

"You've stuffed up three days work. These are just sand."

He shrugged "The jig must'a played up. I never had much confidence in it."

Jim came over. He held up a plastic drink bottle with a straw through its side. "I knew he was up to something. Art's been smoking pot. That's fifteen hundred bucks for the bet you lost plus the cost of repairs for the fire."

"Don't owe youse anything," Art said.

"I can smell it on you. Can see it in the way you look, the way you talk," Jim said.

"That's it," I said. I turned to Chas. "You hired him to us. What's your verdict?"

Chas looked embarrassed. "I thought he would come good. Guess I'll have to take him home."

Jim said. "I'll pick the money he owes when I come through the Towers."

"I'm not paying you nothing?" Art growled.

"Not a problem. I'll collect your wages from Chas."

The bravado left Art suddenly and for once in his life he looked crestfallen. "I like this work. What if I put in a day free to make up?"

"Keep talking," I said. "Three free days to collect the samples again."

"Okay."

"What else?"

"I could give up the grog?"

"Go on."

"The smokes; the pot; swearing?"

"The gambling," Chas volunteered.

"Steady on Ar-Chas," Jim said. "I'll quit too if that happens."

"Keep going," I said.

"Art scratched his head. "Do some of the cooking? Get up first in the morning."

I nodded. "Make a note of these promises, Chas, but I'm still waiting for something."

"No belching during the meals. No dirty jokes? I'll have a shower every night---."

"I'm waiting for an apology, Art. If you want the job back I want all those promises kept and I want an apology."

"An apology to all of us," Jim said. "For making us collect those samples for the third bloody time."

That evening, as we lay on our stretchers under the stars with the smell of burnt bush on the evening breeze Jim groaned. "We've got to collect those bloody samples again," he said, "and you were conned. Art's reform won't last. If you can't do a better job of hiring guys you'd better give the game away."

"It's the story of my life. I'm a sucker for hiring no hopers."

"Steady on," he said. "I'll rephrase that last comment. I've just remembered you picked the world's number one field assistant."

I knew Jim was right. Art would never reform, although he did stay off the pot and mushrooms beer and cigarettes until he became impossible to work with. We collected the samples for the third time and panned them off. They were all barren.

Chapter 7. The Saudi Connection

At the end of our four-week stint at the Sellheim camp, I got word that there was a new project starting up that would temporarily disrupt the team. I was to spend a week or two on the company's hot new mineral sands project.

"How will we get along sampling without a geo?" Chas asked when I broke the news.

Jim gave a sly chuckle. "The shady trees are looking good."

"What if I put you in charge of the camp, Chas? Or maybe you, Jim?"

"The shady trees are looking even better," Jim said.

"Chas would be good," Art said. "Anything would be better than Jim. If he runs the camp then I quit."

"My God," Jim said. "Put me in charge, please."

"Actually they're sending a replacement, another contract geologist called Hermann. Luckily for him it's only for a short while. I don't think any normal geo could take more than that."

"You managed it," Art said.

"Yes, but I built up to it gradually. This fellow comes in at the deep end."

"What will you be doing?" Chas asked.

"Hunter figured I needed a week's R and R by the sea. Word must have got back to them about the appalling hardship I've been under with you lot. I'll be taking samples of beach sands with an old mate of mine, Tony O'Toole, another geologist, who's an expert on heavy minerals. Just imagine it—a five star motel on the beach at Yeppoon, the soft susurration of the sleepy surf sliding over sand and shingle; a cool, salt-tanged breeze blowing gently through my hair; the lonely sea and the sky, the gulls calling ..."

"How can you do this to your old mates? Take us with you," Jim said.

"Yeah," Art agreed. "We're the ones actually working here anyway. Why can't we get a break too?"

"I need a week like this to prove to myself once again that becoming a geologist was not the stupidest mistake I ever made."

Art said. "What, by spending a week working with another geo? You must be joking."

* * *

The canvas chair creak ominously as Art settled his bulk on it with a sigh. He pulled the top off a tinnie, which made a pleasing hiss, and sucked long and hard before wiping his mouth with a none-too-clean hand and surveyed the new campsite he'd largely managed to avoid setting up. "We've done a good job this time," he said as Jim staggered past with an Esky full of food. "Tent is up, caravan is level, dunny's in the shade, generator is going, fireplace is a work of art and we've even got a shower; all finished before sunset. Pity Bob isn't here to see how efficient we've become." He emptied the tinnie and reached for another. "The new geo is going to be impressed if he ever gets here. What's his name again?"

Jim dumped the esky on the ground and sat on it before answering. "Hermann Zeiss or Zeissman, something like that. I rang him this morning to give him directions. He should have been here this morning same time as us."

"Maybe he got lost."

"He said he's worked around here and he told me we were wasting our time as he knew all the best gold areas in Queensland and this wasn't one of them."

Art brightened. "So we can take it easy then."

"How do you figure that?"

"We're not going to find anything so why bother looking."

Jim turned to Chas whose head was buried in the engine of his Toyota. "Why did you bother bringing him?"

Chas closed the bonnet with a clang. "He's not serious."

"You reckon? He's going to get a shock working for Hermann though. He won't be a pushover for bludgers like Bob is."

"You think he'll be hard to get along with?" Chas asked.

"He didn't sound too impressed when I said the camp and the generator ran on flexible hours.

"What?" Art said in amazement. "How else could you run it? It's not a city office where you clock on at nine and off at five. He sounds like a prize prick."

"With that attitude you'll last a couple of days at the most, Art."

"Bull. I know how to handle those types."

"That'll be interesting to watch. What are you planning to do, bribe him?"

"Just be myself."

"Forget what I just said about a couple of days. Make that one day."

"No way. I worked for a German once. "Big guy, six foot four; Rudi Tchac. He had a voice like a bull's roar when he was angry. I was the only one in camp not scared of him. Best way to deal with that type is to show no fear, then they respect you."

Jim groaned. "Art, the dunny is set up and ready to go. I suggest you use it, then dig a new hole for the rest of us."

Later on, with the generator going, they were about to sit down to the meal under the stars when a vehicle drove up, the radio playing classical music. It was a top of the line Range Rover and gleamed in the camp lights as if it were brand new. Even the tyres looked freshly blackened.

A man got out and stretched. "Looks like chow time," he said.

"Blood oath," Art said. "Who are you?"

"Hermann."

Hermann was about forty, with angular features, thinning brown hair and a small moustache. He was of slight build and average height but his pressed Fletcher Jones pants and polished elastic side boots, both light brown in colour, along with his ironed khaki shirt with razor sharp creases gave him a superior edge to the three unkempt field hands watching him. He dropped his Akubra hat on the bench, walked over to where Jim had just set out three plates of food and took one.

"Great timing," he said, sitting down.

Jim didn't miss a beat. "That one was Art's."

"Thank you Ark," Hermann said, reaching for the salt. "Help yourself to some more."

As the dreadful realisation dawned on Art that he was about to miss out on a feed, he made a grab for another plate but Jim was too quick, handing one to Chas and keeping the other.

"There isn't any more." Art's voice had the strangled quality of a man facing starvation.

"That's too bad," Hermann said, cutting into the steak. "You'd better complain to the cook. He knew I was coming."

"The cook has retired for the night," Jim said.

"Well just rustle up a bit more for yourself, Ark." Hermann said, chewing with relish. "This is good stuff."

"Steaks are in the freezer," Jim said. "If you want fries you'll have to cut up more potato."

"Art muttered something unprintable under his breath and stormed over to the fridge.

"Which one of you is the mechanic? Hermann asked.

"We're all prospectors here," Jim said. "There's no mechanic."

"Chas somebody."

"That's me," Chas said.

"The engine misses at low revs. Have a look tomorrow. A vehicle has to be kept in top shape in the bush. Lives depend on it."

"They depend on food too," Art said, slicing up a tomato.

"What was that, Ark?" Hermann said.

Art's voice rose slightly. "It's Art, not Ark. A-R-T. I said lives depend on food too."

Hermann chewed contemplatively before replying. "They surely do. He waived a forkful of steak at Jim. "And this is delicious."

"I wouldn't know," Art said. This bloody steak will take a week to thaw."

"Have an egg," Jim said.

Hermann, seeing an unopened beer on the table reached for it, pulled the ring top off then took a few mouthfuls. "My, that's good," he said.

When Art finally returned to the table with scrambled egg and fried tomato the first thing he did was reach for his beer. As his hand trembled over the spot where it should have been as his eyes followed the line of condensation droplets across the table to Hermann.

Hermann raised the can. "Cheers," he said and took a long draught.

"That's my beer!"

Hermann examined the label. "Fourex? I wouldn't call it a beer, but it's ok under the circumstances; get yourself another one."

Art looked like he could commit a murder but with mouth clamped shut he stomped over to the caravan and returned with two more, which he banged on the table.

Hermann raised an eyebrow. "Is this your beer?"

"Yes, it bl—it's mine."

Herman seemed unconcerned. "I usually get the company to buy beer for the camp; I think it helps morale."

Art, who'd been reigning in his temper with admiral control since losing his meal and his beer, brightened slightly and Hermann rose one notch above zero in his estimation. "This is the only camp I ever been in where a man has to buy his own," he said.

"How many camps is that?" Jim asked.

"Plenty, smart arse."

"How much beer have you got?" Hermann asked.

"Just a few cartons."

"He always brings eight," Jim said.

Chas looked astounded; he turned to Art with a frown. "Is that true?"

"Might 'ave; who's counting?"

"He hides them under the bed so you won't notice," Jim said.

"We agreed you buy one carton," Chas said, sounding both stern and fatherly.

"Yeah—well I did only buy one, the rest I already had."

"My God," Jim said in admiration. "You're smarter than I thought."

Hermann waggled a finger at no one in particular. "I don't encourage alcohol in bush camps unless it's kept strictly under control. A can a night however is very beneficial."

"Two is even better," Art said.

"Field hands turn up with alcohol thinking they can control it but it can get out of hand and then the whole camp suffers. Besides it's not fair to potential alcoholics to have temptation always in reach. There's always one in camp."

"This camp's no exception, that's for sure," Jim said.

"What?"Hermann said, looking shocked.

"I was referring to Art," Jim said.

"Ah!" Hermann relaxed. "You're a joker, Jim."

"Yeah, and a lousy one at that," Art said. "There's nothing worse than a guy trying to be funny but just being pathetic."

Hermann pushed his plate away, pulled out a tobacco pouch and began to fill a pipe before turning to Chas. "Bob tells me you rent out most of the equipment used here."

"Yep," Chas said.

"I like a man of enterprise. If the equipment is maintained I doubt

I'll have much to complain about."

Jim, who had been trying not to laugh at this last remark, had to suddenly swallow his mirth and turn it into a cough as Herman turned to him.

"And you, Jim. Bob tells me you're reliable and always ready to carry out whatever work is required. He also says you're a top cook, which I can vouch for."

"Bob's a good judge of character," Jim said.

"Bob's a bloody dreamer," Art said with a grunt of disgust.

Hermann turned to Art and his brow wrinkled. "I can't recall Bob saying much about you, Ark. What's your background?"

"It's Art." He put on that self-important tone he used when extolling his virtues. "I've done pretty well everything. Drilling, sampling, supervising men, running exploration camps, planning programs—you know. Chas and I are a team."

"Yeah," Jim said. "I can vouch for all that. We haven't been in camp long enough to use all of Art's talents. I'm surprised he bothers with small outfits like Hunter."

"I'm just helping out for Chas," Art said. "They needed another man."

"But instead we got Art," Jim said.

Hermann got his pipe going then looked over to where the tent and caravan were set up. "I hope you left room for my tent."

"The tent's already set up," Jim said.

Hermann shook his head. "I have my own." He stood up. "I'll show you how to erect it. It needs three men."

After hauling it out of the Range Rover, Jim, Chas and Art found that it needed at least four men and preferably six, but as Hermann was fully occupied directing operations the three of them staggered with it over to where he decided to set it up. The new camp site was on top of a low hill with a sharp drop-off on one side and a long slope down to a dam on the other. Hermann pointed to a space with his pipe. "Not much level ground here is there? This is the best spot."

"There's not enough room left," Chas said.

"There's enough if you move the caravan down the hill a bit."

"But we've already set up the annexe," Art said.

"Hermann's right," Jim said with a smirk. It's too close to my tent anyway given the snoring that goes on."

"Fix up the annex tomorrow," Hermann said. "Shift the van a few metres. Let's get this tent up."

With much mumbled swearing from Art, the van was moved down slope, which required chocking the wheels with the few small rocks they could find and lifting the front with the kangaroo jack as the jockey wheel extension was not long enough to get it level. They left the jack in place as a temporary measure.

Hermann's tent was a pentagon with a centre pole and supporting poles for the corners. By the time it was up, with all pegs set at exact measured distances from the corner poles and tensioned, Ringaling's Circus could have moved in with lions and elephants. Hermann walked around it a couple of times examining it critically and then brought in, or rather the exploration team under his guidance brought in a substantial bed, mosquito net and mattress, folding table, several chairs, a suitcase, a radio, two mats (Hermann called them Dhurries) and a Turkish carpet.

"Good work, chaps," Hermann said as he surveyed his palatial establishment. "I learnt a few tips from the Arabs when I was working in Saudi. They know how to be comfortable in the desert and how to anticipate what a geo needs." He turned to Art. "Bring the beer in and stack it up near the bed. It'll make a useful extra table."

"What!" Art said, his voice rising, not sure he was hearing right.

Hermann pointed with his pipe. "Over here. It will keep temptation away."

"What bloody temptation? I always pace myself."

"I'll run the camp my way," thanks Ark. Just bring it in." There was steel in his voice.

Art looked as if he was about to blow up, but he didn't argue further and soon seven cartons were piled up by the bed. He was about to disappear when Hermann said. "Where's the opened one?"

"Oh—Ah!" Art scratched his head. "The opened one?"

"Yes."

"Didn't think you'd want that." He returned with the opened carton, which Hermann emptied onto the bed. "There's only fourteen here," he said. "There should be twenty or more. Where did the others go?"

Chas, who had been looking on with interest said. "They must be still in the van. I'll take a look."

Jim said. "Pity you weren't running the camp six months ago, Hermann. Art would be two stone lighter. You need to get onto his smoking, eating and swearing too. They tried to sort him out in reform school but gave up."

Chas came in with the missing beer, handing Hermann six tins.

"Temptation removed," Hermann said, adding them to the rest.

As Hermann unpacked his two large suitcases and fixed up his bed for the night, Jim joined Chas and Art in the caravan.

"You sure showed us how you can handle Hermann." Jim said to Art.

"What a prize bastard," Art snarled. "The little Hitler should have stayed in Saudi. I was tempted to drop him but he's not worth the effort. And thanks, Chas, for helping. I was really hanging out for that beer. Now I'll be lucky to get to sleep tonight."

"I saved your job," Chas said. "If he'd caught you cheating you'd be on the road out."

"At least I'd have me beer with me. Talking of which… ". He pulled a stubby from his pocket.

"Where did you get that?" Chas said.

"Behind the seat of the Tojo; I think it's from last year." He removed the top and took a swig, then looked at it critically. "It's warm and a bit flat, but whose to complain when a man's got a throat like parched sandpaper."

"I reckon you and the beer will be on the road out tomorrow," Jim said. "He sized you up as a drunken layabout the moment he arrived. Once he sees you working that'll be it." He began laughing. "I thought you were going to plant one on him when he took your steak and drank your beer. That or have a brain seizure."

Chas nodded in agreement. "You came close to losing it."

"No way," Art said. "I sussed him out the moment he arrived. You don't handle those types with force but with skill."

"It's called the brown nose approach," Jim said. "You're a natural."

"Who's a natural?" Hermann said, stepping into the van and making it rock dangerously. He nodded towards the gas ring in the van. "Does that work? I could go a cup of cocoa, there's a chill in the air."

Art, with his stubby sitting in full view on the table, went into shock but Chas was the man of the moment. He picked it up and emptied it down the sink.

Art, seeing this wanton destruction, could barely contain himself. "Wh-what," he managed to gurgle before subsiding again, defeat written in every sagging limb.

"What's going on?" Hermann said, looking at the now empty stubby.

Chas said. "I found an old bottle. Just getting rid of temptation."

"Glad to hear it. I don't want to find I have a crew of alcoholics on my hands. Now, about that cocoa. He turned to Art. "Will you do the honours?"

"Coming up, boss" Art said.

Hermann smiled appreciatively. "Good man". "Make mine on milk." He sat down at the rickety table took a biscuit and said. "We'll have an early night. Lights out in twenty minutes."

Jim said "That won't bother Art but I haven't had a shower yet, nor has Chas."

"Ok, I'll give you 30 minutes given the circumstances. Reveille will be at 6am "

* * *

As dawn brightened the sky a chill wind blew through the camp that sought out any exposed flesh and caused blankets to be pulled tighter. At 6 am on the dot, Hermann strolled over to the kitchen freshly shaved and smelling of aftershave and anti perspirant and banged two pots together making enough noise to drown out even the snoring competition going on in the caravan. Jim emerged five minutes later, then Chas and finally Art, who squinted blearily in the direction of where the sun might rise sometime in the future and pulled a sweater over his pyjamas before joining the rest in the kitchen.

Hermann looked at Jim expectantly. "What's on the breakfast menu?"

Jim, who was about to shake some Cornflakes into a bowl, said. "Whatever you want. Help yourself."

"I always have eggs and bacon."

"Go for it then."

"But you're the cook."

"Evening meal and lunches only. The others wash up. That's it."

Hermann's eyes narrowed. "You're not going to cook breakfast?"

"Not unless you pay me another ten bucks a day."

"I'll cook breakfasts for you for ten bucks a day," Art said, getting up. "Bacon, two eggs and toast. Do you want coffee too?"

Hermann nodded. "Good man; and fried tomato."

After breakfast, Hermann walked about the campsite taking his field crew with him and requesting various improvements, after which they all walked over to examine the Range Rover. "It picked up a few scratches coming in last night," Hermann said. "I might need to make an insurance claim."

"All it needs is a wash," Art said.

Hermann nodded appreciatively. "Good man, Ark. I'll take you up on that." He turned to Chas. "Take a look under the bonnet. The engine runs a bit rough."

By about midday the camp was set up to Hermann's liking. The Range Rover was washed and Chas had found a loose spark plug lead. It was now protected under a dust cover. Hermann sat down at the kitchen table and looked at his watch. "Twelve thirty. What's for lunch, Jim?"

"Nothing; I've been setting up the tarp up for weather protection."

"We'll make 12.30 the official lunch break from now on. That way you can be prepared."

Jim's eyes widened. "Prepared? I just throw a heap of salad things in the cooler. We help ourselves when hungry."

"That might be alright in the bush but you need to do a bit better when we're still in camp."

"My oath!" Art said. "I'm famished. If you're looking for ideas, what about bread and butter, sliced onion, pickles, lettuce, salami, olives, cold sausage and hard boiled eggs for starters."

Hermann chuckled. "You should have been a chef, Ark. Hard boiled eggs and cold sausage require planning the day before. Our cook needs to think ahead but given we've only just set up camp I'll accept that as an excuse."

"Gee, thanks," Jim said. "Will you guys accept a tin of camp pie in lieu of cold sausage and also accept my deepest apology?"

"I guess," Art said. "But keep on top of it. Bob's not in charge any more in case you haven't noticed. You'll need to smarten up."

Later in the afternoon they drove out to one of the creeks I'd previously marked to take a trap sample for gold.

"What now," Hermann said as they stood in the creek bed.

"We're waiting for you to select a site," Jim said.

Hermann looked around. "Am I looking for a golden glow or what?" Art laughed loudly at this clever remark making Hermann smile "So fill me in; what do you do?"

Art kicked a rock. "We dig down in front of a trap like this."

Hermann shook his head. "In front? That's wrong. The winnowing action happens around the back of the rock, not the front."

Art said. "I always thought Bob had it wrong. It's good to work with a geo who can think."

Jim looked over the top of Hermann's head at Chas who shrugged imperceptibly. "So you want me to dig the downstream side then?" Jim asked.

"Of course."

Jim removed a fair pile of sand from behind the rock and finally reached bedrock at which point, Art, with brush and pan, got down on his knees with barely a grunt and began to sweep up the fines. "This is where the gold is if there's any in the system," he said to Hermann. "The ground has to be carefully cleaned or the gold will be missed."

"Good man," Hermann said as Jim raised his eyes to heaven.

After collecting the sample they returned to the vehicles and threw the bags and implements into the back of Chas' Toyota. "Where's the next sample point?" Jim asked.

"We won't know until we check this one." Hermann said. "If there's no gold in it then there's no point in further sampling upstream is there?"

"Course not, it's simple logic," Art said.

Jim shook his head. "But these traps aren't perfect; we could have missed the gold."

"Just let me do the worrying and thinking," Hermann said. "That's what I'm paid for. I'm sure with Ark's careful clean up we won't have missed anything. So what do you do next?"

Art jumped in quickly. "I put the sample through the jig. That gives us a concentrate, which Bob pans off. We also bag a sample for the lab."

Hermann looked at his watch. "Right. That'll get us back to camp in time for Jim to put the billy on for afternoon tea while you show me how the jig works. What are you like at panning off, Ark?"

"No problem. I used to prospect for gold. Even had a small show once but I lost it in a bet."

"Art was born with a pack of cards in his hands," Jim said. "Do you play Hermann?"

"Bridge. Probably a bit over your heads, I imagine."

"A great game," Art said. "I wish I'd had more time to learn it properly."

Hermann sucked in his cheeks for a moment as he looked at the others. "Well, we have a Bridge four. Are there any takers?"

"Chas is out," Jim said. "He doesn't play cards and I only play if it's a betting game. Art thinks you're talking about a way of getting over a river. What about Pontoon or Poker?"

Hermann shook his head. "Gambling in camp is as bad as or worse than drinking in camp. I don't allow it."

"You sure you weren't hired by Chas?" Jim asked.

Hermann looked over to Chas. "Do you back me up on gambling and drinking?"

It was a foolish question but Hermann was not to know. "My word I do," Chas said. "Gambling and drinking are sins."

"But Jesus turned water into wine," Jim said, hiding a smile.

"The Bible is speaking about unfermented juice. Verses that expose the evils of wine are talking about alcoholic wine. In Proverbs it says 'Wine is a mocker, strong drink is raging: and whosoever is deceived thereby is not wise'."

Hermann looked a bit taken aback. "Er—thank you Chas. That's very true."

"God does not lead us into evil," Chas continued, warming to his theme. "He delivers us from it. He does not teach us to practice evil in moderation. "

"Thanks Chas," Hermann said again. " I can see that Ark is in good hands but we need to get back. Afternoon tea is waiting."

While Hermann and Art were down at the river putting the sample through the jig, Jim lit the gas stove to make the tea. "You know what, Chas?" He said.

"What?"

"This Hermann is a dickhead. We're in the middle of the afternoon, we've taken one sample that's not in a trap and now he wants afternoon tea."

"He's got some good ideas on drinking and gambling though."

"But he's lost the plot."

The tea was well brewed by the time Art and Hermann came back. "Any luck?" Jim asked, knowing the answer.

"Just as I thought; there's no gold in the river systems around here," Hermann said, with Art nodding agreement. "This is copper country, not gold."

"Are we going back out this afternoon?" Jim asked.

Hermann shook his head. "It's too late. It'll give you a chance to work up a really good meal. A pork roast would be my preference."

Art chimed in, a great smile on his face. "Yeah, with green peas, baked potatoes, baked onion and apple sauce."

"And only one can of beer," Jim said, wiping the smile off Art's face.

* * *

The 6 am start the next morning was chilly but with lights out at 9.30 the crew were not sleep deprived and at 7 am they headed out, Art to his unsupervised trap sampling and the rest to sample some old copper workings, which were not far away.

They were back in camp by four but there was no sign of Art and he didn't turn up until it was nearly dark. "Only four samples," Jim said, looking in the back of his vehicle. "Did you fall asleep after morning tea?"

Art ignored him and turned to Hermann. "It was a jungle out there. I had to walk about two kilometres for every sample and finding a good trap wasn't easy. I put in a bit of overtime to get the job done."

"Good man. Quality sampling is what it's all about."

"What a load of crap, Art" Jim said as Hermann walked away. "You don't even know how to use an airphoto let alone find Bob's sample sites."

"Course I do. My last boss reckoned if I'd been on the Burke and Wills expedition they would never have died."

"That's because you would never have got them out of Sydney. I bet you got lost. Hermann told me he intends to check your sample sites tomorrow. What's the bet you won't find them."

Art paled."Shit! Is that for real?"

"I knew it," Jim said. "You'll be on the road out tomorrow, just as I predicted."

Jim had cooked up lamb chops and sausages and as they sat down to eat, Hermann came over with four cans of Art's beer.

"As the company would normally be supplying one can per man per day," he said, "and there are only two of us drinking, I guess we could drink two a night."

Art immediately ripped the tab off one. "Beaudy! Does that mean the company's going to pay for me beer too?"

"I'll see you get a credit for what we drink."

"Steady on, "Jim said. "You mean about thirty of Art's beers belong to me and thirty to Chas?"

"Only if you drink them."

"You realise," Jim said, turning to Chas. "That you're now supplying beer to Art. That's disgraceful."

Chas scratched his head in thought for a moment. "No, I'm giving mine to Hermann."

"So am I," Jim said. "Art, give that second beer to Hermann."

"Too late," Art said, throwing his now empty can into the rubbish bin and ripping the tab off the next. "I've already started on it."

The philosophical argument that now started up ended when a small red Suzuki four-wheel-drive arrived. A window wound down, a face poked out and an arm waived. "Yoo hoo, Art. It's me."

"Bongo," Art said, getting up. "What are you doing here?"

A young woman extracted herself from behind the wheel with some difficulty as she was even larger than Art although considerably more attractive. She had on an oversize charcoal grey jumper and black slacks, below which were gold sandals displaying bright red toenails.

"Hi Art," she said, pushing back shoulder length dark hair that was partly covering her pale face. "I thought I'd drive out and overnight, seeing as how you're now running the camp with the geo away." She sniffed. "What's for dinner? It smells delicious." She came over and sat down on the bench and looked around. "Hi," she said. "I'm Julie but my friends call me Bongo."

"I'm the cook," Jim said, pushing Art's as yet untouched plate over to her. "You can have this."

"Oh, but isn't this someones?" She said. She had a husky voice.

"Go for it," It's Art's but he dieting."

"No worries," Art said magnanimously. "I'll make something else."

"Oh thank you. But won't the cook get you something?"

"It's ok," Art said. "I can turn out a top meal anytime."

"Hi Chas," Bongo said. "Art told me you might be here." She turned to Hermann and held out her hand. "Hi."

He stood and shook her hand. "I'm Hermann. Take this easy chair, I'll take the bench."

"Thanks." They swapped places.

"Bongo," Hermann said, clearly impressed by the camp visitor. "What a delightful nickname. How do you come to know Ark?"

"We were at school together."

"Art went to school?" Jim said. "You learn something every day."

"Ignore him," Art said. "Camp cooks are notorious for lack of couth."

"And what do you do, Bongo?" Hermann asked.

"I'm a nurse in the Towers. What about you; are you one of Art's field assistants?"

"I'm a geologist."

"Wow! Art really has moved up in the world. This is quite a team he's got." Her large, dark eyes, set off by mascara, sparkled.

"Hermann is the actual boss of the camp," Art said, somewhat reluctantly. "I run the gold sampling section."

Jim said. "Art is high up the command structure though, just below Chas and me."

"Bongo thought about this for a moment then turned to Hermann."So you're running the camp. I've always wanted to meet a geologist. They must know so much."

Art banged a tin plate on the table and emptied three fried eggs onto it from the frypan as he said. "A geo needs top fieldies if he's to be successful. Without them he's next to useless"

"Ark," Hermann said. "Go get the delightful Miss Bongo a couple of beers from my tent, will you."

There was a natural rapport between Hermann and Bongo and by the time Hermann had recounted some of his adventures as a geologist in the deserts of Saudi Arabia where thirst, heatstroke and marauding brigands had threatened his life on numerous occasions, much beer had been consumed. It was only brought to an end when the generator ran out of fuel.

"Where can I sleep? Bongo asked. "Is there room in the van? I brought a sleeping bag."

"You're welcome to drag a mattress into my tent if the van doesn't appeal," Hermann said magnanimously.

"Or mine," Jim said.

"She's in the van," Art said in a voice that brooked no argument. There's spare pillows and blankets and a decent bed."

"I'll take the van, this time," Bongo said, giggling.

With Chas in the van there was little chance of any hanky panky but as dawn paled the sky there were a few thumps and other noises from the van as Bongo returned from a trip to the loo and climbed back into the top bunk. The excessive rocking shook the jack loose and the front dropped down onto the jockey wheel setting the van in motion down slope. As it gathered speed there were shouts of alarm from inside which roused Hermann and Jim but there was little they could do. By the time they had stepped blearily out of bed the van had cleared a path through the scrub and had entered the dam with a great muddy splash, it's momentum sufficient for it to plane into the middle where is slowly settled until its wheels rested on the bottom, a metre deep.

As Jim and Hermann walked down to assess the problem the door was pushed open and Art's head poked out. "Hoi," he yelled. "Get us out, the water's bloody freezing."

Hermann turned to Jim. "I'll leave it in your capable hands. Try and get Ark out in time to cook my breakfast." He turned and trudged back up the hill.

"How are Chas and Bongo?" Jim called.

"They're still in the top bunks. I'm the only one who got drowned."

"Well wade out and give me a hand."

The water came up to Art's waist as he gingerly lowered himself into it but as he approached the shore the mud deepened and he slipped. His string of oaths warmed the surroundings as he flailed about trying to gain traction.

"Hurry it up," Jim said. "Hermann wants his breakfast."

Art's reply was unprintable but he finally made it to shore, the last few steps on hands and knees.

Back at the camp Art washed and then dried himself on one of Jim's towels and they drove the two Toyotas back and hooked both vehicles up. Chas had appeared by this stage and he waded around to the front of the van and fastened the rope they threw to him.

The van rocked as the two vehicles took the strain but they could gain little traction on the slope.

Art called to Bongo, to try and get her to leave the van but she refused.

"I'll cook you a great breakfast," Art called.

"Stuff your breakfast," came the reply. "I'm not moving."

Art turned to Jim. "What'll we do?"

Jim called out. "Bongo, we don't have a boat and you can't stay there, the mozzies will eat you alive. Art says he will carry you out. That way you'll avoid the mud."

"What?" Art said in alarm.

Jim put a finger to his lips.

They were not sure if this idea was going to work until there was a scream as Bongo splashed down from the top bunk. The van shook and great ripples spread across the water. She finally appeared shivering in the doorway, dressed in bright red but now sodden pyjamas,

"Hurry it up," she said. "I'm fucking freezing."

"Ok, Sir Galahad," Jim said. "Go rescue."

It was never going to work but Art did his best. As Bongo put her arm around his neck it looked as if he might have to make the journey

92

with his head underwater but by lowering her deeper into it instead he got his nose into the air, then made for the shore, nearly deafened by her screams of pain as the cold waters swirled up round her chest. As the water shallowed near the slippery edge he was forced to set her down and to Jim's amazement they both stood, supporting each other, then Bongo took one step towards Jim's outstretched hand and measured her length in the mud; Art fell over backwards.

Back at the camp they washed the mud off under the cold shower and shared the already sopping-wet spare towel. After this Bongo attached her Suzuki to the daisy chain and with three vehicles now pulling the van slowly emerged.

Jim looked at his watch. It was after ten. "I would have thought Hermann would have made an appearance by now."

"The bastard hasn't stirred out of his tent," Art said. "I'm freezing and starving. A plate of hot porridge would go down well."

"I'll cook," Bongo said, finally able to see the funny side to what had happened.

While Bongo ran the kitchen the others attacked the caravan, hosing out the mud and draping the sodden bedding and clothes on various trees and shrubs. Hermann still hadn't appeared and when breakfast was ready they called out to him. He came over to join them unshaved and looking a bit under the weather.

"You look sick," Chas said.

Hermann refused the bacon and eggs. "Jus coffee," he said, slurring his speech a little. "Ish a bug I picked up in Saudi, like malaria. Gives me a nudge occasionally. I'll be right in a while."

You'd better take it easy," Art said. "You've set us up so well we can work without you."

Hermann wiped the perspiration off his forehead. "Thanks Ark. Greatly apprech — appreciated."

"I'll get going," Bongo said as they finished. "Thanks for the hospitality. You guys have a really exciting life; more adventurous than looking after sick patients in a hospital."

"A fine woman that," Hermann said as she drove off with her muddy pyjamas hanging out the window.

Jim nodded his agreement. "She's too good for Art."

"She might straighten him out," Chas said.

Jim chuckled. "She would if she sat on him."

"Make fun," Art said. "But she's just one of several I've got who hang about."

Hermann pushed the air photos across the table to Art with a shaking hand. "Here are a few more sample sites."

Art took them. He seemed a little hesitant. "Thanks—er—you're not coming out?"

"No need. It's all pretty straight forward."

When Jim and Chas returned to camp late that evening, Art was already there. "Where's Hermann?" Chas asked.

Art shrugged. "In his tent I suppose. I wish the bastard would bring out my beer."

"Maybe he would have if you'd cooked a meal."

" I was thinking about it."

"Only thinking? I'm amazed you haven't. Hermann is probably suffering from a sore arse the way you've had your nose up it since he got here."

"That's not brown nosing, its job protection."

When Jim had the meal ready he called out to Hermann but there was no reply.

"He must still be sick," Chas said, getting up. "I'll go check." He walked over to Hermann's tent and called out again, then came back to the table. "He's not hungry."

"What about my beer?" Art said.

Chas shrugged, unconcerned.

"You know how to handle him, Art." Jim said. "Give us another demo of brown nosing."

Art gave him the finger. "Up yours!" He slouched over to Hermann's tent only to return empty handed; he slumped down on the bench looking hard done by. "The flap is tied shut and he told me to piss off."

Chas looked at him sternly. "You drank a week's quota last night. You shouldn't have any more."

Jim said. "And Hermann's charging the company for it. If they finishing up paying for your normal beer intake there will be no exploration budget left."

"I'll be rat-shit tomorrow," Art said.

Jim chuckled. "How will we know?"

In the early hours of the morning, the camp awoke to the sound of mumbled curses, snatches of song, garbled mutterings and occasional screams. "Lemme out," a voice called. There was the sound of ripping and moments later something stumbled over Jim's tent rope.

"Hey," Jim called. Not too keen to get up in case a maniac was on

94

the loose. "Who's that?"

The caravan door opened with a squeak of rusted hinges. "Who's calling?" Chas said.

"Who's running about outside?" Jim called.

Now he had company, Jim ventured out with his torch. The first thing he noticed was Hermann's slashed tent flap, then a body on the ground; it was Hermann.

They crouched over the form as Art joined them. "He's alive," Jim said. "But he might have been stabbed. Look at the slash in his tent."

"Christ," Art said, staring into the darkness fearfully. "There's a maniac in the camp."

Hermann moaned and mumbled a few words and his hands began to scrabble at his legs. "Get away, get away," he said, becoming quite agitated.

"Easy," Jim said.

Chas said. "Phew, smell the beer. I think he's drunk."

"He's paralytic," Art said, recognizing the familiar signs.

"He can't be," Jim said, "unless..."

They pushed into Hermann's tent, it was littered with empty beer cans.

"My bloody beer," Art said, aghast. "He's drunk all my beer; the bastard's drunk the lot."

"We'd better take him into the Towers," Chas said. "He could have poisoned himself."

"All my beer," Art said again. "All my fucking beer."

"We'd better take Art in too," Jim said. "He's in shock."

Chapter 8 Low Tide

While my field crew were working for Hermann, I was catching up with my old mate Tony O'Toole. Tony was typical of what we refer to as a wild Irishman or in his case as a mad Irishman. I had first met him in Mt Isa twenty-five years ago. He was full of quirky humour and friendliness and in those days we were both unmarried and competing for the same girls. He became best man at my wedding a few years later. Tony held a particular fascination for the Mt Isa girls who were attracted and repelled at the same time. His short hair, a straw-like brown, stuck out in front like a halo with a spiky rim. The dark, bushy eyebrows, sufficiently luxurious to invade each other's territory, met in a straight line across his forehead and the deep-set dark eyes that peered out had a fanatical yet humorous gleam. His walk too was different from others. He complained it was due to clubfeet and knock-knees, and it gave him an ambulating, prehensile gait that put one in mind of Neanderthal man. These factors, in combination with his slightly hunched shoulders, meant he had only to bend the knees slightly and it would look as if he were about to drag his knuckles along the ground. Knowing this he would often reinforce the image with a few grunts as he walked past someone he knew.

Despite these attractions it was his strict religious beliefs as a Catholic, his persistent self-analysis and his insistence on romance to the accompaniment of heavy classical music that eventually doomed his love life. Of his girl friends at the time, one became a nun, another stayed single and could only be reached via an unlisted phone number, a third fled overseas and a fourth undertook hormone therapy and changed sex. He disclaimed any responsibility for these events, insisting he was quite *normal*, a word he enjoyed immensely. It would rumble up from his stomach and through the vocal chords in such a manner as to leave no doubt in one's mind that he was anything but normal.

Since our Mt Isa days our paths had crossed a few times, occasions that had added spice to life but which for the most part I'd only been able to laugh about later—much later.

"I'm coming up, hairy legs," he said, when I rang him from Brisbane to organise the field trip. "Set up a bed, get out a bottle of that Plantagenet plonk you cellar away and that tastes like it's been drained through an old sock, and warn your mates—if you have any."

"Are you serious?"

"About drinking?"

"About overnighting here?"

"If I could avoid it I would. No-one wants to stay with an old bastard like you."

"The dog does not appreciate being turned out."

"I know. I'm prepared to share as I told it last time, but I object to it chewing a bone all night. And that reminds me. Tell Judy not to let you near the kitchen. Stewed pumpkin and boiled T bone is not my idea of food."

"I'm preparing a genuine Haggis for you this time. Our pet sheep vanished some time back and I only located the remains yesterday when a neighbour complained of the pong."

"My mouth is watering already. By the way, how is 'She of the beautiful legs'? I'm still trying to work out why she married an old bastard like you. After twenty-years I'm no closer to the truth."

"Judy's great. I doubt you'll see her though."

"The penny finally dropped and she left you?"

"She said she would if you ever invited yourself here again."

He chuckled. "It's good to know who your friends are."

"While we are on the subject, what about your love life?"

"If you want to spew I'll bring up a photo of the current one. She's two pickaxe handles across the beam with a face like a sack full of gumboots."

"An improvement on the last one then. I hear she was recaptured."

"Yes. She's back in the Taronga zoo."

"Tell me. How did you persuade Hunter to hire you to look for mineral sands? It couldn't have been word of mouth."

"The mob I'm working for called Hunter, hoping they'd take me off their hands."

"I guessed some serious money was paid under the counter."

He chuckled again. "You must have been a bad bastard in your youth to deserve someone like me. At least you won't have to spend time in purgatory. A lifetime on earth with me as your mate should be enough." His voice became more serious. "Listen, oh hairy one." (This was a standard expression. I carried no more than the usual amount of hair). "This could be a great project. It's a pity Hunter sent a geo who's a rock short in the quarry to check it out with me but I know even you will be impressed."

"This will be another of your disasters," I said. I'd seen a number of Tony' business projects before. They were great in theory but fell to pieces along the way. He'd have been a millionaire if he'd realised that most entrepreneurial money, money that he needed others to supply to make his schemes a reality, is held by rogues who are rich because they're prepared to—and often do—trample over their mother to see that all benefits from a deal go to them exclusively. Tony never could understand that such people could not be trusted with a simple handshake, which was all he would ask for before doing all the work and losing all the profits.

"This could set Hunter up for life, or longer," he said.

"Doing what?"

"Hang on." There was a long silence before he spoke again. "I'm watching a mad bodysurfer. The waves are great since the last storm. I've got to get down there" He fell silent again. Tony lived with a view overlooking Duranbah Beach and was a bodysurfing fanatic.

"What was I talking about?" he asked, when he finally spoke again. "My short-term memory is not the best since I was donged by a surfboard."

"We're talking about this new deal of yours."

"That's right. Ever hear of a company called Prime something? They're big in mineral sands."

"Never heard of them."

"Not to worry. I've put together a land package for them and they talked Hunter into putting in some money. I need to check out the ground and scrute the bizzos." He was referring to examining the heavy minerals under his binocular microscope.

"What do you hope to find?" I asked.

"Monazite, diamonds, heavy rare earths, rutile, gold—the works. MS Mining originally held the ground until that wonderful PM we had. What was his name?"

"Fraser?"

"Yes, Fraser and his no-sand-mining lackeys booted them out, backed by those green loonies. It's just opening up again."

"And my job will be to keep you sober?"

He chuckled. "Impossible. Not to worry though. I'm a deformed character these days; in fact I'm almost *normal*."

"Tell me about Prime. Have they any money?"

"They're loaded. The carpet in their foyer is three inches thick and there are five secretaries between the toilet and the front desk."

"This is one of your handshake deals, isn't it? Everyone's friendly until you hit the bonanza, then they walk off with the loot and all you've got is some calluses on your hands. You can't even remember their name."

"It's my short-term memory. There's an agreement being drawn up right now. I'm to get twenty per cent."

"And I'll be getting a long stint on a psychiatrist's couch after it's all over."

"If I thought it would do any good I'd have got you one years ago," he said

"A limp handshake, a carton of booze and they've picked your brains for nothing, same as all your other deals. You never learn."

"Listen sludge'" he said. "Surf's up, the waves are calling, and it's two cartons, not one. Take the rough end of a pineapple and manipulate it in the right place. I've lost my car so meet me at the train station tomorrow."

* * *

We headed out of Brisbane the next afternoon with Tony driving. "First stop, Yeppoon," he said. "We'll find a motel that has good TV reception. The State of Origin will be on tomorrow night."

"What's State of Origin?"

His mouth opened in shock. "Only the greatest football competition in the world. It's like the Melbourne Cup of football. They're the best players in the world and tomorrow Queensland is going to stomp over those bastards in New South Wales who've been boasting they're gonna beat us three-nil this year. How can you live in Queensland and not know about it?"

"I was brought up in Victoria where they play real football."

"There's no comparison. State of Origin is where the best Queensland players play the best New South Wales players. Nothing compares to it. Not even your aerial ping-pong. Now if you don't mind I'd appreciate a little peace and quiet." He inserted a tape of Mahler's third symphony in the stereo.

"By the way where's your car?" I asked. "Forget where you parked it?"

"I had a prang."

I raised an eyebrow.

"I get these fits. I was bodysurfing last year; a board took me out and a wave speared me into the deck. A mate who saw me said I was blue. They reckon I was brain dead." He grinned. "And no smart comments."

"Did the doctor twig you'd been like that for years?"

"I said no smart comments, but to answer your question, it improved the brain function about 300 per cent; I became *normal*."

"Who was the moron who pulled you out of the surf?"

"A lot of people ask me that. He's had to move interstate and change his name."

"You get epilepsy?"

"Yes, among other things."

"You've always had other things though. So is it serious stuff?"

"Petite Mal."

"So what happened that you lost the car?"

"I'm not too sure. I think I had a turn while driving. I clipped a car, turned a corner and parked on the wrong side of the road. Least that's what they told me happened. The police thought I was a hit and run. They took my licence and the car. They returned the licence but sold the car to pay for the damages. I found out later the doctor had me on too much Dilantin at the time; about twice what I should have been on."

A thought occurred to me. "You get plenty of warning of these attacks?"

"Not really."

"My God! Would you mind pulling over and stopping?"

"What else is wrong?" I asked as we changed places and I took over the wheel.

He grimaced. "Short term memory's not the best, other than that I'm *normal*, apart from clubfeet, knock-knees, chronic alcoholism ..." He held up his right hand and twisted it to look like a claw. "And *quot* of the right hand."

"It was the left hand a few years ago."

"You're right. Quot of the left hand." He lowered his right hand and raised a twisted left hand. "I've also got ..."

"Enough!" I said. "It's all in the Guinness Book of Records."

We found a motel in Yeppoon and spent some time looking over the maps Tony had brought.

"I'd like to get to these beaches and bore some holes with the hand auger," he said, tracing them with his finger. "They're a bit off the road and hard to get to however. Getting permission from numerous landholders would be difficult and we still may not get close."

"It doesn't look good. The closest ..." I looked at Tony, who had started to whistle tunelessly. It was not that his behaviour was unusual but I sensed something had happened; he seemed older, his face greyer and more lined and he looked at me incuriously. Consciousness seemed momentarily suspended, along with emotion and attention. His eyes slid away and his fingers tapped listlessly on the table for a few more seconds, then he clicked back and was in focus again.

"You all right?" I asked.

"Why?"

"I think you had an attack. You were spaced out like a Martian on Venus."

He pointed to a spot on the map where the road gave access without showing any concern. "What about driving along the beach from here?"

"No way. We could get bogged and caught by the tide. And what about the headlands we have to go around with no beach at all."

We discussed the problem for some time before Tony said. "We'll hire a boat. Then we can cruise to the exact spot. All we'll need to do is walk up the beach with the sand auger and drill a few holes, then hop back in the boat and cruise around to the next site. We'll have a ball."

"It sounds brilliant but there has to be a catch."

"Why?"

"Because you thought of it."

* * *

We had breakfast in the motel dining room the next day and ordered grilled fish. As I began to eat, Tony had another seizure. Humming tunelessly he stared about, his eyes vacant. Then he took a packet of honey, peeled back the top and spread honey over his fish. I tried to stop him but it was as if I didn't exist. Next he took the pepper grinder and shook it over the fish. When nothing happened he examined it for a moment, then unscrewed the nob on top so that the grinder came apart, falling onto his plate; peppercorns bounced across the floor. A moment later he stopped humming, took up his knife and fork, and began to eat.

"You just had another seizure and spread honey on your fish. You became almost normal."

"*Normal?*" He grunted and twisted his left hand into a claw, holding it up in the air. "Please God," he said. "Make my hand like the other one." A throaty gargle came from his throat and he slowly lifted his right hand, which had also twisted into a claw. The waiter, who had come out with the dustpan to clean up the peppercorns and had watched this performance spellbound, did a smart u-turn.

Hiring a small motorboat turned out to be easy. The service station rented them out; but as we didn't have a tow ball, we arranged for Kevin, the owner, to drop it off at the slipway about five kilometres away. "Be back at five or you'll be charged overtime," he said.

"We'll call you from Darwin," Tony joked, which made Kevin raise his eyebrows speculatively, not having been subjected to Tony's brand of humour before.

With our sampling gear on board, we motored quietly down the estuary, Tony navigating with the photos. The morning was perfect with rippling blue water, a light breeze and a gentle sun poking out from small fleecy clouds. The deserted shoreline was marked either by trees and jagged rocky slopes that came down almost to a thin selvedge of yellow sand, or by areas of thick mud and mangroves.

"This is the life for me," I said, as a seagull cruised by with barely a wing twitch. "I would never have believed a job with you could be so pleasant. In fact if it wasn't for the company it would be perfect."

"The company sure sucks," he said. "I'd like to make an adjustment to it with a barb wire pull through."

After motoring for about half an hour, Tony guided the craft into the shore. "This'd be a good place to start," he said.

We dragged the boat well out of the water, then set to work. After completing a traverse of hand-augured holes, which we screwed down into the sand for a couple of metres, we walked along the shoreline and did another traverse. The third traverse would take us round the point and out of sight of the boat so we went back to make sure the tide wasn't going to float it off, but it looked as though the tide was receding, and the boat was not in any danger.

"What do you reckon?" Tony said.

"About what?"

"The boat. It was a bloody brilliant idea. It took us to the exact spot."

"Something'll go wrong. With you it always does. We'll come back and find it's floated out to sea."

"Anchor'll hold the Queen Mary."

"The motor won't start."

"It's only two k from the ramp, we can row."

I laughed at this and he took umbrage. "I was a member of the North Curl Curl surf club for years, I'll have you know. Rowing's in the blood."

"I've heard that story. You don't learn how to row sitting in the North Curl Curl pub."

"It's all lies, I tell you."

We completed another traverse from the shore to the back dunes, sampling down to the water table with the auger, then stopped for a breather.

"I wish there was a bit of surf here," Tony said. He scratched the halo of sun-bleached hair that perched like a loose hairpiece on his thick brown thatch, a legacy of years of body surfing. "We'd better check the boat again."

We returned to find the boat was now about twenty metres from the water's edge.

"I told you we wouldn't lose it," Tony said. "With the tide on the way out it's safe to leave. We'll walk round the promontory, do another traverse then take the boat further round."

We returned to the boat later and found it was now at least sixty metres from the water's edge on the gradually shelving beach.

Tony looked at it with disgust. "Pigs!" he said. "We'll have to drag it out to the water and then load up."

The boat felt as if it had been glued to the bottom as we tugged at the anchor rope to turn it around.

"What about pulling too," I said.

"I hope you're talking to yourself. I've never struck such a lazy, weak bastard."

"I'm doing the work of two as it is. What about gripping the rope with two hands, quot or no quot."

We managed to turn the boat and drag it for nearly twenty metres before we gave up.

"What a bastard," Tony said. "Who'd have thought it could be so heavy. We may as well leave it here and keep working."

"What were you saying before about getting right to the target?"

"Dunno. My short-term memory's not too good."

We returned at three in the afternoon, having run out of beach to sample. Back at the boat we were rendered momentarily speechless, for there was now a vast expanse of sand between it and the sea, which was now so far out it was invisible in the salt haze. "Crap," Tony said finally. "Who moved the bloody ocean?"

"We've got two hours to get the boat back or the owner will think we're headed for Darwin like you said."

He thought for a minute. "Look, It's only two K to the ramp. The tide's way out. I should be able to walk back. You stay here in case the tide comes in and goes off with the boat."

He set off at a fast walk, leaving me on the vast expanse of beach with only a few seagulls for company. An hour later, as the winter sun sank towards the horizon and the mosquitoes became increasingly hungry, he reappeared. His sandshoes, long socks and legs caked in mud. He even had it in his hair.

"What a bloody performance," he said. "There's nothing but mangroves between here and the ramp. I was up to me eyeballs a couple of times."

"It's a pity there weren't any crocs."

"They cleared out in droves. The socks and knock-knees does it. I never made it though."

I stared at him in dismay. "Never made it? We're stuck here then. It could be midnight before the tide comes back and we've no light. The high tide will lift us and the ebb will take us out to sea. You were right about Darwin."

In the far distance, a green cabin cruiser motored into the channel heading for home and Tony took off after it waving madly. He'd always been a great distance runner and he managed to cover the half kilometre or so at great speed. I saw the cruiser stop, then Tony waved for me to join him.

I could hear Tony laughing and talking well before I reached the cruiser, which had pulled into the channel bank.

"This is Allan," Tony said as I came up. He introduced me to a man in his seventies with a ruddy cheerful face. "He's a whingeing Pom who barracks for NSW in the State of Origin. Can you believe it? He lives in Yeppoon too. It's a bloody disgrace. The only thing good about him is he drinks Fourex, the only beer that doesn't taste like cow piss."

Tony had this amazing ability to make people laugh when he insulted them and Allan was no exception. He accepted Tony as a delightful eccentric.

"The tide won't be back in till eight," Allan said. "If you like I could take you back later."

He dropped us at the ramp right on five and we explained the problem to Kevin, who did not seem too impressed. However as he had my credit card number he accepted the situation.

Leaving the ramp later that evening with Alan, we followed the rippled gold pathway of the rising moon. Sometimes we bumped the sandy bottom and once Allan grounded the boat, but the tide was coming in strongly and a minute later we lifted off again. We found our boat rocking gently at its anchor.

"Good on you mate." Tony shook Allan's hand. "This helps make up for you supporting those bloody cockroaches."

"I'll guide you back," Allan said with a laugh.

I started the motor and nosed the boat into the shore to collect the samples as Tony played the torch around. "I don't see them," he said. "They should be on top of a sandbank."

"They probably still are," I said. "The sandbank's under water."

He was silent for a moment, a look of disgust on his face. "And up yours too, mate" he said. "Take me home."

Chapter 9 Short-term Memory

We gave Allan two cartons of Fourex beer for his trouble. The next day we cruised back to the sample site to collect our samples and complete the rest of the auger lines and we made sure we dragged the boat with us through the shallows each time we moved to a new line. We returned to the motel in good time to take in the State of Origin match that evening and when Queensland won Tony was over the moon.

"That will show those New South Wales bastards," he said, lobbing his empty stubby into the bin where it joined a number of others with a satisfying clink. "They reckoned they were going to crap all over us and we gave them a hiding. They won't be so cocky next time. What do you reckon about the game now? Isn't it the greatest?"

"I can't figure out those penalties," I said. "I think New South Wales was robbed."

"Whose side are you on, you one eyed bastard?" he roared. "I've never seen such a woeful bloody bit of one-sided refereeing in my life and we still won. That ref should never be allowed near a league game again."

The next day we set off up the coast, heading for Gladstone.

"What's the go up here?" I asked.

"It's a good place for a decent hot curry and a blue steak."

"Apart from feeding your gut, I mean."

"I want to cruise about the harbour and look at the heavy mineral sand potential of Curtis and Facing Island."

"If that means another boat then it's going to be planned a little better than last time."

"What does your eminence suggest?" he said.

"You organise the boat. I'll get the tide times and buy a chart from Harbours and Marine with the channels and shipping routes. I'm going to make damn sure we know what the tide is doing, what the weather forecast is and where the big ships are going to be before we set off. We will not be relying on the skills of an ex- North Curl Curl surfer this time, no matter how long he stared out the window of the local pub."

"I didn't just stare out the window. I did some serious drinking too."

We found a motel and as it was getting late, we set off looking for a place to eat.

"It's a toss up between a hot Indian curry and a steak," Tony said. "I've never yet found a place that serves a hot enough curry so we'll have steak. There's a good place here run by a crazy Italian. It's called Down Under Steaks. His T-bones are the best this side of the black stump, and the other side too."

"If he's crazy then I suppose he's a mate of yours?"

Tony chuckled. "He's quite a character. The only bloke I know who can turn out a good blue steak."

"By blue you mean underdone?"

"Black on the outside, red in the middle and still twitching."

"You're a bloody cannibal, to eat steak like that."

"You should have seen me before I had my teeth capped."

The Down Under Grille was under new management, which did not seem to have improved the décor or the ambience, judging by the state of the tables and the smell of greasy fat. Tony explained to the chef very carefully how he wanted his steak done, or rather not done. I asked for mine to be well cooked.

We had a pre-dinner drink at the bar while we waited. "Hey bar-st-ard," Tony called as we sampled a beer, making the word sound like an obscenity "A packet of chips for me, and the rough end of a pineapple for me mate here. Preferably inserted."

Fortunately, the man serving was a little hard of hearing and the steaks came before we were thrown out. Tony attacked his and then signalled the waitress. "Excuse me," he said. "I asked for a blue steak, not one like the sole that's been ripped off some old boot salvaged in a house fire."

The waitress, a young gum-chewing blonde with Bessie written on her nametag and who had the appearance of someone working her way through parole, turned down her Walkman.

"Wassat?"

"This steak."

She picked up the plate and examined the red slash Tony' knife had made. "Yuck!" she said. "Sorry about that. The chef must be having another of his hangovers."

"I'd like a blue one, like I ordered. Please return this boot leather to the chef and give him the compliments of the season."

"Blue?" She put the plate on the table and attacked it with Tony' knife and fork, exposing the livid red scar and squeezing a litre of watery blood out of it as she did so. The blood swirled around the soggy chips. "You want him to cook it a bit more? I don't blame you. This is a meal for a vampire."

"I want it cooked a bit less."

"Less?"

"Yes, Bess, less."

"You want a raw steak? Why didn't you tell him?"

"Not raw, blue."

"Never heard of no blue steak. What is it, whale meat?"

"A good blue steak is black on the outside and red throughout. This is only red in the middle. I want one that looks like my eyeballs at six in the morning after an all night drinking session to cure a dose of constipation."

"If you could bring a glass, too," I said. "He likes to squeeze the blood out and drink it separately."

Bess shook her head as she picked up the plate again, slopping watery blood over the tablecloth. "Youse guys." She turned up the Walkman and headed for the kitchen.

"I'm not waiting," I said, tucking into my steak. "Soggy chips and underdone steaks are for whimps."

"It's this new management. I'll soon have them sorted out."

The chef turned up in person. He seemed quite apologetic and listened to Tony' instructions carefully.

"Right," he said. "Black on the outside and red throughout."

Bess returned with Tony' steak almost before the chef got back to the kitchen. "Here you are sir." She set the plate down. "Enjoy."

Tony cut off a slice that was charred on the outside. Sure enough the inside had the bluish look of raw meat. He chewed it reflectively for a moment. "Bleah!"

"What's wrong now?"

"It's still bloody well frozen."

When we got back to the motel there was a message from Jim Shafer asking me to ring him in Charters Towers.

"We need another geo," he said, when I called him up.

"What happened to Hermann?"

"He's in hospital in the Towers. He has the DTs"

"I'm not surprised working for you lot. Not many geos could handle it, but seriously, what's wrong? He's only been there for a week."

"I am serious."

"You drove him to drink?"

"Well ... sort of. He got hold of Art's beer supply and it nearly killed him. Turns out he was an alcoholic. Art knows the nurse in the hospital. Apparently he was in AA and doing all right. I guess he thought he could handle the odd beer but with Art's eight or so cartons right beside him the temptation was too great."

"Why did he have Art's beer?"

"I think he thought Art was heading down the same alcoholic path. Maybe he was trying to help."

"That's too bad. Did you get anything done while he was there?"

"No; he put Art in charge of trap sampling so that will have to be redone and the baseline we put in on the old copper workings jogs in and out like the teeth on a saw. He wouldn't use his four-wheel-drive either in case it got scratched. Can you imagine it? So it sits at the camp all day and he's still getting paid for it the same as Chas and I am. What a lurk."

I pondered the problem for a moment. "I can't get another geo on such short notice, what if I put you in charge. It'll mean a raise too. How does ninety a day sound?"

"My God—Little Jimmy's done it again. I can buy some more shares."

"You're still buying shares?"

"My oath. It's better than trap sampling. The market's gone mad. I've already made about 500 dollars."

"Is Chas there?"

"Yes."

Put him on. Think you can organise him and Art for a few days?"

"You bet. Those two won't know what hit them."

* * *

It was ten the next morning when Tony and I parked at the jetty and loaded up the hired boat. The weather was perfect and the tide was well out so if we happened to get stuck somewhere we were unlikely to be stranded for long. "I don't trust your short-term memory," I said, consulting my list of equipment. "Oars, life jackets, esky, torch, maps, sample bags, auger, splitter?"Tony nodded. "All present."

"Fuel?"

"Full tank. The hire place reckons no one's ever used a tank full yet in a day's fishing."

"Food?"

"Motel sandwiches are packed."

"Radio, flares, distress beacon?"

"Bullshit," he said with a chuckle. "With all the gear we've got on board we'll be more in danger of sinking than getting stranded."

We climbed in and motored over to the south-east side of Curtis Island in moderate swell. "Nowhere to land," Tony said, surveying the acres of mudflats exposed by the low tide. "I'll hop out and have a quick recce. Doesn't look too promising, but."

While still moving he hopped out. As he did, a strange look passed fleetingly over his face and almost in slow motion he pitched forward and with a splash measured his length in the brine. An arm emerged and grabbed the boat, then his head appeared. As I fell about laughing a great grin split his face.

"Forget this performance," he said. "The bloody deck's mud. Stop laughing and help me in you stupid bastard."

When back in the boat he took off his long black socks and sneakers and washed the mud off them in the sea. "These are my croc socks," he said, wringing them out. "Up in the Cape the crocs take off in droves if I've got them on."

"They take off because you never take them off. I bet you've just ruined the fishing here."

"It's all lies. Now look at these shoes," he held one up. "I've got these club feet and I've searched every store from here to Sydney for a comfortable pair and paid a fortune for something that feels like a bear trap. These are the best yet and only forty bucks in Coles."

"Did you ever think of cutting your toenails?"

"They're too in-grown."

We motored around the coastline and then cruised slowly down the west side of Facing Island, making huge detours around the mud islands exposed by the tide.

"We should have waited for high tide," Tony said. "We're so far from the shore we can't check the beaches."

Late in the afternoon, we stopped on a small sandbar near Gatcombe Head and ate our sandwiches.

"This is the life, isn't it," I said as the waves gently lapped on the shelving beach with a steady swish.

"It would be all right if you could get a decent meal and better help," he said. "You remember Dick, that mad geologist who loves hot curries? He's working up here somewhere. I'll see if he's about. If I can sample a decent hot curry tonight it will make up for the lousy company."

"I know him well," I said. "The last time I sampled a hot curry with you and Dick it was a repeat of last night's fiasco with the chef. I thought we were going to get thrown out."

"Well they should learn how to make them hot. There's more to it than adding green peppers." He checked his watch. "Time to head home."

I tapped the petrol tank out of curiosity as we got in; it made that hollow noise peculiar to empty drums and the accompanying hollow feeling in my stomach intensified when I unscrewed the cap and looked in. "The bloody thing's is empty!"

"Not to worry. We've got oars."

I consulted the map then looked up. I could just make out a few cargo ships and tall buildings through the salt haze. "According to the map the coast is nine kilometres away. It'll be dark by the time we get in."

"It will be if we stay here yakking," he said. "Anyway we're not out of fuel yet."

I nursed the motor as we set a course straight back across the bay and squeezed about a kilometre out of the tank before it died. I handed him an oar and we sat next to each other facing the island, then took a few tentative strokes. The boat went round in a half circle.

"If you want to face the direction you intend to travel in," I said. "Why don't you sit the other way and push instead of pull."

"Pigs. It's you, not me. Where did you learn to row, in the bath?"

"Try pulling a bit harder," I said.

"If I pulled any harder I'd break the oar."

We tried again and turned another half circle.

"Why am I the one who has to straighten us out each time?" Tony said. "Back off with your oar while I pull it round."

"I'm just seeing if you can pull. We're turning because you're as weak as a gargled mouthwash."

"You can get drunk on that. I used to bottle the stuff I gargled."

"Well, pull like it then."

We circled for a third time. "Crap!" he said. "Give me the other bloody oar. Let an ex lifesaver show you how it's done. You can take over after fifteen minutes. Relax and enjoy yourself."

He pulled mightily and we circled for the fourth time, although more slowly. "So you were a life saver at North Curl Curl," I said in disgust. "How many people drowned while you were rowing out to them?"

"Plenty. They saw me coming and swam further out."

"With this course you're setting you'll have to cover eighteen kilometres to get to where we set off from. Look at the wake you've left behind before it catches up and passes us. It's like a snake trail on a sand dune."

"It's this bloody right arm of mine. It's shorter than the left"

"Comes from dragging your knuckles on the ground."

"The best way to steer a straight course," he said, zigzagging across the bay, "is to line up two points on the island."

"You've made mathematical history then. First man to find two points not connected by a straight line."

"Pigs," he said, dropping the oars in disgust. "Get your butt back here and start rowing."

"I knew it was just a question of time before you asked for a lesson. I spent three years of schooling doing nothing much else except row and I'm still an expert. You take the right oar so that it favours your left arm. I'll take the left ore and we'll start rowing with intelligence."

"See those two trees on the island, oh mouth of crap?" Tony said. "They're the sighters. Keep them lined up at all times and we'll make landfall."

"You've got to be joking," I said, after checking them out. "I'm not interested in rowing to China. Let's head for Gladstone."

"Okay. You select the sighters."

We managed to get in five or six strokes before we were off course again.

"Look," I said, after we'd lined up our back sights once more. "If the boat moves to the left, slacken off and I'll pull harder. If it moves to the right, I'll slacken off and you pull harder."

"Impressive," he said. "You sure you're not from North Curl Curl?"

We took four strokes before the boat veered right.

"Pull harder," I yelled and stopped rowing.

"Row you lazy bastard," he said, tugging on his oar. "Why should I do all the work?"

I started rowing again as the back sight began to line up again but I left it too late. "Slacken off," I called, heaving on the oar to bring the boat on-line as he did the same. "Can't you remember anything?"

"It's my short-term memory," he said as we stopped rowing and let the boat spin around under its own momentum. "Tell me again."

"If I had a gun it would be more than the short-term memory that was shot."

We started again and ten strokes later veered to the right. I eased off.

"Pull harder you slack sod," I said encouragingly. "Line that back sight up." He heaved mightily and fell backwards off the seat as his oar came out of the water.

"It's a surfing trick I learned," he said, sitting down again. "When those big dumpers hit the boat as you row out you have to lift the oar or you get hoicked into the drink."

"There's only one sort of drink you've ever sampled and it's not found around boats."

He chuckled. "Many is the dangerous bar I've breasted, and not always in the North Curl Curl Club."

By the time it was dark we had almost mastered the art of rowing together and when we finally reached the shoreline our hands were blistered and our bodies were a single fused ache. As we entered the river mouth, a kilometre from the boat hire, the gentle flow of its waters into the sea proved too great for us. We pulled in against some rocks, then tottered down the road.

The boat hire owner scratched his head in puzzlement when we turned up. "Never known anyone to run out of fuel before," he said. "You emptied the spare too?"

Suspicion dawned on me. "Spare?"

"The spare jerry in the locker. I told your mate about it when he hired the boat."

I turned to O'Toole, and he shrugged. We spoke in unison. "It's me short-term memory."

Chapter 10 A Brush With Death

As soon as the mineral sand work was finished I drove back to the Sellheim camp and arrived in the late afternoon. There was no-one about and I had the evening meal cooking when Jim's Hilux pulled up and three grinning faces stared at me.

Jim hopped out and put on a show. "Okay. Chas, Art. Grab the samples and line them up with the others. Chas, you have first shower. Art, you can sweep the back out and put in more bags for tomorrow."

"And you can get stuffed," Art said, going over to the fridge. He turned to me as he pulled out a choc milk. "Thank God you're back, Bob."

"Yeah thank God," Jim said. "What a bloody hopeless mob to try and organise. Between them they couldn't sample a bag of Turkish Delight in a chocolate factory. A creek bed in the hot sun scares the hell out of them."

"For a fleeting moment I was half convinced you'd done the impossible and got Art cooperating." I said.

"Art's as useless as a back pocket in a singlet, but one more day and I'd have had Chas organised for the first time in his life. Right, Chas?"

"Give us a hand with these bags," Chas said, as he hauled them off the back of the Hilux.

"Settle down. The boss is supposed to delegate, not do the work."

"The story of your life, Jim," Art said, squeezing the contents of the choc milk into his mouth until the carton was flattened. "Always delegating and doing nothing, 'cept you're not the boss now, Bob is."

"Has Art put in his three free days for us?"

"Blood oath," Art said.

Jim groaned. "Hunter was ripped off as usual. You ever watched Art taking a stream sample? My God! If that's the best he can do since he reformed he'd be better off back on the booze, fags and drugs."

"It's the flavoured milks," Chas said. "He drinks so many he's become addicted to chocolate."

"How was your holiday?" Jim asked.

"Unbelievably bad. Lousy five star motels, rib fillet steaks only an inch thick and the nude beaches were nearly deserted. The only compensations were the late morning starts and the surfing, snorkeling and swimming."

"Wish I was a geologist," Art said, a faraway look in his eyes.

Jim said. "I hope you thought of your old mates back here."

"You lot were always on my mind. It was all I could do to restrain myself from swapping jobs with Hermann."

"That was one dickhead of a geo," Jim said.

"He was worse than you," Art added. "He acted like we were in the army and he was the sergeant. Up at six, lights out nine thirty, two beers a night if you're lucky." He paused for a moment. "Which reminds me—he said Hunter would pay for any beer he drank and would pay me 10 dollars for each meal. So how about it?"

"Get Hermann to write out a receipt and then send it in to Hunter," I said.

"Would that work?"

"No, but you could live in hope for a few weeks."

"This is bullshit," Art said. "He drank a month's wages. Someone owes me big time."

"If you'd just brought one carton as agreed, none of this would have happened," Chas said.

Jim nodded. "You should contribute to Hermann's rehab too, considering you nearly killed the guy."

As they argued I looked in the back of Jim's Hilux, which seemed roomier than I remembered. What happened to the toolbox?" I asked.

Jim looked over to the vehicle. "I took it out to make more room."

"He means it fell to pieces," Art said. "This mobile junkyard of his takes us twice as long to get to the job as Chas' and we're forever picking up pieces that fall off. The only thing working is the tape deck and you can't listen to that for the screech of things tearing loose and the noise of the clapped out motor."

"Wash out your mouth!" Jim said. "It's a bloody sight quieter than your constant whingeing."

I let out a sigh. "It's good to be back. I really missed you guys."

"Believe me," Art said with feeling. "I missed you too, Bob. You might be a geo but at least you're no little Hitler."

"Amen to that," Jim said. "You might be a geo but you're no dickhead."

Because of the roughness of the terrain and the difficulty of getting about, Hunter had decided to hire a helicopter to help with the sampling and I broke the news to the boys.

Art's eyes lit up. "Beauty."

"Steady on, Ba-art," Jim said, hyped up at the thought of flying. "How many does it take, Bob?"

"Three, plus pilot and samples."

Jim laughed. "Or one plus pilot and no samples if it's carrying Art."

He turned to Chas excitedly. "What about you, Chas? You'll be closer to God in a helicopter."

"The kingdom of heaven is within us, Jim."

"It must be a mighty small kingdom then, although Art's got a fair bit of room. If it's in him he sure keeps any sign of it well hidden."

The Bell helicopter arrived the next morning and circled the camp, barely clearing the trees before it came down in a cloud of grass stems and dust. The pilot, who introduced himself as Darren, looked as though he might have just flown a combat mission in Vietnam. He was dressed in jungle greens with a large leather belt, finished off with calf length canvas and rubber boots.

"What's the go?" Darren asked, after being introduced.

"You'll be leap frogging two teams about collecting stream samples."

"No problem. Who's first?"

Jim said, "I'm game. I think I might be safer working with Chas though."

Chas shook his head. "If you were going to die for your sins you'd be long gone."

Art chuckled. "Bloody right. Jim would have died at birth."

"Settle down Ar-Chas," Jim said. "I'm not working with Art, that's for sure; we'd never get airborne. I'll work with Bob."

Chas and Art went first and managed the chopper managed to lift off, despite Jim's doubts. The doors had been removed and I had a momentary glimpse of Art's white face before they were whirled up and over the trees.

"My God!" Jim said. "It's like Luna Park all day. This is the way to live. It sure beats bush bashing and fixing punctures."

* * *

The sample program worked well, especially as Darren was introduced into the Sellheim gambling club and the art of losing.

"This is the best camp yet," Jim said, looking at his growing pile of winnings a few nights later. "Work is good, cards are good. Even the company's improved."

"I can't concentrate with all this foreign Kiwi lingo," Art said in disgust as he lost another hand. "The way things are going we'll soon have every Kiwi bludger there is, over here. That will be the entire population."

Chas looked up from reading his Toyota manual where he'd been checking out various problems he'd been having, such as an engine knock when in low gear, a whine in the dif in high gear and a shudder in the clutch. "You losing again, Art?"

Jim nodded. "You'd better show him how to play, Chas or you'll be paying his next wage to me like you did last time."

Chas, who'd pretty well mastered the Toyota manual over the years, came and stood behind Art. *"Ye earneth wages to put it into a bag with holes,"* he admonished.

"And Darren, Bob and I are standing at the holes," Jim said.

After Jim dealt the cards Chas gripped Art's hand as he was about to discard. "Don't throw those," he said. "Throw this one."

Art scowled but followed Chas' advice.

Jim grinned. "Your bet, Art. I suggest you fold."

"Five bucks." Art said.

"There's a twenty cent limit, dickhead."

"Twenty cents then."

"Art's got nothing again," Jim said. "Nice try, Art. I can pick your bluff every time. Some gambler; you go cross-eyed every time you lie."

"Raise twenty," Darren said.

The betting continued strongly with Chas taking over Art's hand and before long five dollars was in the pot.

"Hope you know what you're doing Ar-Chas," Jim said, now thoroughly hyped up at the unusual size of the pot.

"Who's Archas?" Darren asked.

"He's a relation of Bar-Chas," I said.

"I'll look," Jim said. "Everyone's looking. What've you got Art?"

"Flush." Art raked in the pot to a chorus of groans.

"What'll I do?" Art said, sounding much more cooperative as the next hand was dealt.

Chas pointed. "Throw these two."

"Don't be daft."

"Do it. Go for this." He pointed.

Jim scowled a few hands later as Art pulled in another pot to swell his expanding pile of winnings. "Nice work Ar -er - Chas," he was interrupted by a cheer from the rest of us as he got the name out.

"Keep this up and Art's only going to lose his shirt," he said. "Didn't really want to take his pants anyway."

"I'm on a roll," Art said. "I've just kissed Lady Luck."

"Yeah. I can hear her throwing up."

"Scoff if you like. Told you I was a gambler."

Jim's upper lip curled. "You're not the gambler. Art is, I mean Chas is." He turned to me. "I don't know about you but it disgusts me that a man like Chas can spout religion yet here he is encouraging a member of his own church to gamble."

"Damn right. We're witnessing sin and temptation in action."

"Yup," Chas said as reality took hold. He backed away from Art. *"The idols of the heathen are silver and gold."*

Art shrugged nonchalantly. "Don't need Chas to skin you suckers. Come on, deal."

Art studied his next hand with a frown then looked up at Chas who was still watching. He fingered a card questioningly.

Chas gave a small shake of his head but Jim was on to him. "Archas, Art—Chas, he said excitedly. "Quit that."

Chas turned a faint shade of pink and turned away. "I'll leave Art alone."

"Don't worry me none," Art said.

Art's good fortune ended at that moment. By the time the generator left us in darkness he was eleven dollars down.

"Lady Luck turned out to be Chas then," Jim said, after lighting a candle. He chinked his winnings loudly in his betting bag. "What do you reckon, Chas? *A fool and his money are soon parted?"*

Chas, amazed at this unusual biblical cognisance, nodded assent. "Yep. *The way of a fool is right in his own eyes."*

"And *a proverb in time saves nine,"* Jim added.

"Honour truth above friends."

"My God!" Jim said. "I've started something. Chas'll be going all night now. I'm off to bed, Goodnight."

"Are you guys for real?" Darren said, shaking his head.

* * *

We were at 900 feet enjoying the rush of cool air through the door-less cockpit when there was a sudden vibration and noise from somewhere in the rear of the helicopter. In a flash Darren hit the switches and the motor died.

"Tail rotor," he said in response to my querying look.

I had that sinking feeling which was not just due to the simple physics of a helicopter falling out of the sky and leaving the stomach behind. This was it! Finality—Finito—The end. Jim, sitting in the back, had gone a greyish white colour and my eyes, like his, locked onto the trees and rocks below.

"Not to worry," Jim said, as rising panic finally loosened his tongue. "We'll just auto glide down and make a normal landing. Right, Darren?"

Darren didn't reply. It was then that I noticed that this Red Baron of the skies was as pale as we were, that a film of sweat was on his brow and that his hand on the control had turned white. It was obvious that Darren was of the exact same opinion as Jim and me: our future was of limited duration.

The helicopter was strangely silent. Through the Perspex bubble, the ground below swung in a slow circle as it rushed to meet us. The noise of the air whistling past with increasing intensity added a sense of loneliness and finality to the scene. I thought of the air rushing past the rotor, turning it. I thought of my long forgotten physics teacher at school trying to explain the difference between potential energy and kinetic energy. The rotor needed to build up kinetic energy to land us gently. This was the example he should have used to impress young minds.

Darren was eyeing a small clearing among the rocky outcrops and trees and I willed him on his way. Some of the trees were tallish. Would we miss them? Would we miss them and hit the rocky outcrops? My past life, I knew, should start to flash before my eyes at any moment. Maybe it had already and I'd missed it. I'd already had some weird thoughts. We should have jettisoned the samples. All that weight was dragging us to our death.

At what seemed to me to be the last instant, Darren moved the control stick to change the pitch of the blades and a huge g force pressed down on us. The roar of the rotor slicing the air became a symphony of triumph in my ears. We were flying again; the cleared space was directly below us, floating gently up. Fifty feet, twenty, ten, five, zero. We touched down like a feather.

Jim was the first to break the long silence. "Hey hey," he said, almost laughing. "You guys all right?"

"Yeah" I said.

"Me too," from Darren.

"We all made it." Jim said.

"We're alive," I said.

"I brought it down," Darren said.

"You can say that again," Jim said.

"And again," I said.

"I brought it down. I brought it down."

We climbed out laughing so hard we could barely stand. We shook hands, then slapped each other on the back, then began to dance around, tears in our eyes, tears of laughter, tears of relief, of the pure joy of being alive. After five minutes, in which Darren's hand was almost shaken off his wrist we sobered up.

"I guess we walk out," I said.

Darren nodded morosely. "We're about ten kilometres from camp. We should make it out by nightfall."

Jim began poking about in the helicopter. "I've lost my notebook. It should be here. I had it with me on the seat, it has to be here."

I started looking too; it seemed urgent that we find it. "Have you seen it, Darren?" I asked.

"What?"

"Jim's notebook."

"No by God, I haven't." He began to search too.

Looking for Jim's notebook was good therapy. After five minutes of diligent but fruitless search Jim thought he must have been mistaken, in fact he pretty well remembered that he hadn't brought it with him and a great load was lifted from us.

"I don't believe this," Darren said. "We're looking for something that isn't missing." The more we thought about it the funnier it became. Soon we could barely stand again we were laughing so much.

"This is the greatest camp ever," Jim said, tears streaming down his face. I can die happy now."

"And with your notebook."

That set Jim off again. "You know what's really bugging me right at this moment?" he got out finally.

"No."

"The thought that Art and Chas will probably have to spend the night in the bush. We've survived but it's going to kill Art."

We burst into hysterical laughter again. "It's good to be alive," Darren said as we staggered light-headedly through the bush.

"Amen to that."

I stopped and picked up a torn piece of paper caught in a tree. It had red and blue lines ruled on it, same as the notebook. "Here's your notebook Jim," I joked, "or a page of it anyway." That set us off again.

* * *

Chas and Art reached camp in the early hours of the morning after walking back by moonlight. Art poked his head inside the tent flap. "We're back," he roared. "Didn't want you to be worrying about us too much, like where we were, what we were doing, how hungry we might be and how tired we might be and whether we might be lost or injured."

Jim shone his torch in Art's face. "You look a bit wet."

"It's bloody raining out here in case you didn't realise. Where's the helicopter? We've walked about seventy bloody kilometres."

"It crashed. Tail rotor failed."

"You should have sent another one to pick us up."

"I'm okay," Jim said. "Thanks for asking. Nice of you to be so concerned. Bob's okay too, so's Darren."

"Yeah—well—we bloody well aren't." He went off muttering.

Chas looked in a few minutes later and shone his own torch in Jim's face.

Jim groaned. "What now?"

"Art tells me the copter crashed. I was just checking that you were alive. Didn't think you would be."

"Why the hell not?"

"No reason really." He shone his torch on me. "I suppose that's the end of the camp then, Bob?"

"Why's that?"

"I didn't think you'd want to keep working. If the job's over I could head into the Towers now and line up another job."

"What, in the middle of the night?"

"It's three-thirty. I'd be home by seven."

"Wait a minute," Jim said, starting to wake up. "What do you mean you didn't think I'd be alive?"

"Well, it's just that with your lifestyle it seems a bit surprising."

"There's nothing wrong with my lifestyle. This proves it."

"It could be a warning," Chas said.

After he had gone, Jim lay back on his bunk. "A close shave like that makes me think there has to be a better way to make money," he said.

"You keep saying that."

"Because I haven't found the answer, unless it's the stock market. My shares are doing really well. I think I'll put in all my savings. The signs are telling me something."

"What signs?"

"I nearly got killed didn't I?"

"So?"

"So maybe it's time to make a killing."

Chas took Darren into the Towers the next morning with instructions from Jim to buy the Financial Review and a book on investing in shares.

"This is shaping up as another really good camp," Jim said as Chas took off. "A helicopter crash will do me though, Bob. Save the next thrill for later in the year or give it to Art."

Art turned to me. "I guess we can have the day off?"

"How do you work that out?"

"I worked eighteen hours yesterday, that's how."

Jim nodded. "That's fair, Bob. Credit Art with an extra six hours but take off 18 for the time he sat around doing nothing the last six days."

Chapter11 Stock Market Guru

After the next break, most of which Jim seemed to have spent with his stockbroker and in research for his now rapidly growing share portfolio, we moved our campsite to the Suttor River. We picked up Chas and Art in Charters Towers and by the next afternoon the tent was set up under a shady tree, Chas' caravan was under another and there was a small dam nearby that the property owner didn't mind us using. It was late in September and the stock market was heating up like the weather. Jim was becoming more and more hyped up as his share portfolio began to accelerate towards the stratosphere and most of his conversation now revolved around mining shares.

"Is this man any good," he said, as we settled in for poker the first evening. "All my shares have increased in value and the market is so hot that my broker now has just opened a second office. Some of my shares have doubled. The 4000 dollars I started with is worth over seven now. If I put this month's pay in I'll be heading for 10,000 and the market's still rising."

"Did you buy some more Hunter shares?" I asked.

"Yes, and they've dropped twenty cents."

Art snickered. "Word got about that you're working for them."

Jim dismissed Art with a superior wave. "They'll be back up soon. The stock market is even more profitable than ripping you off at Manila."

"Bull," Art said. "It's part of me technique for winning long term."

"Long term? I'll be dead before you start to claw back. You've lost over seventy dollars to me, another seventy or eighty to Bob, and the fifteen hundred we let you off because Bob's a sucker." He turned to me. "I bought some Astrik last week. You said they were good."

"All I said was they had a gold mine and were very speculative."

"Same thing."

I shook my head. "Even if all your shares double in value you'll end up making a loss."

"How do you work that out?"

"You won't sell. You'll hang on until they go into free fall. I speak from experience."

"Bob's right," Chas said. *"Labour not to be rich for riches make themselves wings."*

Jim gave a confident laugh. "Not for little Jimmy. I know how to pick the winners."

"Bull," Art said again as he raised the pot twenty cents. "Only thing you can pick is your nose and you still have to practise every day."

"Talking of free fall," I said. "Darren rang me the other day about the investigation."

"Yeah, what happened?"

"The tail rotor had lost its tip. Embedded in the break were fibres of yellow cloth. A bit like the cover of the field notebook you lost."

"What's that?" Art said. "Did you cause the crash Jim?" He burst into raucous laughter.

"Hey, steady on - Settle down - My God!"

"I reckon it must have been sucked out, but unless you want to be even more famous than you are already, we won't say anything."

"What a dick head," Art said.

"Just as well it wasn't you in the helicopter," Jim said. "You'd have committed suicide after seeing your whole life flash past."

* * *

By the end of the week we had a large number of creek samples waiting to be checked for gold.

"We're going well," Jim said, glancing towards Art who was clutching the first of his evening tinnies. "If lard ball over there keeps this sampling frenzy up he'll start losing weight. It's too good to last."

As if on cue Art came over, hobbling painfully. "I've done something to me leg. Can't put any weight on it. Might have to put in for compo. Can't do much more sampling." Art wiped beer froth off his mouth. "What if I spend the next few days in camp putting the samples through the jig to give me leg a rest."

Jim took a pace back in mock horror. "What! You'd be back smoking pot. Besides, it's too important a job."

"I've done plenty of important jobs," Art said.

"Yeah, like you mentioned before, leading hand and drill

supervisor. What a load of crap."

"How would you know? You weren't there."

"I can tell. When you lie you go cross-eyed. I asked Chas too. He said you only had one job, which was painting grid pegs. Isn't that right Chas?"

"Yup."

"Ok," I said. "You can stay in camp tomorrow, Art and check and pack soil samples."

"Beaudy. It'll give me a chance to get my hearing back from listening to Jim rave on about shares."

"I'm 4000 dollars up. All you've done is waste your pay on beer," Jim said.

Chas shook his head. "Art's started saving his money."

Art nodded. "Yeah. Saving to buy a car. While you're paying off your bank manager I'll be driving round in a Merc."

"More like a Ford with a couple of coppers in front," Jim said. "Make sure you don't bludge tomorrow. We'll be back at various times to check on progress."

"Check all you like."

Jim chuckled. "We plan to. Bob brought back a breathalyser kit and a syringe for blood samples. From now on, every time you spend a day in camp on your own we test for drugs and alcohol."

"Pull the other one," Art said.

The next day was hot, with occasional strong westerly gusts. We didn't check up on Art but maybe we should have. When we returned in the evening we found the centre pole of our tent sticking up in the air with the roof sagging onto the beds. It had sawed up and down in the wind and the pole had cut a ragged slot through the canvas.

Jim confronted Art. "You blind or something? First you burn the tent to the ground and now you let the wind destroy it."

"Was working too hard to notice."

"I'll bet. How many samples did you do?"

Art pointed to a box. "All those."

"I can do that many in four hours. What did you do for the other five hours?"

"In your dreams mate." Art pulled his T-shirt off and waddled down to the dam.

"Where do you think you're going now?" Jim asked.

Art kicked off his thongs and waded out through the mud and fringing reeds. "A swim."

"Get out of there. We use that water for cooking and washing."

Art submerged in the brown water with a grunt, setting up a sizeable bow wave, then floated on his back. "Kiwis should be thankful we let them drink stuff like this," he said.

"That fat turd is starting to turn me off," Jim said, reaching for some mud; moments later a fistful of it arched out and lobbed onto Art's stomach, causing him to expel his breath in a surprised swoosh and sink in a gurgle of bubbles.

"Kiwi crud," he spluttered when he surfaced again

"Aussie arsehole," Jim replied, chuckling. "I'm feeling better already."

* * *

After a couple of week's work our supplies were getting low and Chas made his usual late evening trip to be with his family and to buy some more tucker. Jim had given him enough instructions in regard to ringing his broker that it looked as though it would add an extra day to the trip. When Chas returned the next evening he was loaded with back issues of newspapers for Jim.

"You guys will be working for me soon," Jim said, riffling through the business section of the papers and checking his stocks. "All except Art that is, who's unemployable."

Art took another beer from the fridge. "Look who's talking. While we're working you're listening to the radio."

"I rang the office," Chas said. "Craig is paying us another visit. He should be here tomorrow evening."

Jim turned to me. "Maybe we should organise a spotter plane for tomorrow, in case Chas goes walkabout again."

Chas opened his briefcase and took out two letters. "I brought some mail out for you, Jim, from your stockbroker."

Jim ripped them open. Seconds later he looked up in excitement. "Hey! Listen to this. Aurus have a rights issue coming up. One new share for every four held, at a premium of fifty cents. What does that mean, Bob? I've got eight thousand."

"It means that you can buy another 2000 twenty cent shares for seventy cents each."

"That's fourteen hundred bucks? They're at eighty now. I can make a fortune but I haven't got the money." He chuckled. "Forget the meal; get out the cards. You're going to pay for these rights, Art."

"Stupid Kiwi." Art would have said more but Jim held up his hand for silence as the stock report finally boomed out of the radio. A moment later he gave another groan, more painful this time.

"Mt Midas have jumped to a dollar ten. I told my broker to sell at ninety. I've just lost twelve hundred dollars." He turned to me. "That was your fault for telling me to take a profit." He waved the second letter. "This is a buy recommendation. Mt Midas is proving up a major gold resource. My broker says they could go to three dollars. Why didn't they let me know last week?"

"Probably because the directors needed time to massage the figures. Does your broker also warn they could drop back to ten cents?"

Jim wasn't listening; he was chewing his lip in frustration. "I'll buy them back."

"What with?"

"Why not sell the Hilux," Chas suggested. "It would raise a thousand."

Art snickered. "Yeah, if you can find a dealer who's blind and deaf and never been in the used car business before."

"A bank loan," Jim said, brightening. "I'll make out a list of top stocks and go for it. Ten thousand dollars will do. I should have done this a year ago."

"What happens when they crash?" I asked. "You'll be paying interest at nineteen per cent, plus establishment fees, maintenance fees, monthly account fees, loan fees and bank manager superannuation fees."

Jim shrugged. "Life's a gamble."

Art said. "Dumb Kiwi. You'll lose the lot."

"I'm not going to sit around on my fat arse like you all my life, working for somebody else," Jim frowned as a thought struck him. "Maybe I should borrow 20,000. Ten isn't all that much when you think of it." He pulled out a notebook and pencil. "Let's see. If Mount Midas gets to three dollars, Hunter gets to one-eighty, Astrik ..."

The evening meal looked like being a disaster as Jim was torn between the financial pages backlog and watching the cooking pots on the fire. "Gold's looking strong," he said. "Astrik are seventy-five; Hunter's up twenty. Auros has a hot gold property near Cobar and are raising more money; little Jimmy will soon be a millionaire."

"A paper millionaire," I corrected. "Better sell while you're ahead."

"Settle down."

"*He that makes haste to be rich shall not be innocent,*" Chas said.

There was no gambling that evening. Jim was immersed in back issues of the paper and various reports he'd picked up, and checking stock prices as he figured out his new portfolio. Every now and again he would pump me for information on geological and mining terms.

"What's a resource?" he asked. "Aurus has a potential resource estimated at ten million ounces."

I pondered for a moment seeking inspiration. "Imagine that Aurus took some assays of seawater in Sydney Harbour and found it contained one part per billion gold, which is probably quite likely, given the industrial pollution. If they then went out and pegged one hundred billion tonnes of the stuff they'd have a potential resource of one hundred tonnes of gold."

Jim nodded eagerly. "Fantastic. Any one thought of doing it?"

"But," I continued doggedly, "it would cost them the equivalent of ten ounces of gold for every ounce they recovered. In other words it's a meaningless term."

"Gotcha," Jim said. "It's like having Art in the camp. It looks impressive on Chas' books but is meaningless as far as work goes."

"Exactly," I said.

"What was that?" Art asked, looking up from his Playboy.

"Nothing," Jim said. "We just figured out what you are; you're a meaningless resource."

* * *

Craig turned up the next evening with his usual carton of beer and two bottles of high class red. Jim had prepared a pork roast and by the time it was finished the level of the second bottle was dropping. Craig pulled out his wallet. "I came prepared this time," he said, flashing its bulging contents of ten and twenty dollar bills. "The casino owes me about eighteen dollars from the last trip."

Jim said. "I'd be careful, Craig. Art's turned professional since your last visit. That lot won't last more than half an hour, even with a 20 cent limit."

"It'll be nice to take someone else's money," Art agreed. "Jim's so bloody stingy at betting because of his losses that it's barely worth playing."

Jim leaned forward. "I'll give you a useful tip, Craig. When Art is bluffing his eyes cross. That's the time to double the stakes."

Craig smiled. "Thanks for the tip. And what's your winning secret, Jim?"

Art answered for him. "Blind bloody luck. It gives him a few winning hands but I know how to fix that." He stood up, raised his arms skyward, bowed at the waist, then jiggled up and down in an obscene parody of the Can Can. "Lady of love, lady of luck, give me a smile, give me a ...buck." He sat down looking smug. "That should do it."

"You had us going there with that rhyme," Craig said.

"If you hadn't been here it would have been a lot cruder," Jim said. "Chas is supposed to be in charge of Art's career but I think he's washed his hands of him. So what are we playing - Manila?"

As the evening wore on, Art's invocation to the heavens seemed to have met with a response. Although Jim played his usual game, the luck of the cards was not with him and for once he lost steadily.

"Typical Kiwi gambler," Art said, raking in another pot. "All they know about is sheep."

"Let's raise the stakes to fifty cents," Jim said. "I can't get interested in these penny ante pots."

"A dollar if you like," Art said. "What do you reckon Craig?"

Craig counted his pile of winnings, "Fifty cents sounds good. It will have me back in the black that much sooner."

Chas looked up from his motoring magazine. "Don't you go betting too much, Art."

"I can't lose though, the way Jim's been playing. Lady Luck is with me."

"Everyone thinks that, until they leave without a shirt," Chas said.

Jim chuckled. "I'd never do that to Art; what a disgusting sight."

Art began dealing. "Okay, a fifty cent limit. Place your bets."

Art won the next three pots in a row and as Jim cursed, Craig shook his head disapprovingly. "Don't fight Lady Luck, Jim, just cruise along and eke out that dwindling stake until she comes back."

"Craig's right," I said. "It's why I always end up a winner."

"You call being a dollar up winning?" Art scoffed, looking at my unusually small pile of coins.

"Better being a dollar up than being more than thirty down, Art." Chas said.

"I wish you'd keep out of this," Art said.

"Why? It's my money you're gambling with."

"How come it's your money?" Craig asked.

"I had to loan him some after he was fined by Social Security."

"It was just a mistake," Art said. "I got the dates when I worked wrong."

"Any date you put down for working would be wrong," Jim said. He began shuffling the cards so energetically they ended up on the floor. He held up his glass, "A toast to Lady Luck. Come back my beloved. Be with me tonight?"

We all joined in the toast except Art, who patted the seat beside him.

"She's over here, fellas. Eat your heart out."

After Jim lost the next four pots I said. "You'll have to attract her attention with more than just a toast."

That set him off. He stood up suddenly. "Lady Luck," he yelled. "Where are you?" He rushed outside in the dark, flapping his arms and clucking like a hysterical hen until he tripped over the barbecue plate, rolled down the embankment and ended up in the dam. Long after we'd gone to bed we could hear Art laughing.

"That guy really gets on my wick sometimes," Jim muttered, rubbing his bruised shinbone.

"You have to admit though, he makes life more interesting."

"I guess that's right. Contemplating murder is interesting."

* * *

After Craig left, Jim went back to his shares. He had his financial future all figured out. He would borrow 20,000 dollars as a personal loan and buy up a heap of shares; his only problem was how to get set when he was stuck in the bush. Every day he sat in camp saw his hypothetical portfolio increase in value, which also meant it would cost him more to buy. He was going mad with frustration waiting for the next field break.

"Do you realise," he said to me, "that each day I work for you I'm going backwards to the tune of about 300 dollars."

Over the next few days, Jim's concentration fell off and his sleep started to suffer. Art only had to look sideways at him and Jim would take offence. Chas solved his problem finally, when the clutch of his Toyota gave out, necessitating a trip to town to get it fixed.

"You can drive it in, Jim," Chas said magnanimously after we'd discussed the problem in camp. "Reckon you can change gears without a clutch?"

"To get to town I could walk on water," Jim said. "I never thought I'd be glad to see that mobile junkyard breaking down yet again. If I leave early tomorrow I can be back in a couple of days or three."

* * *

It was peaceful in the camp with Jim away. We were used to listening to the stock market report and the next morning, which was Tuesday October 20, the market went into freefall; the bubble had burst. It sounded as though Jim must have just done his 20,000 dollars and then some."

"I knew it," Art chortled. "He thought he was so smart and where has it got him? He's got nothing and I'm on the way to buying a car.".

We were just finishing the evening meal the next day when Jim drove into the camp. After two days of speculation about Jim and his portfolio we watched in silent anticipation, trying not to grin as he got out and stretched, then strolled over to us nonchalantly as if all was right with the world.

"Okay," he said, looking at a row of grinning faces. I suppose you heard the news. My portfolio's rat shit."

"We were hoping you might have suicided," Art said.

"You punted the 20,000 then?" I asked.

Jim turned to Chas. "I take back what I said about that junk yard of yours. I never got to the Towers to buy those shares."

"So what happened?"

"The usual. I'd only gone about twenty k when it broke down. I thought you might have heard me swearing and come looking. I was only in the hot sun for about five hours, trying to fix it along with the meat ants and flies. The station owner came by, luckily. He towed me to his place and managed to get me going again the next day but by then the market had crashed."

"So what now?" I asked. "Early retirement seems to have been delayed."

"Get real. I might have lost a few thousand but it's temporary. When the market hits bottom I'll get that loan and start buying up all those cheap shares."

"I figured that," I said. "What do you reckon Chas?"

Chas thought for a moment. *"God hath chosen the foolish things of the world to confound the wise."*

Chapter 12 Lovers and Losers

We finished working in the Sellheim area and after taking time off, Jim, who'd stayed in Townsville, picked me up at the airport. He was in shorts and thongs and had on a garish Hawaiian shirt. He handed me the keys to the Hilux. "You'd better drive."

"You look as if you're still in holiday mode," I said, as we set off. "Did you make it out of the backpacker's hostel this time?"

There was a dreamy look in his eye and a half smile on his face as he yawned sleepily. "I put in the last three days on Magnetic Island."

"And three nights too from the look of you. Where's that dynamic character I hired? Holidays are supposed to recharge the batteries, not run you down. So what happened?"

"I'm in love."

"Who with this time?"

"A German, mein fraulein; I met her on Magnetic Island."

"You're in love after only three days?"

"That's all it needed."

"Love at first sight?"

He grinned. "They can't resist me."

"What's her name?"

"Katrina." It rolled off his tongue like droplets of quicksilver shimmering in the sunlight. "She's *Wunderbar*." He sighed, selected a tape, then dozed with a happy smile on his face.

It was clear that I would get none of the usual sparkling dialogue on this trip, and for the rest of the afternoon I listened to his new tape, a selection of love songs, which he played continuously.

We returned to the same campsite by the dam but although it was a great site it took a while for the spirit of exploration to be rekindled. Art wasn't happy because he'd copped a hefty fine for undeclared income on his tax return and Jim was suffering severely from love sickness. On the first evening, we made ourselves comfortable in Chas' van and I got out the cards.

"Who's for poker?" I asked. "You in Jim?"

Jim had a small paperback titled Teach Yourself German that he was studying intently and he was oblivious to everything around him. I had to prompt him again.

"Wass is dass?" he said.

"Cards?"

"Yarravole"

"Yarravole? You mean jawohl?"

"Yes err - *nein danke.*"

"Make your mind up."

"Ah, *nein bitte.*"

"Are you turning down a game of cards?" Chas said, an overlay of reforming zeal and hope in his voice.

"Yes. I mean ja, *mein Herr.*"

"Don't get your hopes up," I said. "Jim's in love."

Art looked up from his Penthouse magazine. "Don't tell me," he sneered. "She's fat, fifty and looks like a ewe that missed the shearing shed three years running."

Jim was too far gone to be distracted by Art. "She's beautiful," he said. "Wait'll you see the photos I took; *"wonder-bar;* blond hair, great smile, speaks English, stands about this high." He lifted his arm to chest level.

"A dumb blonde, dwarf, Kiwi," Art said. "She sounds a lot better than most of them. Maybe your taste is improving."

"I kissed her just before she left on the ferry and she waved until I couldn't see her anymore."

Art gave a derisive grunt. "She'll be wanting a new set of dentures, that's for sure."

"What do you mean she speaks English?" Chas asked.

Art broke in again. "It means she can't be a Kiwi. None of them ever mastered the lingo."

"She's German," Jim said. "There'll be a big bunch of flowers waiting for her when she gets back to Berlin." He flipped over a page of his German phrase book. *"Spreken zee Doitch?* I'm learning German to go over there and see her."

"After just one kiss?" I asked.

"Settle down. One kiss from the master is all it takes."

"I thought you were dating a couple of Aussie sheilas?"

"You mean Bev?"

"Who's Bev? Last I heard it was Katy and Kirsty. Didn't Chas post six letters off to them in our last camp?"

Jim opened a packet of peanuts and emptied the contents into his mouth. "Those letters were all for Bev."

"And how many children has Bev got?"

"Just a teenage son, but he's a young criminal. Kids from broken homes have no discipline and no manners; all they've got is cheek. You can't reason with them."

"So Bev's on the way out too?"

He chuckled. "She is now."

"Australian women don't go for Kiwis anyway," Art said. He held up the Penthouse centrefold. "Should get yourself a young Aussie Sheila like this."

"She's not an Aussie," Jim said. "There aren't any like that over here and the young ones who look half decent are too immature."

"You want a mother not a girl," Art sneered. "Any good-looking Kiwi sort who had maturity, would head to Australia where men are men. I wouldn't touch a Kiwi girl anyway, even with a blindfold on in a photographer's darkroom. I'm not that desperate."

"How desperate would you need to get then?" I asked.

"One day in the bush is all it would take," Jim said. "I saw him chasing a kangaroo this afternoon. He'd have caught it except he undid his belt too soon and tripped."

"I'd fall in love with a roo before a bloody Kiwi sheila," Art said.

Jim nodded in agreement. "So I've noticed."

"Look," I said. "No more bickering. We've got a perfect location here. Think positive and we'll make it the best camp ever.

* * *

To my amazement, my words seemed to take effect. The first few days passed with hardly an argument and the nights were without gambling. Art, with a plentiful supply of cigarettes and beer, read through his stack of girlie magazines, Chas worked on his Toyota and Jim would lie on his stretcher after the evening meal, writing to Katrina. He would read me some of his finer efforts when the mood took him.

"Listen to this." he would say. "Since the rain, the bush is a verdant sword and the birds sing like nightingales. My fellow travellers are barely aware of these things but since meeting you I am starting to notice that beauty is all around me."

"You have a penchant for flowery language."

"What's a pong chong? I'll fit that in the next sentence."

During the day, Jim was irrepressible. He bubbled with enthusiasm and at various times he'd test the eardrums with a loud rendition of the current hit— *"Does she love me, with all her heart? Does she worr-r-ry, when we're apar-ar-rt."*

"Ever thought of being a professional singer?" I asked one day, after the fourth rendition within as many minutes.

He beamed. "That good huh?" He whipped out his German phrase book. *"Spreken -zee - doitch?"* He turned the page. "I love you. *Eek - leeber - dish.* You know any German, Bob?"

Geologists know everything," I said. "She might be a dish but c-h is pronounced as in kick but softer without the k; we don't have the equivalent sound."

"Eek - leeber - dick." Jim's face split into a smile. "Is this man any good?" He burst into song again.

"How are you going to afford flying to Germany on a field assistant's pay?"

"Love will find a way."

"If you're serious about Katrina you're going to have to shape up a bit physically. You're giving Art a run for his money."

Jim looked down at his bulging stomach. "I put on four kilos last trip but a few games of squash fixed it."

"The stomach you're building up this trip will take more than just a few games."

He grinned. "When she hears the knock on the door and opens it to find little Jimmy saying *'Eek – leeber – dick'*, it won't matter."

"That will probably get you a slap on the face."

He frowned. "I'm going to get some German tapes. You can help me learn. Maybe I'd better diet too. *Mein Liebchen. Heinz, vi, dry, fears.* What comes after four?"

* * *

Jim's evening gambling interests had been curtailed by letter writing, but one night, sitting in Chas' caravan, with sausages and eggs and vegetables and a huge helping of boysenberry pie and cream inside him, he felt he was due a night off. He stacked the five letters he had ready for posting to Germany to one side and collected the cards, potato chips, packets of liquorice allsorts and other brain food and soon had Art and me involved.

We still had a twenty cent limit for Manila, but despite that the pot was soon around four dollars on one hand as Art kept raising the stakes. When it was called I had a flush, Jim had a full house, Art had nothing.

"You must be a sheep short in the shearing shed to bluff like that," Jim said, munching a fistful of potato chips. "You've been going cross-eyed lying about how you used to clean up at the casinos with no bets under 500 dollars and make a living from gambling, but it's all a put on. You've got a loose lip."

Art drew on his cigarette. "I got me methods."

Jim reached for the jellybeans. "You wouldn't last five minutes in a big game. You can't control yourself."

"Got a hell of a lot more control than a Kiwi queer."

Jim's laugh was short and sarcastic. "Like with your smoking and drinking. You're an out of control piss-pot with a nicotine problem."

"A few cartons of grog a week isn't going out of control," Art said.

"You call two cartons a few? And what about cigarettes, you're a chain smoker."

"I'm not a chain smoker; anyway what about you? You're hooked on junk food, lollies and puddings."

"Maybe," Jim said, peeling the wrapper from a Cherry Ripe, "but I can give it up anytime. You're addicted."

"Bull shit I am."

"I'm not the only one thinks so. Ask Chas and Bob."

"Yeah," we chorused.

Tell youse w hat then," Art said. "For the rest of the camp I'll quit smoking if you give up the puddings and lollies and nuts."

"Not a problem." Jim said. "I need a diet. What's the bet?"

"10 dollars."

"Ten! I thought you were a gambler; you're just a tired turd."

"Okay, fifty."

"You can back out if you want, loose lips."

A hundred then," Art said, going a shade whiter.

"It's a bet." Jim stuffed the Cherry Ripe into his mouth, then went to the cupboard. "Bob, you're the witness."

A look of alarm spread over Art's face. "What're you doing?"

Jim took out five cartons of cigarettes. "Just helping you to win 100 dollars."

Art removed the bowl of mixed nuts, the chips and all the packets of sweets Jim had been munching. "Anything after the main course is a pudding," he said.

Jim looked under Art's bunk and pulled out another two cartons of cigarettes. "Lucky for you I know where you keep everything."

Art began collecting all the tins of fruit and packets of biscuits and lollies, piling them into a separate cupboard and numbering them with a marker pen. It was half an hour before they started gambling again.

The next morning Jim presented me with a shopping list. "Art's leg is playing up again. This is what we need in town. Coffee, milk, rice, steaks, diesel, propane gas, two litres of oil, some fresh fruit and a spark plug. Chas could go into the Towers and get them and take that drop kick Art with him to see a doctor."

"I'm impressed," I said. "What about the chocolate bars, ice-cream and sweet biscuits?"

"I don't want any temptation."

"Very sensible, but I don't see any great urgency to go shopping just yet although I'm touched about your concern for Art all of a sudden."

"It's just that I've been a bit hard on the poor sod. I know he can't help the way he is but his leg does seem bad."

"You wouldn't have anything else in mind would you?"

He shrugged. "Not really, but I could probably think of something."

"I guess Chas could go in. I need to post Hunter a progress report and I want to find out when they plan another visit."

Jim's face brightened. "Beauty. Hey Chas," he called. "Bob wants you to go to town for a few things and to drop Art off at a shrink." He handed Chas the shopping list. "I've got a few things too." He produced another list. "I want the latest Financial Review; there are letters for Katrina to be posted. Also check if my holiday photos are back and get me one of those courses on speaking German. Also, I want you to organise a weekly shipment of flowers to Germany. Reckon you could do all that? Oh—and don't bother bringing Art back."

"Yup. What sort of flowers?"

Art, who'd become rather short tempered since the loss of his cigarettes, sniggered. "If Katrina reckons Jim's good looking then she'll like anything; a bunch of dandelions would do."

"A dozen red roses," Jim said.

* * *

Chas and a more mobile Art returned in time for the evening meal, with news of an impending visit from one of the company's staff geologists.

"Kim someone," Chas said, vaguely, handing Jim a bulky packet of photos.

"I might be able to talk him into a pay rise," Art said brightly.

Jim burst into laughter. "If I was you I'd keep out of sight except it's a bit hard in your case. Nothing that losing fifty kilos wouldn't fix though."

"I'm doing it. You've got to bet money to lose your gut. I can lose mine by sheer willpower, which reminds me." A smirk settled over Art's face. "You left a lot of things off the supply list. I brought back a heap of chocolate, nut assortments and ice-cream for you."

"Not a problem," Jim said. "I don't eat that rubbish anymore."

Jim spilled the photos onto the table to show them off. Katrina had a great figure with looks to match; even Art was impressed. "I'm more her type," he said. "Think I might write to her too and become her pen pal."

Jim selected the best photo of Katrina and kissed it. *"Mein Liebling."*

Art's lip curled. "She won't be kissing when I write her about Katy, Kirsty and Bev and your five illegitimate kids."

Jim pinned the photo to the caravan wall. "She'll bring me luck at cards."

"Lucky in love, unlucky at cards, Jim," I cautioned.

Art said. "He's suffering from lust, not love."

Jim leered. "It's both."

"What do you reckon about all this, Chas?" I asked.

"The price of a virtuous woman is above rubies."

"Blood oath," Art said. "They're worth a lot of money if you set em up right."

Chas frowned. "That's not the biblical interpretation of virtue." He handed a package to Jim. "Your German tapes. You owe me 80 dollars."

"Danke shon mein Herr."

"Are you for real, Jim?" Art said.

"About what?"

"Learning German."

"I want to tell her I love her in her own language; maybe even go over there to live."

"That's all bull," Art said. "The only things you need to learn are 'What about it babe'? Or 'your place or mine'?"

I nodded in agreement. "You should take a few lessons on Art's art of courting, Jim. Instead of drawing it out for weeks it would only take a few minutes."

"It would save a lot on stamps and flowers too," Chas said.

"No thanks," Jim said. "I don't fancy getting a smack in the eye every time I talk to a woman."

We spent the next day putting in a pegged grid over an area where our soil sampling had found interesting gold and copper assays. Jim was curious as to why we banged pegs into the ground.

"The pegs are known points we can come back to," I explained. "We'll take a soil sample at each peg and note its number. If we get a good assay we can come back to the exact spot—*Verstehen zie?*"

Jim's eyes glazed over. *"Verstehen?"*

"Do you understand?"

"Ah, *yarra-vole,*" he felt in his pocket. *"Mine Gott!"* His eyes widened in horror. "I've lost the photos."

We found them back on the track and rather the worse for wear from being run over. "Lucky I pinned the best one to the wall," he said gloomily after checking the damage. It wasn't so lucky as it turned out because we found that Katrina was not looking the best. Art had added a moustache and four o'clock shadow to her.

"Sorry," Art said when Jim confronted him. "Thought you had plenty. She needed a bit of a touch up."

"I'll touch you up," Jim said. He would have liked to, he was so annoyed but he couldn't get Art offside; he needed him for the evening poker games.

Kim turned up after breakfast the next morning. He was in faded blue jeans and calf length boots and looked a bit weedy, with a few pimples, long blond hair pulled into a ponytail and partly hidden under a felt hat. His scratchy voice and a limp handshake made Jim and I look at each other. However, when Jim found he was from New Zealand and knew some of Jim's old haunts they got on really well.

We took him out to the new grid. Jim found it necessary to relieve himself at the gate he was opening and **I noticed Kim looked slightly embarrassed. I also noticed** that he sported a small silver earring and that under the sleeve of his shirt he wore a pink Swatch. Although a few men were starting to sport earrings it was still unusual, but so were female geologists in the bush; they were rarer than good gold prospects. Could it be that Kim was a girl? I was soon to find out.

"Kim and I have been talking about your Magnetic Island attraction," I said, as Jim got back into the Toyota. Show Kim your photos."

"Only have one with me," he said, pulling out the one with the imprint of a tyre. "You got a girl friend, Kim?"

Kim frowned in silence a moment. "Bloody wouldn't want to have. I'm not a lesbian."

Jim turned scarlet.

"You'll have to excuse Jim," I said. "He's been around the woollies too long."

"You unspeakable bastard," Jim said some time later, when the opportunity arose. "Why didn't you tell me Kim was a girl?"

I stared at him speculatively. "Maybe Art is right about you. Can't you tell the sexes apart unless they're in a paddock?"

Kim wanted to see the jig in operation that afternoon so we took her down to the dam. At the time, Art, thinking he was alone, was wallowing about in the water like a bloated and decomposing cow that had been caught in a flooded backwater and was now bobbing about aimlessly. He was not a pretty sight when clothed; naked he was awful.

"Get some clothes on," I called, "and show Kim how the jig works."

Despite boasting of numerous conquests in the Towers, mostly lurid scenes of debauchery, Art was fairly modest in front of people. I threw him his towel, which he caught as he scrambled out. His limp was barely noticeable now and he sucked in his stomach in order to get the towel around it.

"G'day Kim." Art was eager to impress a member of the company staff and he sounded more alert and co-operative than I'd ever heard. "I was just having a late lunch break. Ever seen a jig working before?"

Kim shook her head and Art then went through the operating steps, making it sound as difficult and complex as he could, which was not easy with something so simple in principle. Jim began rolling his eyes.

"Normally Bob and I pan them off," Jim said, when Art finally wound down. "Hunter sent the jig up to get Art off the dole."

"Take no notice, Kim," Art said. "He's a typical bloody Kiwi queer, only interested in sex with sheep."

"Hey!" Jim said. "Steady on. There's a lady present. He turned to Kim. "Sorry about that."

Kim shrugged indifferently and took her hat off, shaking her blond hair loose: Art watched in fascination, his white face becoming a shade whiter.

"I'm a Kiwi myself," she said. It was at this moment that Art's towel succumbed to the pull of gravity. With an inarticulate gurgle he grabbed it and fled the scene.

Jim couldn't wait to have another go at Art, and the first time he had a chance he said. "That was a disgusting exhibition you put on in front of Kim. Is that how you proposition your girlfriends, by flashing?

"Works every time," Art said.

Jim's mouth twisted in a sneer. "If I hadn't grabbed her she'd have fainted. I nearly passed out myself. Not that you've got much there to be proud of."

Art flushed self-consciously. "And you have I suppose?"

"At least I don't need to hide it under wrinkles of fat. You didn't even know Kim was a female. Don't you know the difference?"

"She's a Kiwi, so how could I tell? No wonder you guys end up with sheep if they all look like men." His voice lowered conspiratorially. "But now that I know she's not a bloke, she looks a lot better—know what I mean?"

"No."

"I mean," he bit his lower lip in thought for a moment. "She's not a bad sort. For a Kiwi that is," he added. "She's already taken a shine to me."

Jim leered. "What part of you?"

"That's bloody crude," Art said and stalked off.

"I think Art is in love too," I said.

* * *

Kim stayed a couple of days and was interested in trying her luck at the Sellheim Casino. Art, his performance enhanced by the presence of Kim, who had miraculously succeeded in turning him into a jaunty wit and raconteur to boot, experienced an unusual run of luck, and Jim lost steadily, no doubt due to Katrina's doctored photo staring down at him. He would glance at her from time to time and then look away frowning. Shortly after we started, Kim produced a pack of cigarettes and laid them on the table with her lighter.

"Hope it won't upset anyone if I have a cigarette?"

"Go right ahead Kim." Jim urged. "No one here minds. Art gave it up recently but that man's the original definition of willpower."

"Can start and stop whenever I want," Art agreed, opening a fresh can of beer.

"And he does frequently," Jim added.

Kim lit a cigarette and breathed in deeply. "What about playing

Pontoon. I'm sick of losing at poker. Okay Arthur?"

Art didn't reply for a moment, his eyes were focussed on her cigarette and they seemed to glow with the same intensity, the pupils dilated and lit by inner thoughts that seemed as intense and hot as the glowing tip itself. The hand clasped around his can of beer tightened as she drew in the smoke until with a pop, the tin buckled, sending up a jet of fluid.

"Of course not, Kim," he said, the spray of cold beer breaking the spell. "This is your night. We'll play whatever you want. I'll split my winnings with you later if you like. It's embarrassing to take money off visitors, especially pretty ones."

"Excuse me while I throw up," Jim said as Art wiped down the table. "And Pontoon could be a problem. Art can only count to ten unless he takes his boots off. Even then it only gets him to twenty."

Art smiled in a superior manner. "Don't listen to him, Kim, he's jealous because I keep beating him, although I never push him too far. He has to live, same as the rest of us. But maths was my best subject at school." He looked around as he shuffled the cards. "I hope you lot know what you're in for? Cut. Highest card goes banker."

"Art missed out on schooling," Jim said. "He still thinks a square root is a rude word."

"Bull! My mind is like a calculator."

"Without a battery."

Kim giggled. "You two are unbelievable. Every camp needs a joker. It's good to have a laugh."

I shook my head. "One's all right. Get two like we have here and you'd be better off abandoning the camp."

"Chas is the real problem," Jim said. "He was a gambler and a drug addict before he got religion and I've never known a man to crack so many dirty jokes. That right Chas?"

Chas looked up from the plans of the shed he was building. "Yup."

"And talk," Jim added. "You'd better believe it. And he's still got his gambling addiction. We banned him from playing."

Kim looked at Chas with renewed interest. "Is that right, Chas?"

Chas looked embarrassed. "Nup."

"But you used to gamble." Jim needled.

"A long time ago."

"He gave Art a lesson the other day, Kim," Jim confided. "It was the first time Art had ever won."

"Jim's full of sh—er bull," Art said.

Kim scratched her ear. "Sherbul? What's that?"

"It's one of those words peculiar to the camp," I said, "like Barchas and Archas.

"And what are they?"

"You'll find out if you stay long enough."

Art, who'd won the cut, grabbed the cards. "Right. I'm banker. Let's see some action."

Fortune seesawed for a while, but again Art began to get the upper hand.

"Have another cigarette, Kim?" Jim said.

Kim shook her head. "A couple in the evening does me."

"Mind if I try one then?"

"No, go ahead. I didn't think you smoked."

Jim lit up with a sigh of contentment and Art swallowed the last of his beer in a convulsive gulp.

"These are really good," Jim said. "Think I might take the habit up again. There's nothing like a cigarette to calm the nerves."

Art ripped the tab off another beer can with a jerk. "Come on. Play if we're going to play."

Jim got up and gave Katrina's moustache a kiss. "*Mein libeling*," he said. "That should change my luck." He sat down and parked his cigarette where the smoke drifted under Art's nose.

Art looked at the bets, frowning with the effort of concentration. "Double."

Jim said. "I tried a bit of Pot, Kim, when I was on Magnetic Island. I found it very relaxing. As a kid I used to go for Craven A, then I rolled my own. These filter tips are hard to beat though." He was soon in a discussion of different brands with Kim. During the action Kim and I each bought two cards and then sat; Jim bought three cards. Art, faced with a decision on whether to pay 'twenty or over', flipped too many cards and went bust.

"Expensive hand, Art," Jim said, as he pulled a pile of cash across. "You look as if you're nerves are shot."

"Don't mind losing to Kim and Bob," Art said, scowling. He sucked on his can aggressively as the bets were placed once more. "Double," he said without bothering to look at his hand. Once again he flipped the cards for himself and this time built his hand to twenty. "Pay twenty-one," he cried in triumph, reaching for Jim's stake.

"*Ein und zwanzig*." Jim said, turning his cards over.

"Beauty." Before Jim could react his money was in Art's pile.

"Hey!" Jim grabbed four dollars back. "You deaf or what. I said twenty-one. You owe me."

"Thought you was swearing" Art said. He got up and after rummaging through the cupboard, returned with a bowl of canned raspberries, pressurised cream, a bag of mixed nuts and a several bars of chocolate.

Jim frowned, then reached for another of Kim's cigarettes. "I thought you were cutting back to lose flab, Art?"

"Winning makes me hungry. It's why I'm a bit overweight." Art sprayed a liberal quantity of pressurised cream over the raspberries and dug in.

"What about dealing instead of stuffing your face," Jim said. He dragged on the cigarette and blew the smoke into Art's face, then burst into a paroxysm of coughing.

"I think our luck is going to change, Kim." I said, and I was right; soon it was no contest. Art became too drunk and bloated to think properly and Jim turned green. Kim and I scooped the pool.

"At least that fat drop kick didn't win again," Jim said as he settled with a groan onto his stretcher later that evening.

I chuckled. "You sure fixed him with those cigarettes."

He gave a sigh. "What a disgusting habit. You remember that tunnel we went into once with the bats and the dead roo?"

"Yes."

"Well that's what my mouth tastes like. You'd have to be mad to take up smoking"

* * *

Kim left after breakfast the next morning. "Okay," I said, as Art and Jim began sniping at each other again. "Art, there are plenty of samples to sieve. I want twenty an hour. And you, Jim, just remember you've got a few secrets to hide about Kim, too."

Art pricked up his ears. "What secrets?"

"Nothing," Jim said, "except she took a shine to me. They all do."

"Bull," Art said. "I wasn't going to let on but Kim fell for me. I'm taking her out next time she comes to the Towers. I've got her address and phone number. She said she'd call me."

Jim's lip curled. "When did all this happen? In a wet dream?"

"After you went to bed. Took her for a bit of nooky in the moonlight."

"There was no moon."

"Stars then. What's it matter when you're in love. If she wasn't a

Kiwi I could get really interested."

"You've gone cross-eyed Art."

"You're jealous."

"You said you wouldn't touch a Kiwi in a photographer's darkroom with a blindfold on."

"It was a dark night. Besides she's not like other Kiwi women."

"No. She's the first one to meet you without screaming."

It seemed to me that in the next few days Art actually became slightly more pleasant to live with and that he drank less beer. Maybe there was some truth in his boast and love was indeed having an edifying effect.

On his next trip for supplies, Chas brought back Katrina's first letter. "That was a quick reply," he said. Passing it over.

Jim sniffed it in delight. "I wrote her five pages the day she left the island. The letter would have beaten her home."

"Well what's the story?" I said after Jim had been through the letter a dozen times. "It looks to be fairly short and succinct.

Jim grinned. "Listen to this. *'Dear Jim"*—he paused. "She's calling me dear already."

"It sounds more like the start of a Dear John letter. What's next?"

"Dear Jim. Was amazed to get your very long letter, and so soon. It was a nice group that we met up with on the island wasn't it? I certainly enjoyed myself and I am going to miss all the good times I had. I haven't got my photos back yet. I think you are in one. If so will send it to you. Thank you for the writing. Hope you find my English to scratch. Love, Katryn."

Art gave a chortle. "That's it? You call that a love letter?"

"Not bad for starters. Wait till she gets the next letter."

"And the fifteen after that."

"She has a photo of me."

Chas said. "She only thinks she has. She's not sure and she just told you she can't get rid of it fast enough."

"She means to send me copy, dickhead."

Art said. "When the birds write to me it's full of intimate stuff."

"Sure," Jim said. "Like what for instance?"

Art did a bit of a soft-shoe shuffle that rocked the caravan. "Unless it's happened to you, you can't explain it. Some men have it, some don't."

Jim sniffed the letter again. "Mmm, smell that perfume. She's missing the good times she had. She's missing little Jimmy. Think I'll book my fare over next month."

"You can't speak the lingo yet," Chas said.

Art chimed in. "Why bother to learn a second lingo when you can't speak the first. She's better at English than you are."

"I've already learnt enough German," Jim said. "You two are both *Dickkopffs*. That's German for dickheads." He put the letter in his shirt pocket and turned to Art. "For a guy whose only experience of sex is a cheap grope with half a ton of flab you couldn't begin to understand."

* * *

Initially, Art had seemed to suffer more from the effects of the bet than Jim but after Kim's visit he became less surly and more co-operative. I was inclined to put it down to his reformation due to love but Jim had other ideas. One lunchtime, on a day when we had left Art at the camp sieving samples, Jim started up the Hilux. "Reckon I know why Art has managed to give up the fags so easily. If you guys want to catch him out then hop in. This will be a good time."

Jim stopped short of the camp and switched off the motor. "We'll walk from here so he doesn't hear us. Don't want to warn him."

We found Art sitting in the caravan, reading a Playboy. On the table was a carton of cigarettes.

"Gotcha!" Jim said, jumping into the van and giving Art a terrible fright.

"What?" Art said, going pink.

"Smoking."

"I ain't smoking."

"There's three butts in the ashtray. Where did you get those cigarettes?"

He shrugged. "Dunno. Kim must'a left them. I was just cleaning the place up a bit and found them."

"Cleaning up? This place is a pigsty. It hasn't seen a broom in years. You bought them from her, or pinched them, didn't you. That'll be a hundred bucks thanks."

Art glared at him. "I'm not paying you anything."

Jim turned to Chas. "He's on your payroll. Pay me out of his wages."

Chas nodded. "Yep. Guilty."

Art looked shocked. "You can't do that."

"Just did," Chas said.

* * *

Chas returned from his next trip to Charters Towers with a second letter from Katrina. Jim held it against his heart. *"Mein Leeber chin* Think I'll ask her to marry me next letter." He began to read, then stopped. "Oh - my - God," he said. "Little Jimmy blew it."

"What's the go?" I said. "Maybe there's something missing in the translation. Let us experts decide."

He brightened. "You could be right. What do you reckon? *Dear Jim. I am getting married next month. Please send no more flowers and letters as it annoys my fiance."*

"I think it's over," I said, looking around. "What do you guys think?"

Chas said. *"The Lord giveth and the Lord taketh away.* But I'm thinking that I just posted six more letters for her, and what about Interflora? They'll have to put off staff."

When Art was finally able to get his laughter under control he said. "You might have strung her along a bit more if you hadn't kissed her. No wonder she got married, with single guys like you pestering her."

Jim screwed the letter into a tight ball. "Thanks for the sympathy fellas."

Chas spoke. *"Give instruction to a wise man and he will be yet wiser."*

"Shut up, Chas."

"It is better to dwell in the wilderness than with an angry woman."

"Shut up!"

"What are you going to do?" I asked, before Chas emptied the Book of Proverbs.

"I'm going to burn this stupid phrase book. Anyone want a set of tapes?"

Art said. "I could have been interested if they'd been in Kiwi. I could have used them for getting to know Kim better."

Chapter 13 Wild Animals of the Bush

"What's this next campsite going to be like?" Jim asked, as we headed out of Charters Towers after a few weeks break.

I squinted into the setting sun that touched the desiccated landscape with a brassy lustre. It was mid November and uncomfortably hot.

"Tourists would kill to get to it. It's not far from the great Kidston gold mine and we'll have the luxury of Chas' caravan set up beside the Coppermine River. There'll be fishing, swimming, good tucker and interesting work."

Jim gave a sceptical laugh. "If you reckon Chas' caravan is a luxury I can imagine what the rest is like. Where is Chas anyway?"

"He's coming down from Conjuboy with Art.

Jim groaned. "Art! Just as well that fat sod likes to gamble. Taking his money is compensation for having to work with him. Where are we staying tonight?"

"At the Greenvale Motel; Chas said he'd book us in."

"Motel?" Jim said, impressed. "This is a first. Hunter must have come into some money. Hot showers, air-conditioning, a three-course meal, games of pool, drinks at the bar paid by Hunter. I take it all back what I just said."

"This is one of the perks you get, working for me."

"One of them? What other perks are there?"

"Well for starters you're experiencing the subtle mystique of the Australian bush and the bonding that creates true mateship."

"That's really good, Bob but I'd prefer a pay rise."

"Settle down," I said, using his favourite expression. "Although this is a big budget project it's not that big."

"I might have to hit Hunter for a higher car rental. I fixed the

Hilux; it runs like new."

"You haven't fixed the air-conditioning."

"I was going to but all the extras drained the budget."

Ahead of us, cattle, which were grazing on nothing more than bare dirt beside the road, began to cross over, forcing Jim to brake hard.

"Typical of the animals in this country," he said. They're all brainless. The mob on the right decides it's better to be with the mob on the left and the mob on the left gets the same idea, so they all change positions and achieve nothing." He stared ahead, his eyes narrowed to reduce the glare. "Stupid name too, Greenvale. There's nothing green up here. Place looks dead, like the rest of Australia, but worse. Dead roos littering the road, crows waiting for some poor sod to die of thirst, the horizon blotted out by dust and heat haze, the nights filled with mosquitoes, the days filled with flies. This country is an arse-hole. Mention the colour green to an Aussie and all you get is a blank stare of incomprehension."

"You can get quite poetic when the mood takes you. There must be something you like though?"

He thought for a moment. "Yeah, the sound of this motel. Hope they serve a decent meal, I'm starved."

We pulled into Greenvale late in the evening and went into the pub. The town had sprung up in 1971 to mine the rich nickel laterite deposits and since then it had suffered as chequered a history as any gold mining town. The motel and pub managed to keep going in the bad times, making do with the tourists who passed through.

"There should be a booking for Hunter," I said to the publican.

He flipped open the register. "Nothin' here."

"Amazing," Jim said. "Chas has finally slipped up. Can you believe it?"

"Can you give us two rooms?"

He shook his head. "Only one left. Room 9. Sleeps three."

Jim said. "I'm not sharing with those two. You ever heard them snore? It's no wonder Chas' van fell to pieces."

"We'll take it," I said. "Can you manage an extra bed?"

"I can give you a camp stretcher."

"Could go a seafood dinner," Jim said. "Hunter owes us; and maybe a bottle of red. What time does the dining room close?"

The publican, who was of portly disposition with a stomach that kept him a metre from the bar, frowned. "Dining room's closed. There's pies or sausage rolls. Only red I got is sherry."

We watched the pies circling and quivering in the microwave oven like fat white toads undergoing extreme torture but Jim was unfazed and when they were ready he buried his in tomato sauce.

"This is really good, Bob—Next best thing to a seafood dinner. Hunter sure knows how to spoil a bloke. I think I might join Art on the dole if this job doesn't improve." He yawned. "With a bit of luck, Chas and Art will be broken down somewhere and we'll get a good night's sleep. Could do with one the way I feel."

He fanned his stomach by pulling on the bottom of his threadbare T-shirt. "My God it's hot up here. It'll be good to get into that air-conditioning."

The motel units were a single line of cement-brick boxes designed for trapping the western sun. Ours was the one on the end nearest to the noise from the bar.

We pushed open the door and surveyed the gaping hole in the wall where the air-conditioner should have been. "This is typical of every job I do for you isn't it?" Jim said, his voice rising. Only thing that's gone right on this one so far is that Chas hasn't turned up."

I switched on the ceiling fan that began rotating with mesmerising slowness, making a loud buzzing sound. I turned to him. "When I was a young geo there weren't even motels, you know."

Jim snorted. "And sixty years later we're no better off."

He began experimenting with the fan switch until the blades suddenly took off with a roar. He stood under it, letting the stream of hot air flow over his sweaty T-shirt. "That's better. At least it drowns out the noise from the bar."

"What about having a shower before you do that?" I suggested.

Jim wasn't listening; he was staring at the ceiling. "My God. Look at all those mosquitoes. Where do they breed in a desert like this? There's no water."

"In the septic system, it's just outside. They're good for typhoid, cholera and encephalitis so I hope you had your shots.

"Shots?" Jim looked alarmed.

Life in the outback hasn't improved much over the years when you think about it," I said.

"It's about to improve though." Jim rummaged in his bag for his Aeroguard and began spraying wildly.

Sleep came fitfully. Jim had plugged the hole in the wall with a pillow and the windows were shut to keep out the mossies. The air in the room was fetid but at least it circulated past at great speed. No sooner had we drifted off however than we were awake again. Chas came in, fell over the camp bed, then switched on the light to see where he was.

"I had a bit of a problem on the way," he said, when I questioned him rather crossly as to his lateness.

"I suppose the wheels fell off again?" Jim said.

"I broke a spring. Too much weight."

Art came in with a stubby in his hand. "Yeah. We've got a complete junkyard on board."

"G'day Art," Jim said. "Like to let a few mosquitoes in?"

"What mosquitoes?"

"Don't worry about it. Come to think of it you're filling the doorway better than the door does. Just stand there all night."

"Where's a man to sleep," Art said, as Chas put his belongings on the third bed.

"Outside," Jim said.

Art kicked the stretcher. "How's a body supposed to sleep on that thing?"

"It's easy Art. Shut the door, turn off the light, give Chas a goodnight kiss, then lie down on it and shut up."

About an hour later, when Chas and Art had eaten some of the motel pies and unpacked their gear, darkness was again restored. No sooner had we drifted off to sleep than Chas stirred. "You guys don't mind if I turn off this fan," he said, turning it off without waiting for a reply. "I can't sleep with that racket."

For the few minutes it took the ears to adjust, the silence seemed absolute, except for the drunken shouting in the pub; then the whine of mosquitoes partying began to intrude on the stillness and sweat to soak the sheets. Chas began to snore, quickly followed by Art. When they synchronised the room vibrated.

After a few minutes of this I got up and switched on the fan again. Chas slept on despite the noisy fan and the uneasy slumbers of Room 9 continued fitfully again until Art had a nightmare.

"Get off! Get—Off!" He called.

"Jim?" I said.

"Yeah?"

"Leave Art alone"

"I'm not touching the fat sod, but I'm about to."

Much later, in the wonderful cool moments before the first glimmer of dawn, when the mosquitoes are replete with fresh blood and deep sleep finally can run its course there was a sound like a tree branch cracking, followed by lurid swearing. Even Chas stirred and came close to waking up."

"The bloody stretcher just broke." Art said.

Jim wasn't too sympathetic. "Can't you leave yourself alone? Wank on the floor if you have to."

* * *

"That was a really great night." I said as the alarm, set for six, competed with the snores of Chas and finally overcame them. "I could sure do with some sleep before we hit the road though."

"I'm buggered too," Jim said. "Thanks Chas. Thanks Art"

Chas looked a little bemused. "I had a good sleep."

"Didn't you hear Art yelling?" I asked, scratching mosquito bites.

"Or hear him busting up his bed?" Jim added.

"Didn't the mosquitoes bother you?"

"Or that pub brawl wake you up?"

"Nup."

"What's this about me yelling?" Art said as he extracted himself from the wreckage of the stretcher.

Jim gave a snort of disgust. "You yelled 'get off' half a dozen times. It's no wonder you have nightmares. You were lying on your back. Anyone with a gut like that on top of them would have said the same."

Jim and I left the moment we were sure Chas was mobile, agreeing to meet up near Kidston. We were about an hour into the journey when an emu came tearing out of the scrub and sprinted beside the road just ahead of us.

"Here's a go," Jim said, speeding to catch it up. "It's already doing forty. What can they do?" A moment later it cut in front of us and disintegrated on the roo bar in a puff of feathers and fluff. There was a rattling noise from under the bonnet and we pulled up.

"My God!" Jim said, stepping out into a pool of steaming water and peering under the bonnet. "No wonder they can't fly; emus must weigh a ton. It's pushed the radiator back into the fan."

"That wasn't one of your phantom kiwis, me old mate. That was an Aussie emu and they're dangerous, like most of our wild animals. It's best to keep clear. I speak from similar experience."

"Settle down," he said, removing a handful of feathers. "The animals over here aren't dangerous, they're just stupid. All bone between the ears, like Aussies."

"What about that wild boar you caught. He could have ripped you to pieces, small as he was."

"I wrestled him to the ground didn't I." He bent down to survey the damage. Lucky I welded the roo bar back on or it would have really cleaned us up."

"You could have welded on a few more bars."

"Yeah, but I didn't want too much weight in front. How are we going to fix this?"

"Wait for Chas. The beauty of having him with us is that he carries a complete workshop to stay mobile."

While we waited in the cab the rest of the emu flock gathered in the distance. "Look at that," Jim said. "There's twelve of them."

"If you want to see them close up watch this." I waved my hat outside the window and the birds began to weave about, raising their heads, moving them sideways for a better look, then lowering them again as if in conference. They began to drift closer, occasionally making a deep resonating bong and soon they were on the edge of the road. One was more brightly coloured and Jim pointed it out.

"He's the boss bird," I said. "Get out and say hello but don't upset them. They have a fearsome set of teeth."

Chas turned up an hour later and it took a tube of his Plastibond to seal the leak. We drove on past Kidston to the Coppermine River and picked a campsite on the bank.

Jim said. "This is really good river, Bob. Reminds me of last night's seafood dinner and air-conditioned unit." He waved off the swarming flies. "It's wide, deep and sandy, with plenty of swimming holes." He sniffed. "Even a few dead cattle. It just needs water."

"There are a few damp spots where we can dig down. They can't have had any decent rain this year."

Jim scuffed the boulder-strewn bank. "This year? This desert has never seen a decent rain and never will; I've been sucked in again."

Art sniggered. "Reason you get sucked in all the time is you're ignorant. You Kiwis are a liability in the bush."

Jim walked over to the caravan which Chas had parked under the only tree of any size - an old box gum with a few wilting leaves.

"Nice of you to take the only shade Chas. I was going to set the tent up here."

"That's what I mean," Art said. "Us locals are always one step ahead."

Jim nodded. "That's good. One step ahead puts you behind my

boot." He turned to Chas. "I thought you were going to do the van up a bit. It's still a heap of shit."

"It's got a new card table."

Jim's face lit up as he looked inside. "I take it all back. Well done, Chas."

"Jim," I called from the middle of the Coppermine River. "Bring the shovels; we'll dig down to clean water."

"Settle down. I'm paid to prospect, not to start mining."

The campsite needed quite a bit of work to make it comfortable and the next morning we left Chas and Art putting the finer touches to it while we started sampling. It was a sultry, brooding day with thunderclouds building. The native bees crawled over us in delight at the salty moisture, tickling and irritating us even more than the bush flies, which were reduced to crawling about in a heat-induced torpor. By the time we stopped for lunch, which we ate in the bed of the creek we were sampling, Jim was ready to explode.

"This life is the pits," he said. "Those bloody Charter's Towers pigeons go beedle dup, beedle dup all day driving me mad, the flies drink Aeroguard, the native bees are trying to set up a hive in my armpit and it's too - bloody - hot." He walked over to the Hilux and fiddled with the radio, looking for the stock exchange report but gave it away because of the static. "My God!" he said in frustration. "Wish these clouds would do something." He lashed out at a fly in anger, displacing the five thousand clinging to the back of his T shirt. They swarmed in such numbers that they muted the power of the sun as they circled about jostling into new positions. He lashed out again and then again.

"Steady on mate," I said. "You're getting a bit troppo and this is just the first day."

"I hate flies and I'm not your mate."

I gestured at the purple thunderheads. "Well don't wish for rain, that's really tempting fate. I think we should get out of this creek anyway, there's a storm brewing."

"Rain," he said with a maniacal laugh. "This place doesn't know the meaning of the word."

A few drops, the size of twenty-cent pieces, splattered on the bare rock and Jim stripped his shirt off, stood on a boulder and opened his mouth, trying to catch them. "Send her down Huey," he yelled. "I can take it." There was an answering rumble of thunder, a growing rush of wind and then the heavens opened.

The storm built up with amazing speed but Jim stood there

determinedly until a few hailstones bounced on his bald patch and forced him to join me in the Hilux. A violent wind sprang up, ice cold, and bark, branches and leaves, torn from the trees began to batter the vehicle. The thunder grew in intensity and duration until it was one long continuous roar—a frightening background to the noise of thrashing trees and drumming rain.

"Go!" I said, as the ground vanished under a rising wash of water and visibility dropped to near zero; it was a time for panic to replace reason.

Jim stalled the motor, unable to hear the engine from the noise outside, then revved it furiously and shot forward, only to stop. It was impossible to see a way out; trees, rocks and logs seemed to be everywhere.

"Up," I said, for we were well down a broad valley that over the years had turned into 'badlands' from past overgrazing and erosion. It was a maze of shallow washouts and steep banks—difficult to navigate even in good visibility.

We jerked forward again and the Toyota became jammed between two trees just as a bolt of lightning struck a nearby gum, sizzling in a spiral down the gnarled trunk and exploding fragments over the vehicle like a bomb blast.

"My God!" Jim said as we ducked. He reversed out and then tried to climb again but the Toyota ground helplessly in the mud and rocks, slipping back down the slope.

"Front hubs aren't in," I said.

Jim held his head for a moment and groaned. "I'm not getting out in this."

A spindly gum, its roots waterlogged, toppled over onto the cab, stopping the wipers. "We'll do one hub each," I said, putting my hand on the door. "Ready?"

We stepped out into a mind-numbing deluge of icy rain and hail that alternated in waves trying to beat us into the mud. Thunder roared, lightening flashed and the wind was a lethal weapon, whipping stripped bark and branches about like missiles. I twisted the hub to lock and leapt back inside at the same moment as Jim.

We were both soaked and shivering; the windscreen had fogged over and visibility outside was almost nil but Jim no longer cared. In low range low gear he roared off, flattening anything that could be pushed over. The roo bar kept snagging on rocks and fallen trees and he would back off and try again, and all the time the washouts were getting deeper and the outlook bleaker. No matter where we twisted and turned, the water, now flooding over the ground as a vast sheet, got deeper. Small gullies were dangerous torrents, larger floodways impossible to cross and within a few minutes we had no idea where we were or in what direction we were going except up. Finally, as we lurched across another floodway, a tree fell across our path and we got stuck straddling the trunk.

"What do you reckon?" Jim said, as the front and back wheels turned uselessly.

"If we leave the cab we'll either be hit by a falling tree or by lightning."

"Good point," he said. He switched the motor off.

"But if we sit here, we'll get washed away."

"Good point." He switched on again.

I opened the door a crack, the water was nearly a foot deep and the noise and violence of the storm was indescribable. "I vote we stay here," I said.

The storm centre raged around us for another fifteen minutes and then moved on but the water kept rising. We got out in the downpour with the water almost at floor level and the Hilux beginning to jiggle against the pressure.

"What now?" Jim asked. "The Hilux is going to float off in a minute."

"This is a moment for rational thought and good ideas," I said

"You got any?" He asked.

"No."

"Me neither."

I grabbed the kangaroo jack. "I knew there had to be a use for your roo bar. If I jack up the front enough, the back wheels might get enough traction to reverse out."

"That's really good, Bob," he said.

Kangaroo Jacks are ideal for such situations. They can be set at any height from ground level to a metre high and they can lift several tonnes rapidly. I jacked the Hilux up until the back wheels were firmly on the ground and then signalled. With a rending of metal the Hilux shot back, leaving the roo-bar on the ground once again.

"Leave it there," he yelled. "Heap of useless junk anyway."

I threw the jack in the back and with his reluctant help, the roo bar too and we finally made it to higher ground and switched off. "We're here for the night," I said. "The creeks are too dangerous to cross."

Jim groaned. "Let's make a fire, it's freezing."

As we scouted around for suitable wood we came across a fence with a possum caught in the top barb, hooked by the front leg and through the stomach. It had been blown out of an overhanging tree and now rested quietly, worn out from its struggles.

"This could be my lucky day," Jim said, stroking the grey fur. "It will make a great pet. Think I'll call it Storm."

"I thought you didn't like Aussie animals?"

"They're dumb but nice. This one looks like he's taken to me already, look at those big liquid eyes full of trust. He knows we're here to help him. How will we get it off the wire?"

Getting it off the wire was a bit like trying to get the hook out of a fish's mouth. I had to cut the skin on the front leg as Jim supported it and then nick the skin on its stomach. As it came free it clamped itself on Jim's arm like a fighting cat and sank its teeth into his wrist in a fury.

"Easy, Storm, easy boy," Jim said, gritting his teeth. As the pain increased he began to panic and try to shake it off but the more he shook the tighter Storm gripped. Jim started to dance around in a circle making noises of pain that encouraged the possum to believe it was winning; it tightened its hold further. With a heave of desperation he finally shook it loose. It landed in the mud and immediately advanced on him with menace.

"It's tasted blood and it's dangerous," I said. "Unless you can tame it in the next thirty seconds you're history."

"Easy Storm, easy boy," Jim said.

"I don't think it understands the Kiwi accent."

Fortunately, the possum gave up the chase and climbed a tree.

In the late afternoon as we gathered wood for the fire we observed an interesting phenomenon. Suddenly white ants swarmed over the ground, hunting up small pieces of grass which they took down into holes. They were incredibly industrious but fifteen minutes later, just as other ants were beginning to find and attack them, they vanished.

We managed to get a fire smouldering but as the night progressed so did the hunger pains. "Don't think I can last till morning," Jim said, rifling through the Hilux for signs of sustenance. "It really burns me up to think of Art and Chas pigging out."

"And sleeping in soft beds."

"Yeah—which reminds me. Where are you going to sleep?"

"By the fire. We'll get in plenty of wood. The bush can be dangerous at night. There are ants, scorpions, bats, bush rats, yowies, wild pigs, possums and snakes out there. You never know what's likely to attack."

"Settle down. You think I'm a new chum don't you? I know there are no dangerous animals in Australia. It's like New Zealand."

I shrugged. "Suit yourself."

"If they're so dangerous why are you sleeping out here?"

"Because there's a warm fire."

We dozed fitfully. It's amazing just how much noise there is in the bush at night. A three-quarter moon hung in the sky, casting dense shadows that moved threateningly whenever the breeze stirred through the scrub; some plovers cried out in alarm, then a mopoke started up and seemed to circle the camp slowly during the next half hour. Some roos came by; you could feel the thud through the ground as they took a few hops, stopped to eat and then moved on to the next snack. Something large rustled through the underbrush.

"How is a person to sleep through this racket?" Jim complained. Finally sleep did overtake us for a few hours until a terrible howl rent the night. Although a long way off, it was so haunting and eerie that we were both instantly awake.

"You hear that?" Jim whispered.

"Yeah. Scary isn't it."

"What is it?"

"Dingo, I hope."

"You hope?"

"If it's not a dingo then I would hate to think what it might be."

"Do they attack people?"

"No."

"How do you know?"

"Because you told me there were no dangerous animals in Australia."

"Yeah, but I was thinking more of animals in daylight." He got up and piled a heap of damp wood on the remaining coals and soon a choking smoke enveloped us, forcing us to move. "Bloody hell!" he muttered, fanning the smoke with his hat. "Just when you need a fire you can't even get a spark."

"Nothing will attack through this smoke, Jim. They'll never smell or see us."

"I'm not too worried."

Another howl, much closer this time had him on his feet again and scarcely had it died away when three or four others answered it. "They've got us circled," he said. Moments later the cab door slammed.

"Jim?"

He wound down the window. "What?"

"Are you frightened?"

"Not in here."

I'd always understood dingoes would never attack unless cornered but I kept a stick handy just in case. The sturdy bulk of the Hilux behind me was reassuring too. I was awake, or more fully awake long before the dawn chorus. The kookaburras start exactly half an hour before the first glimmer of light. As the dawn chorus rose in volume I stretched and got up. Moments later the cab of the Hilux opened and Jim fell out.

"My neck is killing me," he groaned. "Those dingoes come back?"

"I had to chase them away. Don't tell me you were frightened?"

"No way. I got in to warm up."

The creeks were still flowing as we set off with me driving, but we crossed most of them without much trouble. The track to the camp, when we finally reached it, showed the storm's effects with its covering of leaves, branches and washouts. We had only just started along it when we came across a beautiful scarlet and green lorikeet fluttering dazedly on the ground amongst a tangle of broken branches.

"Stop!" Jim shouted. "I'll catch it."

"Don't you know when you've had enough pain?"

"A bit of food and gentle handling is all it will need."

Jim extracted a couple of large sample bags from the back, giving me one.

"I'll grab it; you keep the bag ready," he said.

After much swearing on Jim's part he managed to extract it from the branches and get it into the sample bag, exposing just enough of it through the top to stroke the beautiful head while the bird did it's very best to sever his finger.

"I'll call it Rainbow."

"That's too original. What about Storm Two?"

"How about Ruby?" He tied the bag with some flagging tape, leaving a small breathing hole, then we set off again with the bird on the floor beside him. Ruby however showed great determination to return to the wild and within a minute its head poked out the top of the bag and a beady eye glared out.

Jim tried to push Ruby's head back but it caught him on the fleshy part between the thumb and finger and set about having an early breakfast. In great pain, he loosened the top and pushed his hand inside to try and scrape it off. Seeing his chance, Ruby released his grip and escaped into the cabin.

"Wind up the windows, quick," Jim said. It was an unfortunate move, for finding no escape, Ruby settled in the nearest tree-like object, which was my scalp. That bird possessed claws of immense sharpness and it locked them in a death grip of terror as it saw the trees flashing past outside. The Toyota headed off the road and into the scrub as I wound down the window, tried to dislodge the bird and tramped on the brake all at the same time.

The ground was so soft that the scrub we now skidded through side on, offered no more resistance than a lawn in need of mowing. We finished up in a gully with the bumper nudging a large tree and the rear tyre flat. Ruby escaped with a manic shriek.

"I think I'll take my own advice from now on," I said as we extracted ourselves from the gully. "Aussie animals are dangerous. Keep well clear."

We arrived back at the campsite to find the Coppermine River flowing through it. Chas' Toyota was bogged near the caravan, which was on its side; the annex was in shreds and the tent was flattened, looking for all the world like a pile of fresh mud with the outline of our camp stretchers and belongings underneath. Art was cleaning the deep freeze and Chas was readying the winch rope prior to extracting the Toyota.

"You can't trust the hired help these days," Jim said as we pulled up beside Chas. "We give you a simple job of fixing the camp and look at it now."

Chas wiped some mud off his face leaving it dirtier than before. "Some twit said it would never rain. I thought I was going to lose the caravan."

"I wouldn't have bothered saving it." Jim said as he sloshed through the mud and poked his head through the gap of the caravan wall where the window used to be. "This was a good buy Chas. No matter what happens it can't get any worse."

Art came over, glad for an excuse to stop working. "Where did youse two get to?"

"We could have done with your weight in the vehicle." Jim said. "We were nearly washed away. It was unbelievable."

"Blood oath! If I hadn't been here the whole camp would have gone."

"Chas did nothing eh?"

"He went to pieces. Thought he was going to lose his van."

We managed to haul the van back on its wheels but it had an odd lopsided look. Jim walked around it critically. "It'll be nice and cool inside Chas, with the broken windows and the missing door."

"Yep." Chas didn't sound too perturbed. "Reckon I might find the door when the river drops."

Jim walked over to the deep freeze. "I'm starved, what's thawing?"

"Twenty steaks, twelve litres of ice-cream, about two dozen packs of frozen vegetables and a dozen fruit pies."

"That'll do me. What about you lot though?"

We re-stocked in Kidston later, although not quite so luxuriously, and after a couple of days the camp was comfortable again.

"That rain has made one hell of an improvement to this place," Jim said one morning as the bush around us began to rejuvenate. He breathed in deeply. "I could almost get to like the outback. And what's that?" He pointed to the ground. "I see traces of green. Unbelievable."

"Ignorant Kiwi, this isn't the outback," Art scoffed. "You wouldn't last a week in the real outback; this is just the bush. The only way you would survive in the outback is camped in a motel."

* * *

It was a few nights later about two in the morning when a torch was flashed in my eyes.

"Bob, you awake?" It was Jim.

"No."

"There's something crawling on the floor. Take a look." Jim shone the light under the camp table where a whitish centipede about ten centimetres long was crawling.

"Thanks, Jim, I'm glad I didn't miss that. I hate sleeping through the night."

"But what's it doing though?"

"Probably looking for spiders."

"It looks dangerous."

"You said there was no such thing."

"They're only dangerous at night. What sort of spiders does it eat?"

"Redbacks. They'll be everywhere after this rain."

"Redbacks? They're poisonous."

"Yes, they're deadly. Better switch the light off."

"Why?"

"Scorpions are attracted by light."

He switched off.

"Are you mad? I was joking. Let's get rid of it."

Jim switched on again. It had vanished.

"Could have climbed up your sheets and onto the bed," I said.

He put on his boots and began hunting and I checked that my own blankets were not trailing on the floor, then tried to go back to sleep but Jim was now thoroughly aroused. He checked through his suitcase, his bed, the boxes of odds and ends, then searched outside. In the morning I awoke to find the tent empty except for the two stretchers.

"A problem with the natives, Jim?" Chas inquired over breakfast.

"Yeah, a bloody huge centipede. I'm thinking of moving into the caravan."

"Turn it up," Art said. "This is the executive suite and no one gets in without an invitation. Besides, anyone who sleeps near a Kiwi needs a bodyguard."

Chas is the one needing a bodyguard," Jim said.

"I'm safe," Chas said. "Art's not gay, although he's slept with a few who are."

"Good one, Chas" Jim said with a laugh. "I can believe it, but I think I'll stay with the scorpions and centipedes."

The rain brought a few more unwelcome visitors after that, and the following night we were pestered by clouds of flying ants. They dropped off the light, crawled down our necks and joined the dinner, sizzling in the frying pan and drowning in the billy. The same evening, as Chas was walking back from the river with soap and towel, he suddenly began hopping around, his face contorted in pain.

"Scorpion," he said. "There'll be more about so watch out."

"This is an arsehole of a place," Jim said, after searching through the camp and finding two more." He shook a dozen flying ants out of his T-shirt. "I haven't found that white monster yet either. Why tourists would want to pay to see this country beats me. The great Aussie outback is a load of crap."

Art sniggered. "Any chance of you getting the message across to other Kiwis?"

That night, Jim packed all his gear into his canvas duffle bag and left it outside so that his half of the tent was bare. "Anything comes in, it's going to head for your side," he said.

The clouds, which had been hanging about since the rain, vanished the next day, which dawned hot and humid, the air laced with the scent of damp earth and eucalyptus.

"It's like a new world since the rain," Jim said as we walked through the bush. He pointed to a cluster of beautiful metallic green and orange beetles on the branches of a shrub; they shimmered like an exotic growth; then he was distracted by tadpoles massed into heaving black swarms in pools of rapidly vanishing water. Further on, tiny brown ants clung together in swirling balls in the backwater eddies.

"We'll make an Aussie out of you yet," I said. "You're beginning to feel the rhythm of the bush. One day you might even make a useful geological assistant."

"Hey! Wash out your mouth! There's nothing little Jimmy can't handle now."

It was too wet to sample the creeks effectively, and while Art and Chas continued with the soil and rock sampling I took Jim with me to map some old gold workings. A partially collapsed tunnel ran into the hill and the deep trench that had formed as a result of the collapse, was overhung with trees; it appeared to be a cool and inviting place for lunch. Jim walked down the bank towards the tunnel opening where the walls were steepest and where three well-camouflaged kangaroos were enjoying the shade. As he invaded their territory they took flight for the exit, one bounded to the left, one to the right; the third bounded straight ahead.

"You could at least have hung onto the lunch," I said, collecting scattered sandwiches and fruit as he brushed himself down. "Always throw a rock into a tunnel before you go in."

"That's really good, Bob," he said, checking his bruises. "I like to get timely advice. Roos, emus, possums, pigs, scorpions, ants, redbacks, birds; what else do I need to know about?"

"By now I reckon you've pretty well sampled most of the hazards of bush life."

We arrived back at camp that evening to find Chas and Art also facing a new problem. A large branch of the tree they'd camped under had come down on the van, putting a hole in the roof.

Jim looked in. "The table is okay, thank God."

"Yeah," Art said. "But my bunk is under the hole."

"Well what did you expect?" Jim said. "It was a stupid place to camp. Anyone with an ounce of bush sense should know about falling branches."

Art opened his mouth to say something but memories of an earlier conversation constrained him.

A canvas waterbag hung in the camp and the native bees would cover it during the heat of the day in their quest for moisture. They were harmless, but in crawling over us in their search for yet more moisture they drove us mad. One evening, as Jim was taking a drink he began coughing and spluttering.

"I've been stung," he said and spat out something small and yellow, a wasp. "Got me on the back of the tongue."

"I knew an old tin prospector who was stung like that," I said. "His tongue swelled and he used a knife to hold it down so he could breathe. Take it easy until we see if there's any swelling. If you're worried we can run you into Kidston."

"We can watch you die while we eat," Art said, as Jim lay down in the bunk. "Have you made a will?"

It wasn't long before Jim's tongue swelled enough to make swallowing and breathing difficult.

"Why not cut the tongue out and be done with it?" Art said, delighted to find Jim couldn't respond. "A bit of peace round here from now on will be great."

"He might need mouth to mouth," Chas said.

Art groaned. "He'll die then. No one's going to go that far."

After the evening meal, Art stopped by Jim's bunk. "I ate your steak. Hope you don't mind?"

Jim said nothing.

"Always thought Kiwis were dumb. Speak to me. Prove I'm wrong."

Jim closed his eyes, shuddered, gave a strangled gasp and then went limp.

"Hey! You guys," Art said in a panicky voice. "Jim's croaked it. What'll we do?"

As Art turned towards us, Jim sat up in bed and screamed "I'm dead" in Art's ear. Although it was loud enough to wake the dead, it nearly killed Art.

"Stupid bloody Kiwi," Art said, and stormed outside.

"I take it you're better?" I said.

"Tongue's a bit swollen but I'm starving. If Art ate my steak I'll cut it out of him."

"Know what?" Jim said later as we lay on our camp stretchers that night. "Those bunk beds of Chas' are not bad." He got up and went outside.

"Where are you going?" I called "Has the bush battler finally weakened?"

He returned to the tent lugging a foam rubber mattress. "These are three inches thick. I may as well be comfortable."

* * *

When the time came to shift camp and we began packing our gear, Jim let out a grunt of disgust. "Look at this." He had the contents of his duffle bag, which had been outside for three weeks, now emptied out on his stretcher and mould was in an advanced stage of development. "This jacket cost me seventy bucks," he said, holding it up.

"I thought green was your favourite colour?"

"Very funny."

After repacking the duffle bag he slung it over his shoulder. There was a ripping sound and the contents landed on the floor. The white ants had eaten out the bottom.

"I think you upset our wildlife on this trip," I said.

"I take back what I said about no dangerous animals. I'm going to take out life insurance before I come out again."

"And you've only met the tame ones. There's poisonous snakes and spiders, racehorse goannas, wild bulls, not to mention kangaroos and cassowaries that can rip you apart with one kick if you corner them, and that's just a few that come to mind."

Before we headed out, Jim did some work on his roo bar, which Chas had managed to get welded and bolted together while shopping in Kidston. He wrapped a heap of old fencing wire he'd found around it so that it finished up looking like an innerspring mattress.

"No emu's going to get through that," he said.

We didn't see any emus but a baby pig dashed across the road, went right under the roo bar and bounced up into the engine. Chas had to tow us to Charters Towers.

Chapter 14 Bulls in the Camp

We moved to the Bundock area in the last week of November. It was an area of great variety, comprising badlands, where massive erosion had carved vertical walled canyons into the flats that required extensive detours; scrubland, where the bush was well nigh impenetrable, and uplands that were so rugged it was better to walk than drive. It was also very hot. We were there to check out a magnetic anomaly, picked up during an airborne geophysical survey and after seeing the station owner, we set up a temporary camp a hundred metres from a waterhole called Galah dam. We were under the only tree in sight on a dry and dusty plain whose powdery grey surface was like burnt flour.

Jim kicked at a pile of cattle dung as we got out and waved off the bush flies that competed with the dung beetles and blowflies for a piece of the action, then he wrinkled his nose at the powerful smell of droppings

"Beaut spot, Bob. This is more like how a campsite should be: no trees, no shade, no river, no swimming hole, no grass, no drinking water no firewood and a wonderful pong."

"The cow cocky told me we can use the dam water but he doesn't want us camped too close in case we frighten the cattle off. This is the best spot until we push a track through the scrub to the magnetic anomaly."

Art levered himself onto the back of the Toyota, making the springs creak, and extracted a can of coke from the freezer. "This place is going to generate a powerful thirst. I may need to go to town for more beer."

"Do you ever make any money on these trips?" I asked. "By the time you've paid for the grog and the gambling debts you'd be going backwards."

Jim chuckled. "Two hundred for beer and coke and there's the hundred he lost with that bet on smoking for starters."

Art bristled. "Nobody caught me smoking."

"Circumstantial evidence. Jury found you guilty."

"Some bloody jury—all cronies of yours. What sort of trial was that?"

"The best obviously, because I won."

Chas looked up from where he'd been tinkering under the bonnet. "There's ten per cent you owe to the church too, coming out of the next pay."

"What!" Art, who was in the process of opening his coke, pulled the ring tab with such force that its contents, already well stirred by the journey, exploded out in a foaming brown geyser.

Chas was unmoved by the display. "Ten per cent. That's what we agreed."

"That was just for the first bloody job."

"This is the first job."

"Bull shit!"

Jim burst into laughter. "This is the place for it Art, it's everywhere. Let's see. Say you've worked 120 days. No I'll re-phrase that. Say you've claimed for 120 days. That's 120 by 70 dollars a day, which is about 8000 dollars, less 1500 dollars for tax. So ten per cent of 6500 dollars is 650 dollars you owe the church. That's about ten days pay. Then there's 10 dollars for swear words not approved of in camp. "Right Chas?"

"Yup."

"What fucking swear words?"

"That's 20 dollars right now."

"What, for saying fucking?"

"30 dollars."

"What about bloody and shit?"

"They're okay, otherwise you'll be paying Chas for working here."

"I ain't paying no swear tax."

"I could forget it this time," Chas said, "but it's a good idea. No more swearing."

"Fuck me dead," Art said under his breath.

"Hey," Jim said. "Did you hear that, Chas? Ten bucks."

"I said struck me dead. You guys aren't for real."

"Shun vain and profane babbling, for they will increase unto more ungodliness."

"Amen," said Jim

* * *

We had the camp set up by late afternoon. It comprised Chas' caravan, its annexe and the big tent that Jim and I used. Dressed in shorts and thongs we climbed into Chas' Toyota and headed for Galah dam for a swim. The dam was fenced except for an open gate at the south end that led to a black swampy quagmire where the cattle used to drink until the cocky had set them up with a trough nearby. At the dam overflow there was a steep gravel bank and there were two bulls. On the east side was a grey one with no horns that looked pretty docile while a red bull with wickedly curved horns occupied the west side. They sat chewing their cud and eyeing each other across the water.

"I don't like the look of this," Jim said. "What's that grey thing, a bull-camel cross?"

Art laughed. "Dumb Kiwi. It's a Brahman. They're docile. The red one is the danger."

"Any bull is a bad bull," I said. "I did a magnetic survey through a twenty acre paddock once with about forty Black Angus yearlings in it. I figured they were probably still too young to be aggressive so I set a compass course that took me right through the lot without any getting in the way. I was doing well for they watched me go by without much interest, however, by the time I was half way through the traverse they'd moved a bit and I found I was heading right for one. I would take ten paces towards it, stop and take a reading, take another ten paces and do a reading and all the time it just stood there watching. I really wanted to finish the line as I was getting some interesting readings and I thought I had it bluffed, but when I was only thirty paces away, and about sixty paces from the fence, it lifted up a great clod of dirt with its front hoof. Then it put its head down."

"So what happened?" Jim said.

"The fastest sixty-metre dash ever performed by a human."

"And probably by a geologist too."

"It looked astonished. I reckon it was laughing at me."

"I don't intend to get close enough to see a bull laugh," Jim said.

We drove round to the north end, then climbed through the fence and scrabbled up to the top of the bank, which was very steep and rubbly.

"This is too steep," Chas said. "If you slipped in you'd have to swim out the other end or take on a bull."

Jim said. "We could get in on the camel's side. Who's game to try? What about you, Art? You're the man with experience at mustering."

"Well—I dunno," Art said.

"But you just said it was docile."

"It should be." Art didn't sound too sure.

"Well?"

Under this pressure and desperate to cool off Art began to walk around the dam wall. The bull took no notice at first, but maybe it was judging with a practised eye the minimum distance it needed to nail this new territorial rival. With a whoosh of expelled air it got up and headed straight for him.

We didn't stay to watch this drama. A quick calculation showed that by the time Art was back with us, the bull would be too. We disappeared back the way we'd come and Jim actually hurdled the fence, putting himself in great danger as he crossed the top barb. Art must have remembered some geometry from school days and figured a cord was a shorter path than a circumference. There was a yell, the sound as of a small landslide, then a great splash. The bull appeared above us standing proudly on the embankment, once again master of its territory.

"That splash," Chas said. "Was that Art?"

"Couldn't have been," Jim said. "No water came over the wall."

We piled into the Toyota and drove round to the gate, and sure enough, there was Art swimming across. He looked a bit winded but otherwise Okay. As he approached the shore, but still well short of the water's edge he started to wade in but then stopped.

"It's Okay," Chas said. "Come on out."

"How? I'm up to me eyeballs in fucking mud. The… a string of foul epithets followed—water's only knee deep."

"That'll be another forty bucks," Jim called.

"I'll tell you what you can do with your forty bucks," Art fumed, and he did.

"Eighty bucks; I think I missed a few, though."

"If you can get a bit closer we'll throw you a rope," Chas said.

"Why do you think I'm bloody standing here," Art said. I can't bloody move."

"Looks like you'll have to swim back then," Jim called. "Try the red bull this time."

"Come on youse guys," Art said plaintively. "I'm sinking."

Chas threw him the rope, which fell short, but Art managed to worm his way in like a great black eel until he could reach it. We hauled him in quickly, so quickly in fact that a bow wave of mud covered the few remaining spots of white skin, but we were in a hurry as the bull was on its feet again and we didn't want another confrontation.

When finally beached, Art rose to his feet like some monster of the slime with only the whites of his eyes showing. "What now?" he said. He stood there minus his thongs and with his arms held out awkwardly. He could have been the rotting root of an ancient submerged log, recently brought to the surface.

It was a good question. There wasn't enough water in the camp to clean him off. "Just let it dry. It will flake off." Jim said.

Chas shook his head. "He would set like statue."

I felt a bit sorry for Art who looked so utterly disgusted and uncomfortable, not just from the mud but from the stench of it.

"We'll go back to the north end. There's enough rope to reach from the Toyota to the water. That way he can get in and out."

"What about the bull?"

"It didn't bother us until Art invaded its patch. It might leave us alone."

It proved to be the right solution. Back at the camp later, with Art cleaned up reasonably well and everyone refreshed, Jim turned to Art. "I suggest you sleep in the Toyota tonight and park well away from the camp. You still smell like a mob of cattle. Those bulls might come looking to see what the competition is."

Art gave a snort. "If we had a decent bloody set-up here with a proper shower a bloke could get cleaned up."

"Stop complaining," I said. "You'll have skin like a baby's bottom after that mudpack treatment,"

Jim burst into laughter. "It must be working. He already smells like a baby's bottom."

We weren't inclined to play cards that evening, due in part to Art being a bit high so we retired for an early night's rest.

At the first glimmer of dawn I was awakened by the sound of jostling bodies and a pungent smell. Through the flyscreen sides of the tent, many dark forms were visible from which strange mumblings, sighs, and heavy breathings arose. A nose pushed against the flyscreen near my face and snorted, covering me with a malodorous smell of fermenting grass and saliva; a moment later the tent shook violently as a black shape tangled with a rope.

Jim woke up. "Bob? What's that?"

"Cattle. We're surrounded."

There was a clatter of dislodged crockery from the table outside and Jim leapt out of bed. "Bloody hell, they're into our gear." He shot out of the tent. "Get out 'a there!" he yelled.

A sort of rustling sigh came from the herd as a hundred head of cattle threw up their collective heads in alarm, 200 eyes widened in fear and 400 hooves burst into motion. The cattle dispersed outward in a great rush and thunder of hooves, fear adding wings to fright as the rest of the crockery fell to the ground behind them with a crash. A corner of the tent wrapped itself around a pair of horns and it billowed out with a report like a gunshot behind a fleeing steer, slowing it like a giant parachute and causing it to buck and bellow with terror. I was left staring up at the paling stars and coughing in the rank dust. With great presence of mind, Jim leapt on the tent and disappeared after the fleeing herd on his improvised canvas sled.

Art and Chas tumbled out of the caravan.

"Where's the tent gone?" Art said, letting off a few sneezes.

"It's with Jim."

"Where's Jim?"

I gestured into the distance where the faint thunder of hooves could still be heard.

Art let out a bellow of laughter. He was still laughing as he climbed into the back of the Toyota and we went looking. The headlights picked Jim up almost immediately, a ghostly figure dragging the tent. He looked like a dry version of Art from the day before.

Art was still laughing when we pulled up. "If you're going to rope steers, Jim, it's better to use a lasso."

Jim coughed, shaking loose a cloud of dust. "What would you know about it?"

"I've done a bit of mustering. It's best done from the back of a horse, but I could give you a few lessons with the rope if you want to get serious. I've never heard of someone using a tent. Is that how it's done in Kiwi land?"

"You caused this," Jim said. "Those cattle would never have come into the camp if you hadn't smelt like a randy bull."

The business with the cattle was just the start of what proved to be a long and arduous day. The scrub was thick, and although Chas managed to push over most of the trees blocking our path to the magnetic anomaly with his roo bar, there were a few that needed the chainsaw and axe. We dropped into a hole once, crossing a creek, which cost us half an hour. We lost more time when Art jumped on the wheel brace while changing a tyre and snapped it in half; then a stick flew up and pulled out the brake hose and finally we became hung up on a tree and had to winch off. By the time we got back to camp in the late evening totally stuffed, we had made a reasonable track into the area of interest, courtesy of Chas using his Toyota like a bulldozer.

We found we had company; there was a small white Pajero four-wheel drive parked by the van and a one-man tent set up next to ours. Kim was back. There was no doubt that Kim was a woman this time. She had on a blue halter-top, cutaway shorts that revealed long slender legs and her blond hair had been cut a bit shorter than before. With the bit of make-up she'd put on she looked quite cute.

"Hi," she said. "Bob, Jim, Chas, Arthur." She shook each of us by the hand.

"What's this Arthur?" Jim said with a smirk.

"Arthur suits him better. How come you picked such a smelly place for a campsite?"

"It's not the campsite, it's Arthur," Jim said. "He takes a mud bath in the evenings."

"You all look as if you've taken one."

"We're about to head down to the dam," Art said. "Want to come for a swim?"

"I had a look; there are two bulls there."

Art waved his hand nonchalantly. "I sussed them out yesterday. The Brahman's a bit toey but he won't bother us."

"I'll put on some togs and join you then. Would you turn down the stove, Arthur? I've got the vegetables on."

Kim reappeared from her tent wearing a red two-piece and Art leant down from the tray of Chas' Toyota and held out his hand. "Come on up. It's cooler in the back with the breeze, Kim."

She took the outstretched hand. "Ah, a gentleman in the camp. Thanks."

"Art's going to need more than a breeze to cool him down," Jim muttered to me as we joined them in the back and Chas drove. Jim turned to Kim. "Do you think red's a good colour to be wearing around bulls?"

She laughed. "If I get into danger should I take it off?" She turned to Art. "What do you think Arthur?"

This mind-boggling thought caused Art to grip the roll bar with knuckle whitening force and it was some moments before he could comment. "I'd er -I'd er be inclined to—to keep it on, Kim. If the bull goes for you, it'll have to get past me first. You'd have plenty of time to get clear."

"Art has experience in these things, Kim," I said. "He saved us yesterday at great risk to himself."

Kim looked intrigued. "Is that so, Arthur?"

"It's sort of right," Art said, with becoming modesty. "I drew it away from the others and ended up having to swim across the dam to escape."

"My," she breathed. "And you're going back there again now?" She made it sound as if Art was incredibly brave.

Art gave a self-deprecating shrug. "If you don't panic you can usually outsmart a bull."

"It helps if you're full of bull too," Jim said.

Kim laughed. "I'd be panicking, that's for sure."

"Besides bullfighting, Arthur's also done a bit of mustering," Jim said.

"Wish I'd been brought up in the country like you, Arthur," Kim said. "I've never been out of the city. I've had a few riding lessons though. I noticed a lot of horses on this station. Maybe we could go for a ride one evening."

"I'm game," Jim said. "I've never been on one but it doesn't look difficult. What do you reckon, Art? You could give me a lesson."

"Sure. You'd need about fifty, but."

It was quite dark by the time we were back at the camp after the swim. The long day had taken its toll; only Art seemed inclined to stay awake after the evening meal, and when the generator was turned off he stayed up talking to Kim.

"I'm beat," Jim said as he lay on his bunk. "With a four-am start. We were on the job suxteen hours today, which is really good. I need to get some of this flab off."

"You worked like a madman," I said, which was true; Jim had boundless energy no matter how hot the day. "Tomorrow we'll sleep in till the sun wakes us up, then shift camp."

"Beauty." He was asleep moments later.

Well before the sun was due to make an appearance, a distant noise approached the camp and grew rapidly in volume until the raucous shriek of a great flock of white cockatoos destroyed the dawn calm. They circled the camp a few times, obviously suspicious, and after giving us a good stereo effect from all directions, settled in the tree.

Jim stirred and gave a groan. "What now?"

"Cockatoos."

"There must be ten thousand of them."

"We're probably under their favourite tree."

"Of all the shitty campsites you've chosen this is the worst, Bob."

"So scare them off and go back to sleep."

After enduring another five minutes of shrieking, Jim gave up and got out of bed.

"I'll give those feathered fuckers such a fright they'll never come back," he muttered.

"Make sure you hang onto the tent this time."

"Good one, Bob" he said. "Good that one of us has a sense of humour."

Moments later there was a mighty clang of metal on metal, accompanied by Jim yelling at the top of his voice. A great whirring and screeching followed as the cockatoos departed en masse. Jim didn't return straight away, I could hear him running water and generally making a deal of noise in the annexe.

"Are you making a cup of tea?" I called.

He poked his head into the tent. In the dim light it looked like he had some rare spotted disease.

"Look what those bastard birds did. I told you it was a shitty campsite. They all dropped their load when they took off."

"You're determined to prove your point, aren't you," I said. "Clean up and get back to bed, there's an hour's good sleeping time left."

He cleaned himself up and flopped down on his stretcher again but it seemed that we had no sooner dozed off than the cockatoos came back.

"That's it." Jim leapt out of bed, ran outside and began to bang the big frypan. "Everybody up. Rise and shine. We're shifting camp. If I can't sleep no one else is going to. Art, Chas, Kim. Wake up!"

* * *

We relocated the camp to the area of the magnetic anomaly, a relatively pleasant spot with plenty of trees and Kim worked with Chas and Art gridding the anomaly with wooden pegs spaced 50 metres apart. The experience of working with Kim seemed to have a modifying effect on Art for his swearing decreased to zero, even when he mashed his finger hammering in a stake and his cooperation around the camp increased. I complimented him about it.

"Working round a woman makes it different," he said.

"You like her?"

"Yeah. She's got too much learning to be interested in me though. Just my luck."

"Maybe, maybe not. Someone once defined luck as when good preparation meets opportunity."

"What's that mean?"

"Opportunities come up all the time. It means get ready for the next time you meet up."

George, the station owner, drove out to see us as we were having breakfast. He was driving a Toyota about the same vintage as Chas'. His old blue cattle dog, Bully, more grey than blue with the passing years, accompanied him. Kim asked about the horses.

"We have a gymkhana coming up this Sunday. Come on over. There'll be a barbecue and some ring events. Anybody here ride?"

Jim became quite excited at this. "I wouldn't mind having a go. And what about Bob and Art? Do you have a donkey and a draft horse for them?"

"There's something for everybody," George said.

"You in it, Chas?" Jim asked.

Chas shook his head. "The only horses I trust are under a bonnet."

George said, "What about showing me where you're working. Hop in the Tojo and we'll drive out."

Before I could get into the passenger side of George's Toyota, George had to coax Bully into the middle, which he did reluctantly, with a few slobbering growls.

"He likes to ride up front," George said, giving the dog a hug. "He's family. Just like a son. Aren't you boy?"

As we set off Bully leant on me with the pressure of twenty kilos of solid muscle, his tongue dropping a steady stream of saliva onto my knee as he stretched towards the window. I tried to push him back but at this impertinence he raised his head, growled and burped out a suffocating stench of rotted meat and decaying gums.

George chuckled. "Poor old bugger. He likes to ride with his head out the window,"

A branch flicked past and Bully leapt up, his claws gouging into my legs.

"Down boy," George said.

We drove through more scrub and branches sprang through the window, depositing a shower of twigs and leaves inside.

"I'll tell you what, George," I said, as Bully leapt onto my lap and grabbed a mouthful of branches. "Bully can have the window; I'll sit in the middle."

He gave me a friendly smile. "I see you're a dog lover too."

* * *

Jim was so excited by the approaching gymkhana that he had trouble concentrating on his cards as we played Manila that evening.

"The Man from Snowy River will retire when I get going," he said. "I can still remember riding a pony when I was about six."

"Six, sucks and sex," Art said, copying Jim's accent. "They all sound the same in Kiwi lingo."

"I'm sorry to hear that," Kim said. "It's a pity you can't tell the difference between six and sex, Arthur."

Jim burst out laughing. "Art's never been able to find a woman to show him the difference and it's no good you trying. He said he wouldn't touch a Kiwi girl in a photographer's darkroom with a blindfold on."

"Bull," Art said, turning slightly pink.

"Bob will back me up on that," Jim said. "When it comes to girls and sex, Art is about as useless as an ashtray on a motorbike."

"I was talking about Kiwi girls that are attracted to Kiwi men," Art clarified. "The ones attracted to Aussie men are in a different class."

"So which class are you, Kim?" Jim asked.

"I like Aussie men and Kiwi men," she said.

"Would you like another beer, Kim," Art said, changing the subject.

"No thanks. I don't want to leave you short."

Art waved dismissively. "You can have as many as you like. I've cut back."

"You don't seem to be smoking as much either," Kim said. "You were a chain smoker last time I came out. That bet with Jim must have cured you."

"Don't need no bets, Kim. It was a stupid habit. There's more important things to spend time and money on."

"I noticed you've cut back on the food too," I said. "Chas must be quite pleased with your progress."

Chas looked up from some shed plans he was working on. "*The Lord works in mysterious ways*. He still doesn't come to church any more frequently though."

"I know what's got into Art," Jim said, "and it's not religion; but getting back to horses, I guess you'll be showing us how to rope a steer on Sunday, Art."

"Are you that good, Arthur?" Kim asked. Her blue eyes widening appreciatively as they settled on him with renewed interest.

"I'm probably as good as the blokes who'll be there," Art said, "but my crook leg makes it a bit difficult. You need to guide the horse with the legs."

Jim turned to Kim. "Art's fault around women is that he's too modest."

"I like that sort of modesty. Arthur probably prefers to demonstrate skills rather than boast about them."

Jim's mouth gaped. "Come again? He's forever boasting, like with his supposed gambling skills, but he always loses."

Art said. "I'm uncomfortable around amateurs when it comes to cards. I can't adjust to slow, unskilled play and get bored with the small stakes."

"That makes sense," Kim said.

"Yeah," Jim agreed. "I guess that also applies to Art working as a geological assistant when he thinks he should be doing the work of a geologist."

"Blood oath," Art agreed.

"He's so bored that he does nothing," Jim finished.

"Yeah, eh! What?"

Kim laughed. "Would you like to be a geologist, Arthur?"

"Yeah. It'd be good if all I did was what Bob does."

Jim grunted sarcastically. "You'd have to give up reading Playboys for starters."

"And professional gambling," I said.

"And pimping in the Towers, not to mention growing a brain," Jim added.

Kim shook her head. "I think you're all a bit hard on Arthur. He needs encouragement not sarcasm. I see plenty of talent; it just needs the right motivation along with a bit of support and reassurance from you guys."

"Yeah," Art said, looking pleased. "A prophet isn't recognised in his own land."

"You'd need to work on Art thirty-six hours a day," Jim said. "Chas has been trying for ten years."

"Well if Arthur says he has horse riding skills I believe him," Kim said.

"I could be a bit rusty now," Art demurred. "Especially with me crook leg."

"You haven't limped on your crook leg for a couple of months," I said.

"The forces on a leg are quite different when riding," Kim said.

"Yeah," Art said. "There's lat—laterite forces that come into play. The muscles can go into spasms."

"I think you mean lateral forces," I said.

"Yeah, them too."

* * *

Sunday afternoon was hot and humid with distant thunderclouds building to the south. There were about thirty men, women and children from the surrounding stations present and a large barbecue area was laid out under a bottle tree and some shady palms on the back lawn. The house paddock had been set up with coloured jumps and the kids were all practicing, demonstrating considerable skill. Kim was on a black gelding in no time and joined them over the jumps. The rest of the Hunter team sat on the wooden railings by the horse yard eating sausages and watching until George insisted on some action.

Jim was helped up onto a pony that one of the ladies had been riding and shown how to hold the reins. He gave us a nervous grin. "Say a prayer for me, Chas," he called as George led him around the yard so he could get the feel of the animal.

After a few turns, George let the horse go and looked up at Jim. "Now dig your heels in a little and go round the yard."

At Jim's urging the horse broke into a trot while Jim demonstrated the beginner's bounce. "Is this man any good or is he any good?" he called as he circled for the third time. "Should I go a bit faster?"

"Get him up to a canter," George called.

Soon Jim was cantering and the watchers applauded as he hung onto the reins with one hand and the saddle with the other, a look of absolute concentration on his face.

"How do I stop?" he called.

"Pull back on the reins."

Jim reefed on the reins and the horse, which had a sensitive mouth, stopped dead. Jim slid up the horse's neck, over its head and hit the ground.

There was a great burst of applause as Jim dusted himself off. Art had fallen too, but off the railing, he laughed so much.

"You're a natural, son," George said. "We'll soon be able to give you a job mustering. After a fall always get back on."

The horse's owner had ridden off on the pony by this stage but George soon collared another animal and boosted Jim up, bareback this time.

"What about a saddle?" Jim asked.

"You don't need a saddle. Just walk around. Show it who's master."

Emboldened by his newfound skill, Jim grasped the reins and banged in his heels. The horse snorted, put its head down and pigrooted. Jim sailed over its head too, with a yell of surprise.

"That would have to be the shortest ride I ever did see," George said with a chuckle, as Jim got to his feet. "No need to kick start a horse, Jim, that's for motorbikes. Hop on again and sque-eeze him."

I felt for Jim as he clambered back on the horse again. I had learnt to ride on a hard-mouthed chestnut gelding when I was fourteen and I can still remember each painful fall in vivid detail.

"Have you got any sheep, George," Art called as he finally mastered his laughter. "I think he might do better if he can grip some wool."

Jim managed to get the horse to a brief trot but when it came to stopping he had a problem. As he pulled back on the reins, the horse slowed, throwing him onto its neck, but as the reins slackened the horse accelerated again, and this time Jim went over the rear end.

"You've been off the front and the back, mate," someone called out. "You'll be right now, there's no other way to fall."

"That'll do me for a while," Jim said, limping to the rail "Your turn Art."

George appraised Art for a moment. You'd be about sixteen stone, son. Ever ridden before?"

With Kim sitting beside him Art seemed to become even more modest than previously.

"Err—a little," he said.

"He used to muster," Jim said.

"I'll put you on Goliath then."

Art blanched. "Goliath!"

Goliath turned out to be about seventeen or eighteen hands and a bit long in the tooth, but when Art saw a six-year-old girl called Sammy riding him bareback, he perked up. George called to her and with much kicking and use of the whip she managed to get him to come over.

Kim said. "He has a wall eye. Do be careful Arthur."

"No worries, Kim," Art said, as he swaggered across to the horse.

"Art's probably never fallen off a horse," Jim said as he climbed up beside her to watch.

"I'm not that good," Art said. "I can remember falling off on me first lesson when I was about four."

It took a lot of effort to get Art on the horse and he had to use the fence.

"He's a great goer but he's very lazy and needs a stick to start up," Sammy said, as she gave Art her switch. Art hauled on the reins and dug his right leg into the horse's flank to turn him away from the fence. The horse gave no sign that anything had happened.

"Did you have any lessons after you were four?" Jim asked as Art heaved and pulled at the horse.

"Give him a bit of switch," the girl said.

Art gave the horse a cautions smack, then a harder smack that finally got it to move a few paces before it appeared to fall asleep.

Jim said. "It'll be dark in five hours. Show us how to rope a steer while there's still some daylight left."

"You show these doubting Thomases, Arthur; you can do it," Kim called.

Spurred on like a knight in front of his ladylove, Art smacked the horse again. It woke up and moved a few more paces. Emboldened by this success and by the clapping of Kim and the watching riders he smacked the horse again, this time much harder. It broke into a trot.

To a chorus of cheers Goliath headed for the open gate in the paddock, went through, then turned to the right and kept going at a smart trot.

"Art's got the bit between his teeth now," Jim said, impressed by this horseman-like display. "I didn't think the fat sod had it in him."

"See," Kim said. "I thought he could do it. You guys never give him a chance."

"He'd better get Goliath into a canter or he'll never be able to walk again," George muttered.

It was some time before we began to wonder seriously about Art. Sammy was quite upset that her horse had been taken away, but we figured Art would be back. About an hour and a half later though, after an afternoon thunderstorm had rolled through and when there was still no sign of him, the phone rang. It was from the adjacent station to say Art was there and could he be picked up.

"How far did he go?" Jim asked, amazement in his voice.

George scratched his head. "That's about twelve kilometres. A decent ride for a new chum given the nature of the country and the lack of tracks."

"So he's a champion rider after all," Jim said, chewing his lower lip as he pondered this new aspect of Art's character. "How the hell did he manage to go so far and to find the next station?" He turned to Chas. "Does he do a lot of riding?"

"I've never seen him on a horse."

"That's easy," Sammy piped up. "I ride Goliath over here every week. He just thought he was going home."

Kim laughed. "So Goliath headed home. Arthur probably couldn't turn him?"

"He's very stubborn," Sammy affirmed with great seriousness. "Unless you can ride he takes over."

"Oh, poor Arthur."

We collected poor Arthur later in the evening. He was sitting on the veranda in his sodden clothes, looking as if he'd reached that stage of physical exhaustion which presages certain death. He stayed sitting when we arrived.

"What a wonderful ride, Arthur," Kim said, sitting down next to him.

"Yeah." It came out as a long sigh. "It's been a while since I've ridden and I had to fight Goliath all the time just to keep him moving."

Kim nodded sympathetically. "You must be exhausted. What you need is a hot shower and a good rub down."

He turned weary but appreciative eyes on her. "I'd give a month's salary for that."

"How did you find this place?" Jim asked, smirking. "We were about to send out a search party."

"I got lucky. I was about to head back. Then I saw the place and turned in. It saved me a long ride."

"So you're not only a top rider but a first class navigator."

Art shrugged then winced. "Ow—er - I know the bush, sure."

"Of course you do," Kim said.

"Time to head back to our camp," I said. "It's been a great day."

Art made as if to move, then settled back in the chair with a groan. "I can't walk."

It took the four of us to pick Art up, still in his chair and load him onto the tray top and it was a week before Art could do much more than hobble about the camp. I was surprised he didn't make more of a fuss, but then there were some compensations. It's not everyone who gets a massage twice a day from a pretty girl.

Chapter 15 The A Team

The work we had been doing for Hunter had turned up some interesting gold results. Exploration companies work on the principle that fieldwork is carried out in the hottest months. Office work, if required, should be undertaken in the comfort of the tent at the time it is being generated. Final report writing is saved for the cooler months when the exploration manager can discuss the data his field workers have gathered back in the head office without danger to himself of heat stroke. Working on this principal Hunter had its Queensland team back in the bush as soon as Christmas was over.

"This place has bad vibes," Jim said as we set up the camp in our old spot near the Coppermine River, which hadn't stopped flowing since the big storm late last year. He was trying to erect the tent with one hand and use the other to wave off the flies. "If we'd arrived any earlier we'd have seen Santa Claus go past."

"I supposed you asked Santa for a flock of sheep to make up for losing that German fraulein," Art said.

Jim waved dismissively. "We're here now because the Shafer-Woodhouse team came up with the goods. We're going to turn a geochemical anomaly into a gold mine."

Art took offence at this. "What about the A team. Didn't we have anything to do with it?"

A look of incredulity crossed Jim's face and the corner of the tent he was erecting dropped onto to the burning sand. "The what team?" he said.

"The A team, the Art-Chas team. We're the ones what done most of the hard yakka. All you do is follow the geo around brown-nosing and carrying his bag."

"The first rule of a fieldy, Art is to anticipate what a geo wants," I said. "Just as Jim does, and to do it before he has to ask. The second rule—"

"Is to wipe his arse," Art interjected. "Jim puts it first though. Check out his field bag if you don't believe me—it's full of toilet rolls."

"At least I use one," Jim said.

"Getting back to the A team," I said. "We're going to need it for this program; there's a lot to do before the drill rig gets here and we prove up our gold mine."

Chas removed his head from under the bonnet of the Toyota at this comment. "Do you think there'll be a lot more work then?"

"Only if we find something. Our days are numbered otherwise; there are plenty of geos out of work already since the stock market crash. Exploration is dying and companies are running out of cash and can't raise more."

* * *

It was a hot afternoon and getting hotter. Jim and I were working on the gold anomaly that we had christened Kidston Two, after the great gold mine to the north of us. We had already put in a baseline parallel to the trend of the gold mineralisation. Now we were putting in cross-lines, using an optical square to come off the baseline at right angles, and a topofil—which dispensed cotton thread through a measuring device—to keep track of the distance. We had finally run out of wooden pegs to mark the cross-lines at fifty-metre intervals, and Art and Chas, who had gone off to get some more, were nowhere to be seen.

Jim looked at his watch as he fanned himself with his bush hat. "The A team is holding up the S team. They've been gone two hours. What a bunch of dickheads! How long does it take to get a few pegs from camp? Half an hour if you get lost."

"What's this S team?"

"That's the Shafer team. Well ...," he said as I raised my eyebrows. "You're not going to call it the B team are you? It sounds second rate. With Bob, Shafer and Woodhouse to choose from there's not much choice. The WS team has no ring to it and the SW team sounds like a compass bearing."

"I can't argue with logic like that; we'd better go back and see what's gone wrong," I said.

"They'll be in the caravan taking a nap, for sure."

We found them five kilometres down the track. Chas was in the shade under the Toyota, Art was leaning against it looking really sick.

"What's going on?" I asked.

"Water," Art croaked. He rushed over to our waterbag hanging off the roo bar and could barely wait to unscrew the cap before he was gulping it down.

"Save some for me," Chas said, coming over. Art would probably have downed the lot but in mid gulp he was violently sick; it was mostly a greenish fluid.

"Silly man," Chas said. "I warned him but he wouldn't listen. He drank a bottle of lemon cordial."

"What, neat?"

"Yep."

Art grabbed the waterbag back. "I was too thirsty to wait for you guys to turn up," he said as he drained the last dregs. "Jees I was crook after that cordial. It was worse than dying of thirst. We left our water with you guys; never thought we'd need it seeing we were going to the camp."

Jim said. "The A team has just become the B team. So what's the trouble, Chas?"

"A stick came up and put a hole in the radiator. I fixed it but there's no water."

"It's lucky the S team was about," I said. "A useful lesson has just been learned. Always carry water and spare parts. I recall a time as a junior geo working on my own when I became stranded in the ranges behind Tenterfield in New South Wales, when the motor of my Landrover suddenly quit."

"Is this another of those stories of yours?" Jim said.

"It was winter time and I was 3000 feet up in the ranges with the afternoon sun dipping behind the mountains and a heavy frost on the way. I knew nothing about motors and I had no camp gear, no food and no matches, and I was about an hour's drive from a dirt track to nowhere." I turned to Art. "I was out of options Just like you today."

"Bull," Art said. "I was about to jog back to the camp when you two turned up. You were out in Never Never land so you were really stupid. Anyway, what was the lucky break?"

"There wasn't one, only good observation. It had to be fuel, not electrical and I noticed there were several pipes going into what I thought must be the carburetor. I unscrewed them and blew down them all to see if there was a blockage. One produced a strange whistling sound. Tracing it, I discovered it was the line from the fuel tank and a two-inch piece was missing. So I'd found the problem. I was so overcome with my expertise that for a moment I considered giving geology away and becoming a mechanic."

Art gave a derisory grunt. "Pity you didn't."

"So what would you have done, Art?" I said.

"Fixed it of course."

"What with?"

"I'd have found something. If it can be fixed I would fix it."

"I'll give you a clue," I said. "I looked through the tool kit for ideas. There were screwdrivers, spanners, a knife, pliers and a foot pump; that was all. So what would you have done?"

Art thought for a moment. "Err... pumped fuel into a can and fed it into the carby."

"What can?"

Art shrugged.

" I cut off a length of rubber tubing from the foot pump and it was a perfect fit for the missing piece of fuel line; it didn't even need tape. The motor started and away I went. The mechanic was so impressed when I took it in for the next service that he was tempted to leave it as it was."

"So what's your point?" Art said.

Jim gave a groan.

"The point is, Art that you don't just jump into a vehicle and take off when you're working in the bush, especially in summer. You could have been here another two hours before we came looking. You might have died."

Jim turned to Art. "If you tapped some of that water on the brain, you'd not only think clearer, you'd never get thirsty."

* * *

We kept the assay laboratory in Charters Towers fairly busy processing our soil and trench samples. When the first batch of results came back I began to plot them up the same evening on a large sheet of expensive, metric graph paper. The table in the van had a warp in the middle, which made drawing straight lines with a ruler virtually impossible. The warp acted like a black hole in space, which sucked nearly everything into it. Anything that was too distant to be trapped was then ejected onto the floor when the table leg wobbled. While this was going on, a million insects buzzed around the light globe like the cometary fragments of the Oort cloud. Some of these would be set free in a steady stream to pepper the plans I was working on. I had to wear a hat.

Jim came into the tent after an evening dip in the river, followed by Art, who was hopping on one leg to clear water from his ear.

"What are those lines you're drawing?" Jim asked, pulling up a chair.

"Isograds, contours of the gold values. This tells us where the best values are and how big the mineralising system is. Using this we can lay out the drill holes."

"So how do these contours work?" He ran a damp finger over one.

"Careful. This is a precision drawing and a work of art to boot."

"It looks good enough to be a work of mine," Art said. "Bloody good for a geo too, that's for sure."

I pointed. "This contour in the middle outlines values above five parts per million."

"And is that any good?"

"It's promising."

"And what are these round things?"

"The proposed drill holes, to test the values below the best surface grades."

"So where would the Shafer open pit be?"

"Probably right where that contour is."

"You mean the Arthur Fenman Pit," Art said.

Jim looked up. "Did you hear a voice just then, Bob?"

"When this mine gets going," Art continued, ignoring Jim's sarcasm. "I'll be in charge of the gold room." He poked a finger in his ear to clear the water.

Jim stifled a laugh. "The police would check everyone working there for a criminal record. You'd end up in jail before you could steal the first bar. Just remember, when you come crawling to me for a job in the Shafer pit that the S team got onto this by panning gold in the creeks."

"Just like the old prospectors," I said. "We followed the gold up into the hills until the trail stopped."

"What was that?" Art pulled a finger from his ear and hopped on one leg, tilting his head. A shower of water sprayed the plan. Not content with this act of sabotage, he overbalanced and leant against the table, which collapsed. Art followed it down.

"My map," I said aghast, as Art rolled on it, then scrunched it further, getting up. When it was laid out on the table again it had two rips, copious dirt and water stains, and worst of all, a great crease running across it like a major fault line.

"You bungling moron," Jim said. "Look what you did to Bob's map."

"I'm not drawing it again," I said. "If we miss the lode with the drilling it will be because of you, Art. If Kim complains about it I'll tell her that this crease is Art's Fault."

"Hey, good one," Art said. "The Art Fault. I get something named after me."

* * *

While Chas was away organising a bulldozer, I rang Kim in Townsville, to organise a drill crew. As there was not much work about for drilling companies there were plenty of rigs available and she soon had a crew ready to start in a few days.

"What if the drill rig gets here before the dozer?" Jim said as we discussed the program timing.

"There's no chance of that. No drill crew anywhere in Australia ever starts work the day they arrive and they always arrive late. In my experience it usually takes two or three days, sometimes a week before they get into serious drilling. They like to do their maintenance on the job rather than in the workshop for some reason."

"How long is the bloody drilling going to take, anyway?" Art asked. "The sooner this arse-hole job ends the better. I can't sleep, can't eat, can't work, can't see for the glare and can't piss 'cause I can't drink enough; it all goes in sweat. A man should be on two hundred a day for working in these lousy conditions."

"A man, yes." Jim said.

"A thousand metres at 150 metres a day is seven days," I replied.

"Great!" Art said. "So we could be out of here in a week."

"That might be a bit optimistic."

"Is Kim coming out?" Art asked, a spark of animation in his eyes for the first time in the three weeks since we'd arrived.

"I was going to ask you?" I said. "I thought wedding bells were about to ring."

Jim chuckled. "There's no doubt about Art. As soon as a woman comes into the camp, he cons her into running a massage parlour. Marrying her will be the last thing he wants."

"Those massages were bloody marvelous," Art said. "I wonder if I could talk her into giving me a few more?"

"If you can," Jim said. "I'll take over your camp duties for the rest of the month." He turned to me. "What do you reckon, Bob? If she only massages people in pain, you and I should get one every night for having to work with Art."

* * *

Chas managed to find a dozer from a place near the Oasis, a D4 that was just powerful enough to do the work. Drillers are mighty particular when it comes to drill pads. The pads have to be dead flat and very large. If a light plane can put down on them they are generally held to be satisfactory. Despite this we had them all prepared by the time the drill was due to arrive, but the cloud of dust that announced someone was coming turned out to be Kim.

"Where's the rig?" I asked as she pulled up.

"What?" It was blowing a gale, about a thirty knot westerly and she had trouble hearing me.

"The rig?"

"I passed them on the road just out of Townsville. Their trailer broke down."

Art came across. "I've just put a brew on, Kim, would you like a cup?"

"Arthur! You're a lifesaver. Thanks."

We moved to the caravan, as it was too windy, dusty and hot to sit in the annex. "This is a terrible wind" Kim said as Art poured the tea.

"At least it keeps the flies off," Jim said. "We're really earning our keep out here. I reckon Hunter should pay a hardship bonus, but they couldn't afford to compensate us for what we've put up with the last three weeks."

"The weather's not that bad," Art said. "You have to learn how to take the bad with the good."

Jim's mouth opened in shock. "You two faced liar. You've been complaining the most."

Kim shook her head in amusement. "I can't believe Arthur can be that bad. At least he made us a cup of tea."

Jim, who never touched the stuff, looked at the tea leaves circling in her cup. "That isn't tea Kim, it's hot water and tea leaves. You have to boil the water to make tea, Art."

"Pick, pick, pick," Art said. "Lucky I'm easy going."

"You got that right," Jim said. "I've never come across anyone going more easily than you."

"So what have you all come up with?" Kim asked. "Some interesting assay results have come over my desk."

"This is the Shafer pit," Jim said, pointing to the contour outline as I spread the plan on the table. Found and developed by the Shafer-Woodhouse team, better known as the S team."

Not to be outdone Art leaned over. "And these are the proposed drill holes Kim. Drill pads prepared courtesy of the A team."

"It was the A team," Jim said. "It was demoted to B team status after they nearly died of thirst."

Kim looked startled. "What's that?"

"Just Jim exaggerating as usual," Art said.

"The A team broke down without any water on board. Art drank the coolant and then started on the cordial."

Kim laughed. "I guess the truth is out there somewhere, so what is this S team and A team?"

Art was quick to jump in. "The S team is Bob with Jim as his assistant. The A team is me, with a bit of help from Chas."

Kim looked over to Chas who was sitting on a bunk listening. "Would you agree with that Chas?"

"'When he speaketh fair, believe him not for there are seven abominations in his heart.' That translates as no."

"The A team has a good ring to it," Kim said.

"The A team's done a lot," Jim said. "This crease in the map here. We call it the Art Fault. That was put in by the A team. These tears too and this footmark, these smudges. That's the A team."

"I never did all those," Art said, getting up to hand Kim a packet of biscuits and knocking his cup of tea over. The milky liquid and floating tea leaves jetted across the plan and onto the white shorts Kim was wearing."

Kim arose from her seat with a cry, spilling her own cup of tea on the floor. Chas came to her rescue with a tea towel.

"Jees, Kim, I'm sorry," Art said. "Can I get you another cup of tea?"

"Give her a break," Jim said. "It's obvious nobody wants to drink the stuff. And this big brown stain that's just appeared on the ore body. That was put in by the A team."

When the plan had been sponged and Kim had dried off and settled down with a fresh cup of tea, she looked at the plan again. "So the area of interest is at least 350 metres long and maybe 40 metres wide. If it goes down 50 metres we've got …" She looked at Art. "How many tonnes Arthur?"

"Err—A bloody lot?"

"Yes. Nearly two million. How many ounces is that Jim if it averages five grams?"

"Two million by five grams. Five grams is about a sixth of an ounce; that makes it about 300,000 ounces."

"And if gold is worth 500 dollars an ounce?"

"150 million dollars."

Kim nodded. "That's the in-ground value. Very good, Jim. Give the man a cigar."

"I think he'd prefer a sheep," Art said.

"It's hard to believe, Kim," I said. "But Jim had never used a compass and never been in the bush when I hired him. Within a week he could navigate with the air photos, put in a grid, take samples, pan gold and cook,"

Kim. "And he's learnt to ride a horse."

Chas. "And caused a stock market crash."

Art. "And a helicopter crash."

Jim. "And he even ran the camp when the geo was away. Any chance of a raise?"

Art. "If you want one the toe of my boot is ready for lift-off."

Kim got up. "Let's go look at the site."

Kim and I drove to the site in her vehicle with the rest following in Chas' Toyota. I had the plan and all the drill sections with me. Each drill section showed a plot of the proposed hole, with the outline of the surface and a projection of the mineralisation marked on it. We parked on a drill pad where we could see the layout of the drill holes fairly well.

There was no hope of getting out with the paperwork as the wind was far too strong and the dust from the freshly dozed surface was swirling wildly about, so we discussed the program sitting in the cab. We'd only been talking for a few minutes when Art appeared and Kim's door and wrenched it open. This would not have mattered if my door had been closed, but being on the lee side I had it open to reduce the stifling heat. There was the roaring of a mighty wind, accompanied by a snowstorm of paperwork and in a flash the contents of the cab were emptied except for its startled occupants and one corner of the map, which I still grasped in my hand.

I leapt out to retrieve whatever I could but the plans were well on the way to Charters Towers with Jim and Chas in pursuit. I heaved the door closed again as Art let Kim's door slam shut. Kim wound down her window.

"What is it Arthur?" Her voice had a certain edge.

Art had gone red. He passed her a pair of safety goggles. "I thought you might need these, Kim. There's a lot of dust about."

* * *

Kim had to go to another project and left before the drill rig turned up. The drillers were a day late and after spending half a day doing some running repairs they started the first hole. The rig used a tungsten-carbide bit to grind its way into the rock and it brought the cuttings to the surface by using what is called 'reverse circulation'. This blows the rock chips up the inside of the drill rods and into a large container called a cyclone that separates the fine dust from the coarser material. The coarse material then drops into a large plastic bag, which is the limit of the driller's responsibility; the mining company then takes over.

Jim and Art had the job of processing the bag of cuttings, each of which represented a one-metre advancement of the drill bit and which weighed about 15 kilos. They then split the sample into smaller parcels for assay and storage. It is heavy work, made worse by the noise of the rig and the copious dust it creates, but Jim revelled in it and Art was forced to keep pace or lose face. Chas looked after bag numbering and sample storage and kept me supplied with samples of rock chips for logging and panning.

After an hour, Art looked ready for a retirement program, but before he could conk out the compressor beat him to it and expired with a gasp. It took the drillers the rest of the afternoon to fix.

The next day began well and we finished the first hole and had started on the second when a hose burst. Shortly after that a swivel on the mast broke, then the collar around the hole collapsed and the hole had to be re-started. It was another easy day and the third was much the same when the rig hydraulics had to be repaired and the radiator of the compressor needed to be cleaned out. The following day the crown wheel and pinion went and the differential on the rig had to be pulled apart. On the fifth day the crossover sub blocked up, the rods got stuck in the hole and the off-sider fell off the mast and hurt his leg.

"It's just as well we have all these breakdowns," Jim said that evening. "Five days and only sixty metres a day. It gives Art a chance to get fit. By the time we finish he'll be able to lift a sample bag by himself, maybe even empty it into the splitter."

"What are you talking about?" Art said. "I've been working around drill rigs since I got into the mining game. I know how to pace myself. You'd never last in a full day's program the way you tear into everything."

"Good one, Art," Jim said. "I'll tell you what though. No way would I be a driller or driller's off-sider. What a shithouse job lifting those heavy rods and working in all that dust and forever repairing something when you're covered in diesel and grease."

"Piece of cake," Art said. "I put in some time off-siding on a rig working at Pajingo doing 200 metres a day. Once you get the hang of it, it's money for jam. Timing is half the battle. You use the weight of the rod as you swing it round to get it in position to screw into the hole. When you're pulling out you do it in reverse. If you can handle a woman you can handle the job."

There was a knock on the van door and Clive the driller came in. He was better known as Pud, due to his build, which was like Chas' but with a beer belly attached.

"Me off-sider can't work. It could be a couple of days before we get going again, as I have to get a new one." There was a collective groan from all of us.

"Unless one of you guys want the job. There's only 600 metres left."

"Art's had some experience," I said.

"Sixty metres a day is all we're doing," Jim said, as Art didn't seem too responsive. "Come on Art. You reckon you handled 200 a day and Christmas will be on us again if we're here much longer. Think of the rig as your girlfriend."

"I dunno," Art said.

Pud said. "You don't need any experience for this job. The pay's 120 a day and there a bonus on top of that for metres drilled, not that we've seen anything of that so far."

Jim whistled. "One twenty a day and bonus! I could be tempted for that."

"I'd prefer somebody with a bit of experience."

"Go for it Art," Chas said.

"I'll make it 130 a day," Pud said.

"Yeah, okay," Art said. "If it gets youse guys out of a hole I'll do it."

"Good on yer, mate," Pud said. "I'll get the paperwork started." He left.

"Talk about money for jam," Jim said. "There's ten days work if the rig does sixty metres a day. It could break down for a week. That's over 2000 dollars in the pocket. If I was as brain dead as Art I'd have taken it on."

"Eat your heart out," Art said. "When you learn how to negotiate a deal by playing hard to get you'll start to make real money. Tomorrow youse guys will be putting boring samples through the splitter for peanuts while I'm raking it in."

Pud appeared again. "I forgot to tell you, Art. Be on site at five."

Art's jaw dropped. "But we don't start til six?"

"You're a driller now, mate; this is real work, not some cushy field assistant job. The rig has to be greased, the compressor serviced, the oil in the rig dropped, the rods pulled and the bit changed."

* * *

By the time the S team and the other half of the A team arrived on site at six the next morning Art was well on the way to looking like a typical driller. Diesoline and dust coated his clothes, black grease covered all exposed parts, and a large wad of cotton ragging hung out of his back pocket. He was sitting on a pile of dirt and he looked up wearily as we parked.

"I knew I should have taken this job," Jim said. "Have you been sitting here since five o'clock?"

"Do I look as if I bloody have," Art said.

"What's that new dark sunscreen you're using? I don't go much for its colour."

"Hey, Art." Pud called. "Give us a hand here."

It is a feature of nearly every drilling program that the slower they start the faster they finish. Everything that could have gone wrong with the rig had gone wrong; now it was ready to perform. At the end of the day we had completed just over 150 metres. It probably would have been 200 but Art slowed the production somewhat and several times Pud abandoned his rig to storm over to Art and set right some tangle. Only the good drilling conditions preserved Art from death and dismemberment.

An hour after we were back at the camp, Art stumbled in and headed for his bunk. Chas forestalled him. "You're not going to 'black stick' in my van," he said. "Clean up, then eat."

"Only three more days to go," Jim said cheerfully when Art, a little cleaner, flopped down at the table. "You're only fifty metres short of your record too. It's amazing how the rig's performance has improved with an experienced off-sider on the job. We've gone from sixty metres to 150; I'd never have believed it if I hadn't seen it."

Art didn't respond.

"What about a game of poker?" Jim said. "You're earning enough now so's you can afford to start losing to me again."

Art put his head on his arms and fell asleep.

* * *

The next day the rig achieved 180 metres and Chas and Jim began to take pity on Art and help out with the rods in between splitting samples. Art was moving about like a zombie and in danger of getting himself injured by either Pud or the rig. When he dragged himself in for the evening meal he was unable to eat and after cleaning up he just fell on his bunk in a semi-coma.

Chas had wisely set the alarm for 4am the next morning and it took nearly an hour to get Art out of bed. Luckily for Art there were a couple of breaks during the day as Pud had to make some running repairs. Even so, Art barely survived and seemed to be fading fast. It looked as if he wasn't going to be able to finish the job. Every time he clung to a rod to swing it out or into the hole, he appeared to fall asleep.

As the sun began to redden in the west near the end of the shift, Kim turned up again. She came over to the rig and smiled in surprise to see Art as drill off-sider. The effect on Art was extraordinary. Pud's obscene swearing was no longer needed for Art now pranced about alert and in control. Sweat beaded his brow, his breath laboured in his chest but he manfully swung the rods, flicked off the monkey wrench and remembered to grease the threads, which he did with a flourish. As the final metre was drilled and the rods pulled back he flopped down on a sample bag, totally exhausted but triumphant.

Art returned to the camp long after we were back, his feet dragging and his shoulders drooping wearily. Kim was full of sympathy. "I didn't know you were a driller," she said as he sat down.

Art let out a long sigh. "I'm beat, Kim. It's a few years since I did any drilling. It sure takes it out of you. Pud needed an off-sider and nobody else would do it. I did it to save the program."

Jim managed to hold his tongue and began to serve up the meal. Art shook his head when he was handed a plate.

"You've got to eat, Arthur," Kim said.

"And wash-up," Jim said. You've already missed two nights."

"I feel like death. Every bone in me body aches."

"I'll tell you what, Kim said. "Have a shower, have something to eat and I'll give you a massage."

That massage and Kim's presence at the rig the next day did wonders for Art. Pud worked an extra hour, doing 210 metres and finished the job, but Art, with a bit of help from Chas and Jim, stayed until the end. Another massage that night and again the next morning, after a long sleep in, had him back on the road to recovery.

"You know, Arthur," Kim said as she put her bottle of liniment away. "You should become a driller full time. It would burn off the flab and put on some muscle. You could have the Charters Towers girls falling over themselves if you took a bit of pride in your appearance."

"What about the Townsville girls, Kim?"

She smiled but shook her head. "There are enough in the Towers without going to Townsville." It was the brush off but done with style.

"I don't believe it," Jim said, after Kim had gone back to Townsville. "How does Arthur do it? He conned Kim into another massage session?"

"You heard her," Art said. "The girls fall over as I walk past."

"Only when you bump into them. A rhino would do less damage than you waddling down the street."

"I think Jim's a bit jealous," Chas said.

"They like the feel of me," Art said. "Smooth skin, rippling muscle."

Jim groaned. "They feel sorry for you. A lot of girls are like that when they see a loser."

"Loser? You're the loser?"

"How do you figure that?"

"Because I just won our last bet, remember? You're doing all my camp duties. I'd like some lunch thanks. Make sure the plates are clean too. The last guy you had washing up for you was a bit careless."

Epilogue

When a mining company moves onto a property to explore for minerals it is immediately assumed by the property owner that a mine is about to spring up, the water table will be destroyed, there will be shafts that his cattle will fall down, a large open pit will encroach on the house block, there will be constant noise, sleepless nights and trucks going back and forth raising huge dust clouds, not to mention gates left open and vast heaps of rubbish covering his paddocks when the mine is finally closed.

Only about one in a thousand prospects gets to become a mine however and the Shafer orebody could not beat the odds. The drilling found very little gold and the geochemical anomaly was attributed to the concentration of gold values in the iron and manganese-stained weathered zone. Although Hunter International survived the economic downturn it was forced to curtail its exploration and disband its field crews.

In the years that followed, Chas managed to finish building his shed in Charters Towers and with this as security he went on to build another one in Townsville. Both of these returned a good income and he then formed a construction company, which has prospered, as did his family with four boys and four girls; the only material sign of his success however was a relatively new, second hand Toyota. He has not forgotten his roots however. In one corner of his Charters Towers shed is a battered caravan with rickety table and ancient carpet surrounded by various bits of exploration equipment. Whenever the mining cycle turns positive he rents it all out.

Art, impressed by the blandishments of Kim and the lure of big money and to a much lesser extent by the realisation that physical labour might be beneficial to his love life if not taken to extremes, stayed with Pud for the next contract. He then became a fully-fledged driller and made enough money not only to pay for his beer but also give him a surplus. With help from Chas he bought his own rig, a small Airtrac machine, and secured a long-term contract drilling blast holes at the nearby Mt Leyshon gold mine although he soon found it was far easier to let others do the actual drilling. He sold out ten years later after expanding the business and then ran a luxury charter boat operation near Proserpine that promised "Romance on the Reef" and was crewed by bikini clad girls. He was named recently in a Senate inquiry into gambling and prostitution in Queensland but no charges have been laid as yet.

Jim moved to Hobart for six months and found work at the casino where he polished up his gambling skills and his memory for card sequences until he was politely asked to leave. He then worked his way around Australia trying his hand at everything from crocodile wrestling to barman. He eventually found a wonderful Aussie woman with three grown up kids and settled in Perth. There he picked up an ice cream run, became a water contractor, had a part share in a butchery and ran a small business selling tourist artifacts, many of which he made himself. He also improved his squash game. Ever the gambler, but wary of mining shares he eventually had a share in a winning lottery ticket that netted him nearly half a million dollars. Since then he has taken to cruising around Australia with his partner on a Harley Davidson searching for gold nuggets in remote areas with the latest in metal detectors.

Kim took a contract job in New Mexico, working in a gold mine. She made headlines a few years later when she was ambushed by bandits one Sunday evening as she entered the mine compound through a locked gate and was forced to hand over the keys to the gold room. She retired from geology after that and married the owner of a ski lodge in Canada. Her husband was killed in an avalanche a few years later and she sold out. She now works for the US government in the National Parks and Wildlife Service.

Tony, fed up with 'handshake deals' that earned money for others but not himself, retired from geology to volunteer his time working for St Vincent de Paul on the Gold Coast. He died the way he wanted to and with joy in his heart in the Summer of '92 from a petit mal seizure, while he was body surfing a three metre break in wild seas at Duranbah.

Hermann never overcame the effects of trying to empty Art's

stockpile despite several rehab sessions and he was last seen sleeping under a bridge near Mt Isa just before the wet broke and dumped five inches into the creek. His body was never found.

Bob became a geological consultant and roamed the world disseminating practical advice until his retirement. Inspired by the legendary golfing feats of his brother in law, which he later discovered were entirely fictional, he then spent considerable time road testing Greg Norman approved courses to get his handicap into single figures. After a neck injury affected his game, he took up writing and to date has published several successful novels.

END

ABOUT THE AUTHOR

Robert graduated in Geology from Melbourne University in 1961and spent many years first as a field geologist and later as a wide roving consultant travelling to many parts of the world. He still runs a consultancy and has drawn on his experiences to write two light hearted books with a strong geological theme. This is the second one he has turned into an e-book. The first book "Meekatharra. From Gold Dust to Bull Dust" was also published in 2014.

Robert has two grown up children and apart from writing his main hobby is singing. Robert is a baritone who has sung bass solo roles in many places during his travels as a geologist and combined with Peter Krenske on piano to record two CDs of classical songs. He has also produced a CD of Australian ballads.

15378149R00115

Printed in Great Britain
by Amazon